DEVON C. FORD
EREBUS

www.aethonbooks.com

EREBUS

©2017-2020 DEVON C. FORD

Loving you always,
Forgetting you never.

PREFACE

All spelling and grammar in this book is UK English except for proper nouns and those American terms which just don't anglicize.

In loving memory of sleep.
Loving you always,
Forgetting you never.

PROLOGUE

She came awake almost imperceptibly. Her eyes opened slowly, but no other movement betrayed her transition from sleep into consciousness. Her chest maintained the same steady, rhythmic rate of rising and falling, showing no noticeable change in her behaviour.

But she was cautious and alert.

Her senses, although instantly watchful and wary of her hostile surroundings, zeroed in on the feeling that something was somehow *different*; something had changed significantly since she had fallen asleep. Still, her body remained seemingly unchanged to any outside observation.

Her eyes found the source of the disturbance within seconds; the trapdoor in the high ceiling, the portal through the heavy glass separating her prison cell from the world above where the scientists roamed free, was open. Not just unlocked or slightly raised, indicating that it had malfunctioned when last closed, but wide open.

Sensing an obvious trap immediately, she remained still as she thought. Her eyes roamed carefully around the scene, her brain spinning all the while at impossible speeds as she formulated the plan to escape.

Escape.

She had dreamed of nothing else for the entire time she had been there. She had no idea how long it had been, as the permanently lit room disorientated her; as such brightness would for a young girl who had lived her whole life underground in the murky, subterranean darkness. Her only measure of the passing of time was the intensity of the foot traffic above her, where the men and women wearing white coats went past, mostly ignoring her. Occasionally she would see the reflective black visor of a soldier watching her, usually when they opened the heavy hatch to give her food and water. But try as she did, she had quickly lost track of the days.

All she knew was that she had been there a very long time but could not say with any certainty whether it had been days or weeks or months.

Slowly, careful to show no obvious sign that she had seen the potential of freedom on offer, she made believable but overt signs of waking. Stretching her back on the white sheet over the cot she lay on, she raised her hands to her face and rubbed her eyes, feeling the thin crust on her eyelids yield instantly to a light touch. Spinning lithely to rest her bare feet on the warm ground of her cell, she wiggled her toes as she arched her back further and extended her arms stiffly to stretch away the inactivity of sleep. Bending her neck from side to side to alleviate the tightness in her muscles, and to offer a better view of the glass ceiling, she satisfied herself that nobody was present. Careful to act as she always did when she woke, she stood and stretched again, rising to her tiptoes, before shuffling towards the partially screened corner of the room, where she slipped down her white pyjamas and sat on the steel toilet. She stood, washed her hands and then ran the water to make it hotter before splashing her face. No working parts were vulnerable to damage in her prison cell; there was no toilet seat to break off and use as a sharp instrument, and even the fixed faucet was activated by a waved gesture of her hand.

Turning away from the small sink, she did as she always did in the morning or what she assumed to be the morning and dropped easily into a handstand against the wall where she did vertical press-ups to maintain her strength for the opportunity of an escape attempt. She did less than usual, mostly because she was not exercising now but merely warming her muscles in case the offered gift of freedom was not snatched away imminently. Dropping away from the wall, she extended her legs into a split and leaned her upper body forwards to lie flat against her outstretched leg as she leaned her head sideways to watch the trapdoor again.

Rising to her feet almost nonchalantly, she bent her head to her knees to stretch her lower back and legs and looked at the wall from her upside-down perspective. She gauged angles and heights, calculating her required effort to reach freedom.

Knowing that the smooth walls would offer her bare feet sufficient purchase, she stood tall from the stretch and turned. Three quick, long strides saw her accelerate to a speed fast enough to carry her momentum upwards. Running two steps up the far wall she sprung away and twisted her body in mid-flight before her feet met the wall above head height on the other angle of the corner of her cell, which she used as a launch pad. Bending her legs slightly and reversing the impetus, she bounced lightly off the second wall and reached upwards with both hands to grasp the very edge of the exposed lip above her. Swinging twice as she steadied herself, she tightened her grip and pulled her upper body through the gap and switched her grasp to turn the pull into a push and raise her straight legs as she spun again to land her backside onto the floor above.

The entire sequence of calculated movements had taken less than three seconds.

Rolling backwards and lowering the trapdoor, she froze, all senses on high alert for any response to her escape. She stayed still for five seconds. Ten seconds. Nothing. Her escape had taken her less than a handful of heartbeats, and she knew that the responses to her behaviour when she had first awoken in the brightly lit cell were rapid enough to warrant an armed response within the time she had spent outside of her cage by now.

Satisfied that she was not about to face an incoming squad of faceless soldiers, she rose and lightly tiptoed her barefooted way through the corridors. She knew that every inch of the facility where she was being held would be covered by cameras, but that knowledge would not dissuade her from exploring or from attempting to escape the clutches of the Party's scientists who had drugged her and poked and prodded her when she was barely conscious. Her eyes scanned left and right, searching for anything she could use to arm herself against the impending discovery and confrontation she expected at any second.

After the tenth glass window she looked through, she froze.

Standing immobile as a statue, she stared intently at the occupant of the small glass box and could not believe what she was seeing.

Sitting on a chair in front of a small, bare desk was Cohen. She was reading something on a computer tablet and was wearing a pair of glasses. Eve knew that was a new development, as the woman who had raised her always squinted at the words and had to hold things at arm's length to make them out with any clarity. The woman had not seen her, and she raised her hand to tap lightly at the glass before she stopped herself.

Why does she look happy? she worried. *Why isn't she trying to escape like me?*

Her fingertips rested a hair away from the glass, but she could not bring herself to tap and announce her presence. Slowly lowering her hand, she decided to continue on and come back for Cohen after she was armed and had found a way out of their prison.

Her prison, at least, as Cohen seemed to be more guest than captive.

She carried on, rounding the next corner and seeing an expansive room the size of which she had never seen before. The ceiling extended far up into the gloom, and an array of apparatus towered before her.

The loudspeakers set into the walls crackled to life.

"Detain her," a bodiless voice said aloud.

She detected movement to her left and right simultaneously, causing her to settle into a crouch and raise her hands. Two people dressed in the same simple, white linen pyjamas showed themselves; one male and one female. Their faces showed no expression, no emotion. They both stalked towards her, keeping their eyes fixed on her but moving their feet inexorably closer as she was flanked on both sides. She could not keep both of them in her sight where she was, and to withdraw into the corridor would limit her options to move, so she sprinted forwards to leap desperately and pull herself high onto the apparatus to try and obtain some kind of advantage over their superior number.

No sooner had she gained the top rung than she glanced to her right and saw the female standing on the same level. Sounds behind her told her that the male had gained the same height with alarming ease. Changing her approach, she dropped and began to lower herself though the framework to ground level like a primate. As soon as her feet hit the mat-covered ground, a thud to her left told her that the male had taken the direct route down and now stood too close to her for escape. Uncoiling herself from her crouch like a striking snake, she advanced on him, forcing him backwards with each attack as he deflected her blows, before stamping his foot back towards her in anticipation of her next attack. As she responded, a brutal blow to the back of her left thigh dropped her to the ground, the limb instantly useless and numb. Rolling urgently away and back towards the direction of the blow, she wrapped up the leg of the female and took it with her as she spun, trying to wrench the joint unnaturally and return the maiming she had been delivered, just more permanently.

The female came with her, dropping her knee painfully into Eve's abdomen and rolling over her to break her grip. Gasping for air, she tried to rise to her feet but managed only to get to one knee before the female was back on her feet and advancing. She stopped, recoiling a step and giving Eve the time to rise up painfully. As she did so, a powerful arm clamped around her neck and pulled tight.

Eve responded instantly, instinctively, spinning her head so that her vulnerable throat was nestled into the crooked elbow of the male with the dead eyes, allowing her precious breath to fill her lungs. She lashed out backwards with an elbow, forcing her attacker to arch his torso away from her and she pushed his head forwards. She was under no illusion that this would free her, but it was designed to set him up for her real counterattack and it worked perfectly. Flicking up her right leg high behind her, a feat only possible for someone who had trained to be strong and flexible from the moment they could walk, her bare heel struck the male on the bridge of his nose and broke his grip momentarily.

It was enough for her to strike three savage blows in the confined space between them into the vulnerable parts of his upper body; one to the lower ribs of his left side into the nerve cluster, one to the throat and one hard strike downwards with her elbow onto his collar bone. As he fell away, her almost lifeless left leg threatening to collapse her, more hands grabbed her from behind and wrapped her up tightly. With one arm around her neck and a strong hand clamped onto her forehead, she felt both of the female's legs impact on her narrow hips and hook together around her waist. The additional body weight on her one good leg toppled her backwards to land heavily, driving the remaining air from her lungs. Her struggles rapidly faded out to become weak twitches matching her narrowing peripheral vision as the oxygen supply to her brain was being stifled.

"Father," announced the voice from the speakers, only this time it did not come from the speakers in the wall, but from a man.

She was released to roll away and lie gasping on the ground as her hazy vision saw a man in a leather coat stride towards her. He was flanked by another man, similarly dressed, and she watched as the first one held the chin of the dazed male whose nose she had broken with her foot.

Nathaniel inspected the damage done to Shadow with evident amusement, then dismissed him to receive treatment for the injury. He glanced at Reaper who, although undamaged, was breathing heavily and was covered in a sheen of sweat from the brief, violent combat. Twitching his head, he dismissed her too and bent down to regard Eve up close. He smiled at her, a gesture she did not mirror, before rising and turning away.

"Clean her up and put her back," he ordered, just as Eve's awareness abandoned her and she lapsed into unconsciousness.

CHAPTER ONE

A DEEPER TRUTH

Adam felt much of the same frustration he had felt before. He had been kept underground beneath the city streets of the Citadel for his entire life, until finally being allowed to go above ground and use the skills he had spent that lifetime honing. Events had rapidly unfolded, giving the Resistance an edge they had never experienced before, but they promptly squandered their resources. The Party had responded brutally, targeting the population in their self-awarded official capacity and bringing terror to the citizens; the majority of whom knew nothing of the Resistance, nor did they want to.

Most people were just happy to trudge through their short lives under the heel of their oppressors, choosing to believe that they were instead their protectors.

It had all gone wrong when he and Mouse had made their own decisions and had acted outside of the established chain of command. They were tools. Weapons. Resources to be used and deployed where Command saw fit, and they weren't entitled to know the reasons why they were and were not allowed to act. But they had acted, and now they had lost one member of Command as well as Adam's counterpart, the other half of the whole of his project, and Eve was trapped in the Citadel with the Party doing who knew what to her.

If she still lived, that was.

Adam still didn't know how his escape was made possible, after he and Mouse had been captured with the young woman who was being tortured for information on the Resistance. But the transport they had been placed in had been hijacked by the Resistance, by his gruff mentor, Mark, and they had received orders and authorisation to flee to the Frontier.

Where he now sat alone, waiting underground for other people to make his decisions for him.

He was deep under the inhospitably rough terrain in the south-west of their island, a place that the Party had been in active service ever since the age-old civil war had ended and all other parts of the British Isles had been destroyed or conquered; this one small bastion had defied them ever since.

Their technological advances and advantages over the downtrodden citizens held no advantage there, tipped no balance of power, and on the Frontier they had long since given up losing valuable hardware by sending their drones into the wilderness to never be seen again. Retreat was not an option, as any ground yielded would be mined with vicious traps designed to maim and kill any Party soldiers sent to reclaim the territory. The two eternal foes were locked in an endless cycle of raiding their opposing sides and holding their lines, a battle quietly self-perpetuating through three generations in its current form, and little seemed likely to change on either front.

Unless one of them found their hand forced.

Adam paced restlessly, exercised rigorously until the

depression of endless inactivity and boredom removed his will to be constructive, and then threatened to remove his will to live. He had been effectively imprisoned and dragged through dark tunnels where he constantly hit his head on the low ceilings; dragged there by small figures wrapped under cloaks, their small hands digging sharply into his flesh where they gripped him.

He had been separated from Mouse, from Mark, and from the girl they had brought with them for days on end and left alone, ignored with the exception of a delivery of food to his room every day. He referred to it in his head as a room, but in truth it was a cell.

Any room you can't get out of is a prison, he told himself angrily.

He was used to being underground, to being in the dark, but this dark seemed more absolute. More natural. He lost track of days, just as Eve did, unbeknown to him, although for different reasons. Hers was because of the clinical, bright, alien atmosphere; his because of the changed routine. He realised that he had grown used to his life being dictated by the comings and goings of others and marked time by the expected sounds of his door opening. After he knew not how long, the daily delivery of food differed in that it was brought in as normal, but the person delivering it did not leave immediately.

The small figure walked into the room and placed the tray down on the bare table dimly lit by the single, weak bulb in the ceiling, then sat on his cot and looked at him from under its hood. Adam saw the small shape, the mess of cloak folds making it impossible to discern any real figure inside and was mesmerised by the glow of the eyes deep inside the shroud. They were elliptical, almost feline, and larger than his own. The slant of them made them appear in his imagination more feline than human, but the way the figure moved was inescapably human. He towered over the sitting figure at over six feet tall and would have done even if the figure had been standing. The heavy cloak moved, and the legs crossed over with a rustle of fabric, almost demurely, as the eyes never left his own.

It's a she, then, he told himself, unable to switch off his hunter's instincts for assessing a potential target.

"Sit down, please, Adam," she said haltingly, carefully pronouncing the unfamiliar words. To reinforce her point, a fold of the heavy material slunk out sideways from the mass and patted the thin mattress gently. Adam hesitated, his indecision being taken for refusal.

"Do what she says, *boy*," came a gentle command from the doorway.

Adam spun to look at Mark, who was leaning casually against the doorframe and obscuring nearly all of the dull light coming from the low-ceilinged corridor beyond. Adam said nothing, and Mark just nodded to him once before turning and leaving them alone.

Adam looked back to regard the small pile of material concealing the large eyes on his bed, and slowly lowered himself to sit beside her.

Carefully, hesitantly, two small hands appeared from the cloak. He held his breath, watching as the thin fingers of the hands moved upwards to lightly clasp the edge of the hood before slowly drawing it back to expose her head.

Adam still didn't breathe as the pupils of the large eyes narrowed visibly at the slight increase in light hitting them. As best he could make out in the low light, the iris of her eyes was a morphing mixture of hazel and green, and the eyeballs themselves seemed larger by half than his own. The face was small and very pale to the point of seeming fragile and thin, but the strong, narrow jawline suggested that the petite female was anything but weak. She smiled, an unconscious gesture either designed to put him at ease or else to demonstrate that she was no threat. Either way, the sudden flash of teeth made Adam catch his breath and begin to breathe normally again as though he had temporarily forgotten how.

"Hello, Adam," she said, again uncertainly, "You have many questions of us, I know, but please wait for your others?"

He was mesmerised by her. He opened his mouth to respond, assimilating the words and rearranging them in his head to double-check their meaning, before answering her simply.

"Yes."

She rose suddenly, almost startling him with the smooth speed of her movements and walked soundlessly towards the open door. She stopped at the door and gestured back for him to follow her.

"Holya my," she said, as though he would know what she meant, before remembering herself and adding, "Follow me".

Adam stood up to follow, hitting his head on the ceiling as he did and cursing, before walking after her, pausing only to grab a sandwich of roughly cut bread and a thick meat filling.

His education on the Frontier had been as thorough as other matters, in that he was told what Command thought he needed to know. As any child, he trusted what he was told unquestioningly and was now realising that he had been greatly lied to by omission.

He had been told that a band of people like them, Resistance fighters, lived underground and kept the Party at bay by preventing them from invading the small peninsula at the south-western tip of their island. That much was true, but it rapidly became obvious to him that there was a world of information on the subject which people hadn't deemed it necessary for him to know. The small, low corridors wound in a seemingly illogical manner without any signs to indicate their destination, until they evened out and became more uniform, as though this new area he was progressing into had been tunnelled out later than where he had been housed, and with apparently more modern techniques.

His assumption was factually correct, but that piece of knowledge would not have chipped even the smallest peak from the iceberg of information he didn't know about the place and its people. He could stand to his full height after a while, escaping the permanent annoyance and discomfort of having to reduce the length of his body by a mere couple of inches, and he leaned around Mark to try and see the small figure who had restored the heavy hood of her cloak and now swept along ahead of them. Her short legs were moving at twice the rate of his own which now seemed ridiculously long in comparison with their hosts and his surroundings.

On one of his awkward leans for a view ahead, he saw the that the tunnel suddenly opened into the expanse of a wide, rounded chamber which was the single largest room he had ever been in. It felt as big as outside had felt to him the first time he went above ground, and the slight chill of the open air hit him suddenly. Wishing he was wearing his black suit in place of the rough-spun outfit he had been given, the legs of which stopped at the top of his calves, he soon filtered and sorted the riot of senses he experienced. Closing his eyes briefly, he stood and tried to catalogue the individual elements.

Cold air, warm ground.

Smoke, a fire?

Cooking. Maybe meat, but not quite right; there was

something different about the smell, almost unpleasant but not entirely unappealing.

Voices, only low and hissing, but no words he could make out.

"Oi," Mark snapped, breaking the trance he was in with a gentle poke into his ribs. Adam recoiled, gritting his teeth at the annoyance of his mentor seeming to know every single part on a person's body which could make them feel like they were being electrocuted. A useful skill he also employed effectively, but at that moment he was less than impressed and his face showed it.

"Focus," Mark said, scanning the figures in the room and easily locating Mouse on the other side of the chamber; marked out by being a head taller than the two shrouded figures he was talking to. Their odd companion seemed to be thoroughly enjoying himself as he appeared to be miming his way through some form of explanation. He didn't see their approach, wrapped up as he was in his interactions, but Adam felt the gaze of every other cloaked shape in the room fix surreptitiously onto him as he strode tall across the space.

Mouse noticed them as he neared, and his face lit up further. He stopped giving his animated description with a small bow of apology to his audience, and took a pace towards them, casting his eyes back down to the ground as he always did when speaking to people.

"You're better!" he announced to Adam as he stood in front of him. Mark cleared his throat quickly to head off any counter question and left Adam dumbfounded as he struggled to comprehend the need for a ruse explaining his absence.

"You've got to see these," Mouse said excitedly, ignoring the thought that anyone else might have something to say, "they have some great pieces of kit.

Remember this?" he asked, holding up a small device for inspection.

"It's the same as the one you used to knock out the tower," Adam answered. "What did you call it? A *pinch?*"

"It's a *crunch,*" Mouse corrected him, "and the Nocturnals have stuff that's even better than that."

Adam's face scrunched up in confusion.

"The what?" he asked, giving Mouse a curious look.

"Not what," he replied, eyes searching the ground for anything to focus on except the person he was speaking to, "*who.*"

Adam opened his mouth to ask another question but stopped as Mark's hand rested on his elbow. The two exchanged glances briefly and the flicker of Mark's eyes to their small guide conveyed a great deal more than he could put into words. The message was clear; *mind your manners.*

"Dren?" Mark said, turning to face the slight woman who responded by turning her face up towards his. The muted glow of her eyes shone out from the darkness of the shroud, making Adam catch his breath again as the eyes reminded him of time spent with Eve.

"*Ya?*" she responded immediately, flashing a white smile from inside the hood.

"Can we speak to the *Myghtern* now?" he asked respectfully, pronouncing the uncertain word as *migshtern* and prompting Adam to pull yet another confused face.

The smile under the hood disappeared but the eyes still shone slightly. "*Ya,*" she said again, only with an intonation which let them know she was not entirely happy to lead them to her King right then. She did, leading the way in silence out of the large chamber and not looking back to check if the three outsiders were following.

Adam followed behind her, as Mark stood aside and held out a hand to gesture for Mouse to fall in line. As the awkward and excited young man walked past him, Mark plucked the improvised electro-magnetic bomb from his hands and handed it carefully back to the small figure who had been talking to their technical specialist before he and Adam had arrived. Giving a small bow to simultaneously convey his thanks and apology, he took three long paces to catch up with the procession.

The same feeling Adam had when they had first entered the large chamber now crept into Mark's brain through the back of his skull, as he too felt all the hooded faces in the room swing to bore into the back of his retreating head.

CHAPTER TWO

THE INFECTION OF REBELLION

Cohen had held out far longer than Nathaniel had suspected the small, seemingly frail woman would. She had responded with a stoic silence, and that silence had been repaid with brutal physical abuse. Nothing too damaging; just the application of electricity to the body in controlled doses every time she refused to answer a question. Those questions were asked quietly, politely, and the responses to her refusals to cooperate were also administered with a similar calm and professionalism.

Nathaniel had not dirtied his own hands with the interrogation as he didn't want any prisoner to ever think that they were important enough to warrant his personal attention; he wanted them to believe that they were at the mercy of the interrogators until such time as they said something of use.

The man who had been wounded, shot in a diversionary attack when the small squad of killers were doing something at the Citadel hospital, had recovered from his wounds, thanks entirely to the expert medical care given to him by the doctors and nurses of the Party. He had not lived long after that, much to Nathaniel's annoyance at the waste of resources spent bringing him back from near death, and his interrogations had been conducted under a different set of parameters. He had yielded information, they all did eventually, but by the time he had regained sufficient strength to be questioned, the relevance of his information was useless. He gave up time-sensitive facts, but from a timeframe that was weeks behind their own accelerated schedule.

"He was a dead end," Major Stanley mused aloud as he flicked though the report of the prisoner's confessions for the third time. "A *dead*, dead end now, I suppose."

Nathaniel gave only a slight snort in answer to the poor joke, leaning back in the high-backed chair at his desk and interlocking his fingers over his chest as he relaxed.

"He cracked too soon," he offered, "he was an amateur. Disposable. Just one of their pawns; he knew nothing of use."

"Not like the old woman though…" Stanley answered, intentionally trying to provoke the Chairman.

Nathaniel snorted again, only in derision this time instead of mild amusement. "No, she's no amateur. She still needs to be handled carefully, though…" he trailed away, thinking of the moment when she finally broke.

She had been restrained, her hands bound by cuffs and shackled to her waist with her ankles similarly chained. She was shuffled along the corridor, watched on the monitors by Nathaniel and Stanley, and dumped to her knees on a glass floor. They watched, both holding their breath unconsciously, as the old woman froze. She placed a single hand flat on the glass and stared, finally drawing a lungful of air and screaming the girl's name at the top of her voice.

She wasted her effort. The girl had been sedated; the

subtle pumping of tranquilising gas into her cell carrying her off into a deep, unrousable sleep in preparation for the act designed to break the woman.

And break she did.

All of her stony defiance, her tight-lipped silence, her seemingly endless strength and tolerance for pain, all of it abandoned her in that moment and she screamed the girl's name over and over, willing her to wake up and escape. To fight. To never give in to them.

They had told her that Eve, now that they knew the girl's name, had turned and wanted to experience all that the Party could give her.

Only then did Nathaniel intervene, walking into her cell with Stanley and no armed guards in sight. Cohen's red eyes focused on them, switching between their faces as she assessed their importance and guessed what horrors they would inflict on her next. Her eyes flickered towards the brutish revolver strapped to Nathaniel's left thigh, her intent evident should she get the chance.

Nathaniel saw her gauge the distance to his weapon, the only firearm in existence he or anyone else knew of that could be fired by anyone not authorised by the chips inserted into everyone's necks. He smiled at her, knowing that if she could, she would snatch the gun and kill them both. The final, suicidal, shred of resistance left in her. He broke that final bastion of her original self, speaking softly and factually, explaining what would happen to the girl if she did not answer their questions.

He didn't threaten; he promised.

He promised that, if Cohen complied and helped them, then Eve would live.

He promised that, if she didn't comply, then Eve would be forced to fight for her life every day until she finally succumbed, and even then, her death would not be slow.

She had broken. She had given up names, locations, plans, stores, and collaborators. That was what worried Nathaniel the most.

"Party members and soldiers are helping the Resistance?" Stanley had asked him incredulously.

"No," he growled back at the young Major to correct him, "they are helping the *terrorists*, and that makes them guilty of terrorism also."

Just as each day went by and Cohen was granted more comfort and safety from the aggressive questioning she had survived since they had taken her from her home, more and more people were rounded up and taken into custody. Terrorists, collaborators, it made no difference. Each of them was interrogated, and each of them spoke of everything they knew before being imprisoned again to await their sentences.

Those sentences were carried out publicly, and the residents of each block were marched to the steps of the Citadel where they were forced to brave the worsening weather and watch as the executions were carried out. So, as the two senior officers sat in the Chairman's office and made careful assessments of the plethora of intelligence the interrogations had revealed to them, Cohen and Eve sat confined far below ground.

Safe, for the time being.

———

Cohen smiled as she sat at her small desk. She had traded the cold fear of a bare cell for the warm comfort of a sparsely decorated room, although the door was still locked, and she was still effectively a prisoner. The tablet they had given her, not connected to their mainframe, obviously, contained some reading material and games.

The reading material was mostly Party propaganda, and tales of fearless Chairmen from history who bravely fought the vicious and wild Scots in the Civil War before leading the Party to freedom after the world had torn itself apart. She read the stories, keeping her face neutral the entire time, as she knew at least one camera studied her every move, filing them all away in her head. Finishing another grand tale of the first Chairman, who apparently killed one hundred men in hand-to-hand combat, she filed that away too.

I'll just put that under B, she thought to herself, *for bullshit*.

In truth, she had suffered massively in the early days after she was arrested. They had no idea that she was so involved with the Resistance, let alone that she was a member of Command, but Eve's actions in trying to rescue her had sealed her fate. If she had not broken, the girl would be dead. Her reaction to seeing Eve in the glass prison was real. It tore her heart to shreds, seeing the baby she had delivered and nurtured locked up in a box, even worse that the girl was at the mercy of men devoid of souls. So she hid her true self, grew an outer layer of the person they wanted to see, and gave up the information.

People died. Lots of people died, but they were all committed to the cause in their own ways. Some died believing that they were fighting the good fight against the tyranny of oppressive rule. Some died believing that their actions, even if it cost their own lives, saved the lives of others. Some died full of self-pity and regret, cursing the day they were ever recruited to fight for a side they never believed could win.

Most of those who regretted their involvement were the collaborators, who Cohen knew could be replaced over time. They were all recruited through greed, which made them easy to manipulate and easy to control. They wanted *favours* from the citizens, mostly, and the growing trade of underground prostitution was a lucrative industry. That level of supply and demand would never go out of fashion.

The real secrets she kept to herself.

Long-established protocol dictated that any member of Command being taken constituted too high a risk to continue with their current hierarchy, and the transfer of control would cycle to the redundancies. The beauty of that system was that not even she knew who would be leading the new Command now, and she only hoped that James was brave enough to fulfil his responsibilities as leader. She knew she would have been able to do it herself, to be able to hand over control of everything and then take her own life to prevent her secrets being plucked from her brain one by one.

———

She had no way of knowing, but James had indeed lived up to his responsibilities. He had invoked the collapse of Command, transferred control of all assets to the redundancy, including Fly and the Twins, Jenna and Jonah, as well as their piggy-backed system allowing access to the Citadel mainframe. After that he had waited in his meagre apartment until he finally heard the sounds of boots on the stairs coming in force.

Slowly, he reached to the small coffee table beside his chair and picked up the glass containing the last of the alcohol he owned. He had been saving the half-empty bottle for some as yet unknown reason. He finally realised that the reason was to give him the courage to do what he'd sworn he would when he'd accepted the job of leading Command almost three decades before. As the weight of the glass left the table, it wobbled marginally, almost uncertainly, on its uneven legs. He drained the liquid, grimacing as he swallowed it down and felt the fire burn into his empty stomach. Walking slowly to the window, he took a moment to stare out over the expanse of dull, grey concrete and the empty wasteland beyond at the far reaches of his vision.

That's all life is above ground, he told himself as his eyes swam out of focus briefly. *It's grey, it's lifeless, and everything here dies.*

Opening the window and letting in the whistling chill of the wind so high up in the residential tower block, he turned to face the entrance to his apartment and sat on the window ledge. Just as the two shots sounded almost in unison and the door hinges blew violently inwards, allowing a squad of black, reflective face plates into his small home, he smiled sarcastically and held up the middle fingers of both hands.

Then let his body fall backwards.

CHAPTER THREE

THE ART OF PROMOTION

Lieutenant Jasmin Blake accepted a mug of coffee with thanks and a smile which made the young officer blush a deep crimson. She knew the effect her personal appearance had on men, and also on more women than many would expect, and she used that to her full advantage.

She was never overt about her manipulations, never vulgar in making promises, but she simply exuded an air which engendered the instant adoration of almost everyone she met. She did that with the young officer, only slightly her junior in rank and age, and it worked perfectly, because he always made sure he had added the precise one and a half sugars to her coffee that she liked, along with the perfect amount of milk, just before she was due to arrive on duty.

She always arrived thirty minutes early, releasing the officers on the night shift to steal an extra few minutes head start on getting to sleep. This engendered yet more respect and admiration from people she didn't get to have direct contact with. She took the brief handover, standing in interim charge of the control room until the Captain arrived usually thirty minutes late, and bid the small team sleep well as she gently placed a hand on an arm here, or flashed a brilliant smile there.

Because Lieutenant Blake was thirty minutes early, Second Lieutenant Toby Baxter arrived thirty-five minutes early to ensure he could hand over her morning coffee with an air of casual nonchalance. He was the only one of both the day and night shifts who did not know how obvious his infatuation was, but still he fought to control the instant warmth in his chest and face as Blake walked in. She offered smiles of greeting, asked polite questions about how they were feeling and gave light touches to the tired officers, riding on a wave of good feelings that she brought with her everywhere.

It was common knowledge that Blake wanted her Captaincy, and her extra efforts were rewarded with the devolved authority of the Captain of the day shift who held no enthusiasm for his role or posting.

It was rumoured, not that Blake would engage in seditious gossip, that Captain Solomon was at a dead-end in his career after some mistake when posted to The Citadel. If such a rumour were true, Blake knew any serious error in judgement would have resulted in Solomon's transfer to the Frontier and not to the soft, safe command of a unit in one of the mining districts in the north. But some element of it had to be true, she thought, because the Captain held poor standards of uniform, arrived late and left early every day he was on duty, and seemed not to care about anything.

There was a Colonel in the base, but he was rarely seen. Three Majors were posted to the area; one from the Adjutant's Corps who oversaw the administration of the mining base, one of six such bastions, and who reported to the Colonel directly whilst leaving the day-to-day running of operations to the Captains, and two troop Majors who were in charge of the soldiers stationed there. Blake's additional efforts were seen as her attempt to make Captain, also rumoured to be the reason for her transfer, but Solomon's apathy allowed him to accept her dedication without question as he slowly devolved the running of his team to her piece by piece.

Keeping her eyes on Baxter, waiting as he always did to see her face when she took the first sip of her drink, she smiled in satisfaction and shot him a playful wink.

"Perfect, thank you, Toby," she said in her velvety voice, allowing the blushing boy to resume his duties, before raising her voice to the room. "All stations, report, please."

"Perimeter clear," came a female voice.

"Comms, nothing to report," said another.

"Drones, NTR," croaked the voice of a young man who always seemed to take until mid-morning to be fully awake. He was a different animal entirely when their rotation gave them night duty, and never seemed to suffer any tiredness during darkness.

"Accommodation security, all clear," announced Baxter in his best big-boy voice.

Blake nodded and sipped her coffee again.

"Okay, Drones: request a morning sweep, push it out by five kilometres," she said confidently, giving an order as though the operator at the drone terminal would be doing her a personal favour by complying. No answer came, but she heard the order translated as a request over the communications network to the drone operators based at the highest part of their sprawling compound.

"Itinerary?" she asked, waiting for Baxter to swipe his finger over a tablet and find the information she needed. She already knew that information, but she liked to go through the morning routine publicly, as it made her feel like the captain of a warship from the stories she had read as a child.

"Three outgoing convoys for loading and dispatch," Baxter began, "one incoming from Western district. They're escorted and will take their own fuel load back. Two convoys going south, one of which is requesting additional troops to escort them back to The Citadel." He looked at Blake for approval. She nodded, sipped her drink, and cast her eyes to the communications operator.

"Signal the duty troop, Major," she said smoothly. "Give them Captain Solomon's compliments and say that he would be obliged if they could accommodate the request." The operator nodded and began to hail the barracks command.

Satisfied that the challenges of the day were minimal and appropriately dealt with, Blake leaned back in the command chair in satisfaction. Two fuel loads to be sent to The Citadel, some troops on loan to escort them, who weren't really needed in the mining district anyway, a food delivery in from the west and a fuel load to go back with that detachment, and little else to manage throughout their twelve-hour rotation.

Close to an hour late, Captain Solomon walked in looking as though he had slept in his uniform. He stumbled into the doorframe as he entered and returned the collective looks of everyone in the room with an uncertain sketch of a salute. Blake respectfully stood to vacate the command chair but was waved back down by Solomon as he paced a sedate lap of the control centre.

"All quiet, Sir. Nothing to report," announced Baxter, eager to impress his commanding officer. Solomon stopped and regarded him, then simply looked away and resumed his inspection. His circuitous tour of the command centre took him back to the door where he turned to speak over his shoulder.

"Carry on," he said simply, then left for the day.

Lieutenant Jasmin Blake kept her face wearing a suitably worried expression, but inside she smiled wickedly. Some put Solomon's behaviour down to a problem with alcohol, but she alone knew that the Captain was taking a small dose of psychotropic drugs each and every night. Solomon didn't know. He merely woke each morning thoroughly exhausted and each day saw him more confused than before.

Blake had been slowly poisoning him, night by night, totally undetected.

There were many ways to earn a promotion quickly, but she could hardly attract the attention of The Citadel's senior officers, let alone hit the radar of the Party Chairman. She would surely be recognised, and her efforts to disappear would be for nothing.

Better to make herself indispensable, well thought of, and subtly undermine her superior officer. She would no doubt be put in interim charge of the team and be breveted as Captain subject to some low-level formal administrative ratification.

"Comms," she said softly, receiving a raised eyebrow from the operator, "please signal the Adjutant Major with my respects, and ask that I can see him at his earliest convenience."

The operator nodded, then tapped at his screen to submit the written request. Within an hour, Blake had been summoned and had given her brief report with evident reluctance. It was regrettable, she told the Major, but she could no longer in good conscience continue to cover for the actions and behaviour of her superior officer. She was thanked and dismissed, returning to the control room in time to relieve Baxter before the first convoy arrived.

Before the end of that shift Blake had been summoned again, then escorted to the Colonel's office, where she was awarded the interim rank of Acting Captain and given a half-hearted speech about stepping up to her new responsibilities. Her first act as Captain was to arrange for a vehicle to transport Captain Solomon back to The Citadel under escort provided by the troop major.

Quite the career climber, she thought to herself as she kept her face neutral on the way to join her team in the mess hall, *Corporal Samaira Nadeem to Acting Captain Jasmin Blake in just a few months.*

CHAPTER FOUR

THE CARROT AND THE STICK

Eve gasped as she awoke this time, throwing her body up and off the cot in her glass-ceilinged cell and dropping into a defensive crouch. Her breathing came ragged and fast, her hands shook as her body responded to her last memory of being in combat. Taking precious seconds to comprehend that she was alone and safe, safe from any attacker at least, her body began to relax as her mind raced to catch up.

Lowering her hands and releasing the cramped tension in her muscles, she dropped her chin to her chest and stepped back to the cot to settle herself on the crisp, white sheets. Above her, the lights still shone brightly but the movement of people was absent.

Night-time, she thought sullenly, *which means I've missed two meals.*

As though her stomach had heard her words, she felt a pang of emptiness and a gurgling growl from her midriff. Rising to her feet, she padded across the room and checked where the tray of food usually sat when it was lowered in and out three times a day. Finding the area devoid of anything to eat, her face dropped into something resembling a hybrid of a scowl and a sulk. Her belly growled again, making her clamp a hand to the flat surface as though physical contact could stop her feeling hungry.

Hunger was not a new concept to her. She had grown up living on whatever rations could be purloined and donated by those aware of, and sympathetic to, the Resistance's cause. She turned to the sink to try a trick that had served her and others well in lean times and waved her hand under the faucet to start the cold water flowing. Cupping her hands and bending her head down, flicking her head to send her long hair over one shoulder away from the flow, she drank water until she could no longer cram any more liquid into her body. Standing upright and wiping her mouth on the bottom of the white top she was wearing, she shook the excess water from her hands and wiped those on her clothing too.

Turning away from the sink, she felt the cold water sloshing uncomfortably around in her stomach and threatening to upset her natural equilibrium. Lying back on the cot carefully, she cursed aloud as no sooner had she settled, than the effects of consuming so much water took control and forced her back to her feet to empty her bladder.

Returning to the bed, she stared up at the glass roof and the gloomy darkness above. She closed her eyes and concentrated on her breathing, making it rhythmical and steady, passing the time and changing her breathing rate to force her heart to slow down and transition her into sleep.

———

"What exactly do you mean by *'switching it up'*?" Nathaniel asked carefully, instantly making the ugly scientist quail before him. As though to make the pressure he felt worse,

Major Stanley leaned in closer to hear the response with evident interest, but only intimidated the chinless man further.

"I… I mean, Sirs," Professor Winslow stammered, "that you should consider a variation in the behavioural responses. Provide a positive outcome for the desired behaviour, in this case non-hostility and acquiescence, and allow the cause and effect to solidify in the subject's subconscious…" he trailed away, realising that his unnecessary use of scientific jargon had annoyed the two men asking the questions. He cleared his throat and tried again.

"You should get her to do something that you want and reward her for it."

Stanley straightened, glanced once between the bespectacled man quivering in front of him and back at the Chairman, then slapped the terrified man on the shoulder.

"Easy as that, then!" he said with faked satisfaction. "Thank you, Professor, you can go now," and watched as the small man fled as fast as possible without actually breaking into a run. His own smirk of enjoyment at the man's discomfort was mirrored by Nathaniel, who had only just allowed the man to remain on staff with Special Projects access after he'd failed to account for the circumstances of his being found unconscious when Eve had been captured. Professor Michael Winslow, known amongst the science staff as 'The Weasel', was a man of disturbing proclivities, but he was the best behavioural scientist they had.

The circumstances unaccounted for, as obvious as they were, had still not been satisfactorily explained. Worse still, not only had the Professor been found unconscious in a room which had been used to restrain a young female for interrogation, but their newly appointed Sergeant Major

Du Bois had been discovered in that same room with even more explaining to do.

"So, the official advice," Nathaniel said acidly, "is to treat her like a puppy?"

"Seems that way," Stanley answered. He didn't need to add a 'sir' when they were alone and rarely did, unless they were around officers or soldiers who weren't viewed as part of the inner sanctum. Still, the two held a respect for each other, and hardly considered themselves to be friends.

"So," Nathaniel asked thoughtfully, "what shall we do with our puppy? Treats and tricks?"

"Yes," Stanley said, all trace of humour gone from his voice.

———

Eve woke to the sharp sounds of high-heeled shoes clipping loudly over the glass ceiling to her cage. She opened her eyes to see a white lab-coated woman stride past, tablet in one hand and a steaming mug of something in the other as she hurried to be somewhere. The water she had guzzled to settle her hunger pangs had left her stomach empty once more, hitting her senses with the simultaneous need for both sustenance and relief. One symptom she could manage, the other was at the mercy of her captors.

The walkway above her began to echo with sounds again. *Three or four pairs of heavy boots,* she imagined as she cocked her head to one side to focus her ears on the approach, *and something else. Bare feet?*

It was three pairs of boots, and one pair of bare feet padding casually along with them. She looked up at where the procession stopped above her, seeing the big man who had called off her attackers when she had escaped *or had been allowed to escape,* she corrected herself and the male wearing the simple white clothes and a look of blank obedience. She recognised two of them; one she had tried to kill with a throwing knife in the holding facility where she had been captured, and the other had saved him from that fate with a shield he had activated on his forearm.

She stared at them and they stared back at her, an impasse, until the man in charge spoke once.

"You must be hungry," he said. Not a question, but not entirely a statement. It was as though the solution to that problem was within her control. He nodded to the other two men wearing boots, one of whom was dressed as a regular soldier although without a reflective black visor, and he activated a switch panel to pop open the glass trapdoor.

"Step forward," he instructed. Eve did not move but glanced back to the man in charge and then to the human animal she had fought. His nose was bruised purple, the very edges of the injury already beginning to fade to a sickly yellow hue.

She smiled in satisfaction at the injury she had caused, attempting to goad him into a response.

He did not respond. Did not smile. Did not scowl. He just simply stared.

Giving up, Eve glanced back to the big man who had spoken first. He said nothing but gestured her forward. She waited a few heartbeats, just enough to show that she wasn't inclined to take orders, then slowly stepped closer.

The ground in the corner of the room, the exact size of the trapdoor above her, began to rise silently.

That's how the food gets in and out then, she thought, glancing to the control panel but unable to see what buttons were pressed to activate it. Her strong legs kept her stable as she rose up, never taking her eyes from the men, until her ground level became theirs and she had to keep her head leaned back to look up at them.

"Food," said the other booted man simply, "this way," and he walked away with the man in charge. The soldier and the barefoot man with the broken nose waited for her to move, setting off slowly after the two men, and fell in step behind her as they watched her like hawks.

She followed uncertainly, casting cautious looks behind her, expecting an attack at any moment. Given her last and only experience of Citadel life outside of her glass prison, she wholly expected this latest interaction to be another trick. Her heart pounded and the blood coursed through her veins carrying the oxygen supply from her lungs which inflated and deflated at a fast rate.

She tried to keep her expression neutral, to not show fear or wonder at the new and unexpected things she saw, to demonstrate control and retain some power, but completely failed to control her response when they arrived at their destination.

Following the men through a doorway, her eyes shot wide at the spread laid out on the table before them. Her mouth opened, her jaw dropped, and she uttered an involuntary sound which was mid-way between a gasp and a choke.

She had never seen so much food in one place. Plates upon plates lined the long table, containing some items that she recognised and many things that she didn't, but was desperate to try. She saw bread. Fresh bread that was still warm and not the hard, stale samples she had experienced. She saw thick slices of meat; the streaks of fat running through the flesh glistening in the artificial light and making her mouth water. She saw fruit; fresh and healthy and not the dried, paltry treats she had grown up anticipating.

And then the smell hit her.

The glorious riot of aromas of the different foods mingled together in her nostrils and made the synapses in her brain erupt like an artillery barrage bombarding her into a loss of self-control.

She broke, not sparing a glance to the two white-coated scientists in the room or the soldiers and threw herself towards food utopia. She snatched up bread, meat slices, a block of something cold and pale yellow which felt slippery and greasy in her hands. She thrust red berries into her mouth, not bothering to remove the small green leaves on the top.

She crammed as much food into her mouth as she possibly could, turning her body to keep it all away from the others and protect her property. She told herself that she was still fighting them. She was taking the opportunity to gain strength before they took it away again, and she wasn't the slightest bit sorry.

Eyes darting nervously around, she watched carefully as the two men sat down and picked up small, white pieces of cloth from the table and shook them out. They laid them in their laps and spoke quietly to one another in casual conversation, whereas she, in stark contrast, acted like an animal.

Still she wasn't sorry. She could barely chew fast enough to swallow down the food before she threw more into her mouth. Her hands and chin were covered in grease and juices from the fruit. Her chewing began to slow down as she watched what the two men did.

The tall one seemingly in charge selected a fresh bread roll and used his fingers to pry it in half. He looked around the table for something, finally resting his eyes on the greasy yellow block melting in her hand.

"Eve," he said politely, "could I please have the butter?"

She froze, cheeks puffed out full of food and her white top already stained with different residues. Chewing the remainder of her mouthful down, she swallowed and hesitantly reached forward to put the block on the empty plate where she had snatched it from. The man thanked her nicely, then carried on talking to his fellow soldier as he reached out with a small, blunt knife in his hand and scraped the block a few times. She watched in awe as he wiped the butter on the insides of the bread roll and then used a small set of metal tongs to select three slices of the streaky meat. She watched as he carefully laid these into the roll, closed up his creation and took a careful bite before chewing slowly.

She was suddenly aware of how she looked.

She wasn't a feral animal, despite how the Party treated people like her, but she felt as if she was not only embarrassing herself but making everyone else on her side of their quiet war look bad. Slowly, hesitantly, she put down the squashed and misshapen contents of her hands on a plate set out on the table. She reached out for another square of white cloth and carefully wiped her hands clean before rubbing the sticky mess away from her chin. Looking down at her top she let out an involuntary tut of annoyance.

"Don't worry about that," said the other man as he smiled at her. Eve's eyes scanned the room to see that the lab coats had left, and the soldiers hadn't followed them inside. She was alone with these two, and she was suddenly embarrassed by her actions. The men carried on talking, saying something to each other about a project and talking about new buildings as if she were not even there; as though she were not their prisoner.

She sat, never taking her eyes off them, and resumed eating at a more sensible rate. She turned over a glass, clean and clear, and picked up a jug of orange liquid to pour herself some. That sensation when it first hit her mouth was unlike anything she had ever experienced before. The sharpness and the sweetness struck her simultaneously, making her eyes half close. The small bits suspended in the drink gave it a texture and a contrast that she wasn't expecting, and she coughed into the glass spraying it upwards into her eyelashes and making her set down the glass to cough again. Wiping her face clean with the stained cloth, she tried again and drank more slowly as she relished every gulp until the glass was drained. She poured herself another and ate shining red berries with fruits adorning the outer skin. She carefully picked up a small, blunt knife identical to the one the man had used on the butter, her hand resting on it and waiting for a response.

None came, so she used it to cut the green leaves from the top of the fruit and put the berries whole into her mouth one by one and let them burst as she chewed. Her eyes closed as she enjoyed each one more than the last, until her mouth craved something different. She copied what she had seen, pulling open a bread roll and feeling the heat of the inside. That smell of fresh baking wafted to her nose and struck her on an emotional level, making her open her mouth and breathe it in loudly with her eyes closed again. She scraped thick wedges of the butter and smeared it on the warm bread, then followed it with four slices of the meat. She dropped the last piece she picked up with her fingers as the heat scalded her. Shaking away the small pain, she tried again and made her movements faster to minimise the amount of time that her skin was in contact with the hot meat. Sucking her burnt fingertips, she was rewarded with a hint of the taste to come before opening her mouth wide and taking a huge bite. Leaning back to chew slowly and let the salty tastes swim around her mouth, she heard the big man speak.

"Have you ever had bacon before?" he asked. She opened her eyes to see them both looking at her. She sped up her chewing to empty her mouth and answer them, remembering that Cohen had always admonished her for speaking with her mouth full.

Cohen.

That memory brought back the emotions of capture and imprisonment like an icy wave and her face dropped.

"Yes," she said with hostility, "but it was always cold and stringy. You obviously keep the best for yourself."

Both men chuckled lightly.

"Yes," the smaller one answered with amusement, "I suppose we do," before taking another bite of his own breakfast. The bigger man had finished his and leaned over to lift a small platter of glazed, brown things to offer it to her.

"These are sweet pastries," he told her, "and I'll admit they are my favourites."

Eve was torn. She wanted, no she *needed,* to try the glistening treats offered to her with their promise of sugary goodness with the hidden fruits she could see embedded in the doughy centres. She fell back on sullen resentfulness, barely overriding her obsession with the opulent food on offer and leaned away to fix them both with a stare of hatred.

"My name is Nathaniel," said the big man before pointing at the other one, "and this is Major Stanley,"

"Why am I here?" she snapped at them, making the two men exchange glances of confusion.

"For breakfast?" answered Stanley. "Would you prefer to stay in a cell forever?"

Eve would not, but nor would she admit that and play into their hands.

"What do you want from me?" she asked testily, fighting her urges to snatch up more food with all of her resolve.

The big man, Nathaniel, looked at her, or more appropriately *through* her as she felt a shiver of cold under his gaze, before rising from his seat and turning to a machine behind him. Picking up two plain mugs, he poured black liquid from a full, steaming jug and turned back to offer her one. She didn't take it, just stared at him until he set it down before her with a sigh.

"What I, what *we*, want from you is to hopefully change your mind about us," he answered, regaining his seat and sipping the drink. Placing the cup down with evident approval, he regarded her again.

"We want to show you what we really do, who we really are, and then you can decide what to believe for yourself," he said.

Eve stared for a long moment, assimilating this information and trying to decide how best to respond. Leaning forward to pick up the cup, she stared down into the dark contents and watched as the light film of small bubbles swirled in a clockwise direction.

"Show me then," she said, sipping the drink and contorting her face into a rictus of repulsion and disgust before spitting it back into the cup and utterly ruining her achieved air of power.

CHAPTER FIVE

THE NEXT WAVE

Residence block one, not that many people knew it, was the original seat of the Resistance in The Citadel. The very first collective of Citizens unwilling to bow down to the nationalised Party rule had met in that block innumerable years before, and the irony was that little had changed in all that time.

Command had been passed between the various tower blocks over the years, sometimes far more often than was reassuring, and now it had returned to its spiritual home once more. The flash-burning protocol of a compromised Command was a violent process, and the redundant members of the Resistance knew nothing of the structure and operations until they were activated, only then having to catch up on the recent history and ongoing projects.

Helen Randall had lived all of her forty-one years on the fifth floor of Residence block one, and when she had received the coded message from James, her heart sank. Not because of the responsibility she now held, but for the fact that sending the message to her had likely been his final act and that he was probably already dead. The battered piece of paper in her hand bore only two words.

Phoenix
James

Phoenix was the activation signal, and the name was proof of authenticity. She didn't know what she expected if she ever even *got* the call to activate, but she felt such a feeling of sadness at the unknown loss of life, that she allowed herself to cry. Wiping the few tears away, she looked at the words again, then went to the single burner on her small gas hob and sparked a flame. Touching the edge of the dried paper to the flickering blue glow, she turned off the gas and walked to the window to let the fiery ashes drift away on the wind.

Closing the window, she put on her thick coat and gloves before leaving her apartment to get to her work placement on time. After the brief walk to the cold warehouse and her twelve-hour shift spent organising the allocation and rotation of food supplies, she made the brisk walk back to the block and went down instead of up; heading through a basement door into the labyrinthine tunnels beneath The Citadel. Offering a nod to the small, elderly female sitting near to and watching the door, a hard-bitten woman widowed by the Party soldiers many years previously, she stepped into her new world of subterranean darkness and subterfuge.

This knowledge was part of her selection as the redundancy leader. She and a hand-picked few, all activated separately through different methods, were now in control of the secret fight against their oppressors. And she had a lot of catching up to do.

She naively expected her transition into leadership to

have some sort of training setting, and hoped for a long report on recent activity and their next planned steps; instead, she found three scruffy young people and a mess of computer hardware, all arguing over what lead went where.

They stopped arguing as she walked in, staring at her, and she stared right back at them.

"My name is Helen," she began as confidently as she could manage, "Helen Ra…"

"No surnames," interrupted one of them. He looked different from the other two, and as she looked at him, she found herself startled that the difference she had noticed was that the other two looked very similar, and only his individuality made him seem like the odd one out. Recovering, she nodded.

"Of course, then if anyone is taken, they can't give up any information they don't know," she said, hoping to demonstrate her understanding of the operational security protocols, but instead she found herself facing three hostile stares. Realising her tactless mistake, her face flushed with colour and she mumbled her apologies.

"Forget about it," the same one said before introducing himself, "I'm Fly, and these two are Jenna and Jonah," Helen looked to the others, obviously twins or at least very closely born siblings, and exchanged nods with them.

"Has anyone else arrived yet?" Helen asked them in a business-like tone.

"You're the second to arrive," the girl, Jenna, said, "there's a man in there already waiting," she finished as she held up a finger to point towards a dark alcove. Helen nodded but the three had all returned their attention to the mess of wires before them. Walking towards the direction that had been pointed out, she stepped slowly and mentally prepared herself for the meeting. She had spent all day inside her own mind as she had worked, wondering who would be part of her new Command and what they could bring to the fight. She, like the others, would have been intentionally insulated from any Resistance activity in case they had become a person of interest to the Party.

That's how this works, she told herself, *it's how we stayed alive and, more importantly, un-tortured.*

As she walked into the room, she found a younger man than she expected. He must have been ten years her junior at least, and her look of unveiled confusion took him aback as he stopped arranging chairs in a circle and looked at her. He smiled, a brilliant flash of white in the gloom, and took two confident strides towards her, extending a hand.

"Harvey," he said simply as she took the offered hand. She felt the strength of the grip, not a painful squeeze or an assertion of dominance, just the enveloping feeling of a strong grip holding hers. She answered with her own first name, looking into his eyes and feeling grateful for the poor light as she felt her cheeks flush with colour. He had a square jawline, neat facial features even if they were a little on the small side, and a wide mouth which showed the white teeth behind the lips.

"I'm on a construction team," he told her as he let go of her hand. "We've just had orders for a refit of one of the factories. We're going to pull it down and build a bigger one, apparently," he went on. Helen found herself missing the contact immediately and thrust her hand back into the pocket of her big coat to retain the warmth that the brief contact had left her with.

"What is the factory for?" she asked him, taking one of the seats.

"Not sure," he answered, almost annoyed, "but it's rumoured to be something military and larger than the drones," Helen nodded in answer, not sure what else to do with the snippet of information just yet. She knew that the secret web of information would spin itself back and would start to feed her with morsels very soon.

Better to keep quiet until then, she thought to herself, *no point in letting everyone know I have no idea what I'm doing yet.*

She was rescued from the prospect of making small talk with the attractive man when Fly walked into the room escorting another three members. They were introduced and ran through their allocated employment, detailing what information they had access to in their day-to-day experiences. Small talk ensued between different people, until Fly poked his head back around the door-frame and caught her eye.

"You ready?" he asked her. She fought down the urge to respond with, *for what,* as she nodded.

Fly returned her gesture and called the others in. He stood in the room and spoke softly but confidently, filling them in on the facts of recent activity. Helen's mind wandered as she realised that the four others comprised her Command, but she brought her attention back to Fly.

"We still have a successful tap into Citadel computer systems," he said, detailing a few for clarity's sake, "drones, troop rotations, CCTV… but after recent compromises, we can't make any direct changes and have to be very careful about how we mine the data," he finished.

"What compromises?" Harvey asked, leaning forward.

Fly looked down as he spoke, as though he read from an imaginary sheaf of notes.

"Mouse, he was our computer person," he explained, realising that nobody present would have known about his existence, "he went on a mission with the other two people of Project Genesis to rescue captured Resistance members from a holding facility. None of them came back."

He let that hang, seeing the shock and worry on the faces of everyone assembled, and went on.

"Adam and Eve," he said with a hint of a choke in his voice, "went with Mouse without Command approval. From what we've seen, they were all captured but somehow, Adam was smuggled out to the Frontier with Mark and another person. I don't know how, nor does the Party by all accounts, but we can only surmise that it's either an outside influence or was a Resistance redundancy that was activated."

Silence met his report. They had lost nearly twenty years of planning and training, according to the briefing on Project Genesis, in a single unplanned and unauthorised mission.

"And the other one?" Helen asked, "Eve?"

Fly met her gaze and didn't look away.

"Captured," he said, "no sign that she made it out. Also taken was a member of the previous Command, hence the redundancy and your activations," he finished, sadness evident in his voice.

No longer able to stand the silence in the room, Harvey asked a question.

"The Frontier? Why would they be there?" he said quizzically.

"Because," said Helen slowly, silencing the room with her recently acquired knowledge, "the Party is fighting an enemy on the Frontier, and that enemy is our friend. They are called The Nocturnals. Now," she said to Fly, "please bring us up to speed on everything else."

"I'm glad we started with The Frontier," Fly began, "because they've sent word that we are to do nothing until instructed."

———

Fly was annoyed. He was annoyed because any handover protocols should have been the main responsibility of Mouse, only he had gone and got himself captured, then subsequently rescued, such was his luck, and was now out of The Citadel doing who-knew-what, who-knew-where.

He was left in charge of the remnants of the Genesis project, and lacking the three with skills which could barely be replicated to any level of adequacy stuck in his throat and wouldn't budge. They could all fight, they could all tackle locks satisfactorily with the exception of himself, who had become something of a master at the task and all of them could fumble their way through a computer system. The weird ones, as he thought of them, Adam and Eve, who had been raised and trained separately from him and the others, possessed a lethality with weapons which they could not expect to match. Fly had personally proved that when they had fought the unique, and uniquely dangerous solider who had descended on them from an oversized drone and had knocked him insensible within seconds. Without Mouse trying to save him and ending up almost as broken as he was, and without Adam fighting the terrifying creature, Eve would not have had the opportunity to intervene and remove its head.

He had, with help, searched the Citadel computer system and pored over every report submitted but still found no trace of Eve. He had seen the irregular change in the outbound vehicles and correctly assumed that someone else had hacked the system to allow Mouse, Adam, Mark and the girl they had rescued, Georgina, to escape south. He also assumed that whoever that hacker was, they weren't Resistance, at least not the type of Resistance who lived in, or underneath, the tower blocks. They had watched the internal CCTV from the holding facility and watched the grainy images of Adam cutting down a platoon of soldiers single-handedly, but that footage suspiciously stopped recording shortly afterwards, confirming Fly's fear that the Party knew of their covert tap into the mainframe.

He had made an executive decision after that and declared that the system link was to be used unobtrusively, and that no changes could be made to alert the Party that they were still active. Better to let them think that they had captured or killed their enemy.

Now, their numbers halved and with a uselessly new Command in place, they had to try and patch together their operation to find another way to topple the generations-long reign of control without the consent of the people.

CHAPTER SIX

REGROUP AND REASSESS

"Good morning, Sirs," said the young female adjutant in a small voice as she hurriedly rose to her feet and smoothed down her tight uniform skirt. She had been detailed as the replacement for her predecessor for three reasons; namely her face, her youth and her figure.

Nathaniel waved an irritable acknowledgement as he strode past her and into his office. Stanley, following three paces behind, loitered wearing a wolfish smile which he thought made him look roguish.

Rebecca Howard did not think the smile aimed at her was at all roguish, and she barely stifled the urge to shudder from head to toe. Instead, she returned the smile as professionally as possible, hoping that her own said that she wasn't open to his obvious and predatory advances.

Stanley followed Nathaniel into the Chairman's office, not even breaking step as his eyes drank her in again when he leaned back to order coffee. She smoothed her skirt again and tried to keep the fear and disgust from her facial expression as she went to fetch their drinks.

Inside the office, both men removed their coats, both

cut like uniform jackets but neither bearing any badge of rank or other insignia. That alone dictated their level of power to their subordinates.

"She's fairly useless," Nathaniel told him, not caring whether his words carried through the open door, "but she looks better than most I've had sent here."

"Apart from the last one," Stanley said with evident sadness. Fearing that he might give away a little too much, he straightened and offered his opinion on her reassignment.

"Samaira," he began, then coughed and tried again, "Corporal Nadeem should never have been sent to the Frontier," he said.

"No, but the transfer was at her own request, evidently," Nathaniel answered, watching the younger man carefully.

"That's what I don't understand, Sir," Stanley continued fervently. "I think the terrorists must have faked those orders. I think…"

"Major," Nathaniel interrupted, his use of Stanley's recently acquired rank silencing the man as he intended it to, "if she didn't request the transfer, then why did she not send word to either of us to question it?"

Stanley said nothing. To protest any further would potentially open the floodgates and give the Chairman an indication that his relationship with the former adjutant corporal was anything but professional. In itself that wouldn't have been an issue, save for the fact that he knew Nathaniel had intentions in that particular direction. He swallowed down his next words, instead falling back on the unwelcome news of her demise. He had sent an immediate order to the commander of the Frontier, demanding that she about-face on arrival and be reassigned to The Citadel.

"Just dumb luck that her convoy was attacked," Stanley finished.

"Again," Nathaniel said with a sudden additional depth to his voice, "I don't believe in luck. No, something more sinister happened there other than *dumb luck.*"

The hint of steel in his words ended the conversation, leaving the two men regarding each other in silence until a weak knock at the door broke the deadlock.

"Come," Nathaniel snapped as he looked away.

Corporal Howard walked in bearing a tray and appearing with all her strength to make herself as small and unnoticeable as humanly possible. She felt the eyes of both men burning through her uniform as she set down the tray and fled with all the dignity she could muster.

The girl fleeing the room seemed to signify an agreed ceasefire between the two senior men, and both helped themselves to coffee from the pot in silence. Nathaniel's brain spun fast, as it always did, only this time he couldn't unwind the puzzle he faced. He sipped his coffee, deep in thought, and stared into nothingness as he worked through the sequence of events logically. He had done exactly this more times than he could count in the few weeks since the last terrorist attack and finding out in the aftermath that his adjutant, the first one he was actually pleased with, had been deployed to the Frontier during the chaos. Before he could even make direct contact with the commander, a disgraced Colonel who had killed a junior officer he had found in bed with his daughter and who had been reassigned quietly to prevent the spread of scandal, Nathaniel had been given the news that the transport going south had been attacked, with no survivors. He listed the elements of the array of facts which scratched at his logical mind as they simply did not make sense.

Why had the transport been travelling alone and unescorted?

Why had Nadeem requested the immediate transfer?

Had Stanley made advances to her that had forced her to take desperate measures to escape?

How had the prisoners disappeared without a trace, from right under their noses just as Nadeem had?

As much as he hated to think it, he could not get past the facts that this unusual activity had all taken place just when they had captured the terrorists and broken them.

The information forcibly taken from prisoners, at least the prisoners they still had who had not inexplicably escaped, had led them to assault residence block six and drag every man, woman and child from their homes until every piece of the block had been searched. The information they had been given by one man in the foolish hope that his life would be spared if he told them his secrets led them to the underground chambers. Evidence that people had been living there in secret, clearly for many years, right under their noses annoyed him even further. He had personally inspected those rooms and found that they had been stripped of anything useful. The only thing that hadn't been cleared away and was left either in the vain hope that the girl locked away below his headquarters would escape and make it back there, was a sword. A long sword, straight-bladed and sheathed in matt-black polished wood. A sword with a razor edge that had maimed and killed his soldiers. A sword that had ended a third of the Project Erebus resources in a matter of seconds.

Nathaniel suspected that it wasn't left there in the hope that she would return, but as a warning that they knew he had taken her.

The overwhelming stench of strong chemicals burned his nose, eyes and throat, forcing him to accept a respirator mask as he delved deeper. Access to other chambers had been prevented by collapses, the engineers called in to make the area safe assuring him that the tunnels under the city were long disused and could not possibly have been accessed from there.

He reserved his own judgement on that fact.

"Sir?" Stanley prompted, breaking his reverie.

"Major?" he responded, his eyebrows knitting in question. Stanley gave the slightest shake of his head, unwittingly coming dangerously close to sparking The Chairman's rage.

"I asked what you wanted to do next," he finished.

Nathaniel leaned back in his chair and regarded the bland ceiling for a few heartbeats before he spoke.

"We go slowly with the two prisoners in Special Projects," he said quietly, "and we burn down the residence block and relocate everyone elsewhere. Give Du Bois control of the holding areas," he added with a small smile.

———

Sergeant Major Owen Du Bois had been frustrated by his enforced bed rest, but he'd had no choice in the matter. For the first two weeks, walking had been an impossibility, and since then it had merely been a pure, all-consuming and fiery eruption of agony. He had regained consciousness in the aftermath of the raid on the holding facility and when the pain of his injury first hit his consciousness, he had bellowed like a wounded animal, screaming fit to wake the dead. A medical team, who had first seen his unmoving body and incorrectly assumed that he was dead, rushed to him as he convulsed and were forced to sedate and restrain him to prevent him hurting those trying to help.

When the extent of his injuries had been explained to

him by a shaking doctor who fidgeted constantly with the collar of his white lab coat, the man keeping his distance in evident fear, he had raged until they had sedated him again.

"The electrical burns were almost catastrophic," the man stuttered, "and the muscle spasms caused by the attack had caused crush injuries which couldn't be fully repaired with surgery…"

Du Bois fought against the wrist and ankle restraints holding him to the heavy hospital bed as the doctor continued his explanation that he was now left permanently damaged.

Damaged and very incomplete.

As soon as he could walk, he insisted that he be released from the hospital with strong painkillers. He reported for duty, relishing the task of terrorising the Citizens to make himself feel better for the partial loss of his manhood. Everywhere he went, he saw the occasional look of muted humour; the people smirking and averting their eyes made it clear to him that his injuries, and possibly the circumstances of his discovery, had become common knowledge outside of the medical unit.

He bit down the anger and humiliation he felt, instead channelling that rage into useful action against the people it was in his power to hurt.

———

Relocating everyone from Residence six was not as easy a task as the casually given orders made it sound. Over a thousand citizens had to be assessed and prioritised into categories of jobs which could easily be replaced and those which could not. The more important or short-staffed roles were allocated new residences in the other five blocks, running the risk of overcrowding the remaining towers. Those who were more disposable were sent west or north to bolster the mining and farming colonies.

All that administration took time. It split families. It caused unrest and minor revolt at times, each such outburst being rewarded with punishment or immediate execution for those who raised their hands to the Party soldiers.

To raise a hand against anyone wearing our uniform, Nathaniel's father had instructed him solemnly many years before, *is to raise a hand against you personally. It is to raise a hand against the Party, and that cannot be allowed to go unpunished or they will all refuse to know their place.*

As expected, the commanders of those remote bases, who had to suddenly find rations and work allocations for a hundred or so more citizens, contacted The Chairman's office with their legitimate concerns and respectful protestations. Each and every one of them was told to make it work and follow their orders, with the promise that a new residence block would be under construction in the immediate future, and that they could send back other citizens to fill the void left in The Citadel's industrial production sectors. It would mean a slight downturn in drone production and maintenance, as well as other military equipment, but the years of solid production had created enough of a stockpile that no shortages should be suffered. The additional food which the colonies would require would be rectified with a reduced amount delivered to The Citadel and diverted to where it was required.

All of these problems were simple, logical, cause and effect issues which Nathaniel grumbled could be solved by a child.

The enforced refugee status of block six Citizens lasted for almost two weeks until the daily convoys dwindled the numbers to zero. Losing fifteen percent of the Citizens populating the Citadel had some effect on the general feeling and production of the city, and the reduced foot traffic going to and from work allocations each day was noticeable.

Whether it was a trick of the shifted dynamic, or an actual increase in deployment, everyone noticed the squads of soldiers roaming the Citadel day and night just that little bit more.

CHAPTER SEVEN

THE KING AND HIS SECRETS

Adam followed Mark, still in quiet awe of his surroundings and the shock of being amongst people who bore such little resemblance to him and the people he had grown up with that they might as well have been from another planet. They were like children, or more like teenagers in size, but their features were of fully-grown adults, with the exception of their oversized eyes.

Behind him, Mouse kept turning to ask the small woman questions. Mark had called her Dren, which was unlike any name he had ever heard. He didn't know if it even was her name or whether it was a kind of title like the unpronounceable person they were now apparently going to see. After the first long corridor morphed into the rougher, lower type of tunnel like the ones he had first seen, Dren had taken the lead, forcing Mouse to stop nagging her for information.

He tugged at Mark's clothing, the action being more insistent after he had been told to shush twice. Mark eventually stopped and turned on him, hissing "What?", evidently annoyed.

"What's going on?" Adam hissed back, trying to convey more than the simple question really meant. He wanted to know who these strange people were. He wanted to know why they were on the Frontier. He wanted to know why they looked so different. He wanted to know everything and that was the exact reason that Mark refused to tell him anything.

He had always been like that, even when he was very young, and every answer led to three more questions so that it became never-ending.

Mark said nothing in response, merely turned away and carried on, forcing him to follow or else be left behind in the near-dark labyrinth, until they stopped at an unmarked door and the small, blonde woman from the Citadel joined their procession.

Dren, if that was her name, had stopped to watch the brief interaction. From within her hood Adam was sure that he could see her wide, elliptical eyes shining with amusement at him. Minutes later, after walking through probably half a mile of tunnels utterly devoid of any directional markers, twisting and turning in a seemingly illogical pattern, they arrived at another large chamber. This room, a hollowed-out dome with a flattened earth floor packed hard by feet over innumerable years, seemed older still than anything he had seen before.

Dren waved them back, then walked forwards and sank to one knee with her head bowed low. Above and ahead of her was a raised dais atop which sat a figure similar to her, only with a fierce grey beard flecked with irregular streaks of jet black. His hair was fully grey, and slicked back over his high forehead. He wore a thick robe like the others Adam had seen, only this one seemed to be made of dark fur. The chair he sat on was polished black, made of some material Adam had not encountered before and it seemed to glitter in the low light of the small fires burning on either side of him. In his right hand, its point resting on the ground, was a straight sword of a pattern Adam had never seen before. He could not see it clearly from that distance, but the weapon emanated a sense of great age; older than anything he had ever seen.

"Ow Myghtern," Dren said in an almost ceremonial voice which seemed louder than was possible from someone so small, *"komendya an erel."*

The man on the throne shifted, then stood to reveal that his true height was only marginally taller than when seated. He swung the blade up, reversing the grip with practised ease and rested the edge on the fur-covered shoulder of his robes. Stepping down from the raised platform, he stalked forwards until he stood over her. In a blur of movement, he switched the sword to his other hand and placed his right palm on the back of her bowed head, as his eyes found Adam in the gloom and seemed to fix him to the spot in paralysis.

"Thank you, Daughter," he said in accented English, "I think we can speak their tongue now?"

She rose, turning to see Adam's open-mouthed look at the revelations bombarding him at every turn.

"Please," she said as a slim hand emerged from her robes to gesture them forward, "come."

The four outsiders walked hesitantly forward until they were bathed in the same flickering glow in the centre of the chamber. A subtle hand gesture from Mark made Adam and Mouse follow his lead to sink to one knee and bow their heads hesitantly.

"Ow Arlodh," Mark said uncertainly, hoping that his pronunciation was at the very least understandable and did not translate into any kind of insult.

The King erupted in a belly laugh so genuine and loud that all three of them were startled.

"Very good," the King chuckled on with evident amusement and pleasure, gesturing them to get to their feet. Adam stood, locking eyes with the powerful, squat man as he rose. The King's neck continued to crane upwards as Adam rose to his full height and the amusement continued to flow freely from his wide smile as he laid eyes on the full extent of the alien giant before him. He kept his eyes on Adam but bent his head slightly and muttered something into Dren's ear which made them both laugh.

The sound struck Adam in the chest. The hissing, sibilant sound which reverberated around his head like an echo was as strange to him as the rest of his surroundings.

"You may call me that, but I speak your tongue so simply, *Lord* will suffice," he announced in his larger than expected voice, "come, first we have a feast."

———

The Nocturnals knew how to throw a party.

Adam had tried throughout the formal festivities to ask questions, and each time was either hushed by Mark, who kept a wary eye on their surroundings, ignored largely by Mouse, who was having an uncharacteristically immense amount of fun, or else deftly diverted by the Nocturnals themselves.

His mood was guarded at first, then dropped off into something bordering on sullen when he wasn't given the information he craved, but then melted away into a sense of enjoyment.

They sat around a long table, which seemed to have been carved into a flat surface from a single, massive tree.

The wood was so worn and stained that its surface was a dark slab of smoothness which had been adorned with platters of foods that Adam had never seen before. A robed figure, eyes and teeth flashing from the depths of the hood, asked what he preferred to drink and he answered with the only thing he had ever had.

"Water," he said hesitantly, before adding a hurried, "please."

The teeth had flashed again, making the young man feel that he was being the point of a joke he didn't understand, as the other similarly shrouded figures around him made their strange hissing noise of soft laughter. Instead of water, he was poured a cup of something slightly thicker, and far sweeter but with a hint of some strange sensation which made his body tingle. He liked the taste of it, relishing the difference from the harsh and inadequate rations he had spent his entire life surviving on. After his third cup, Mark gently placed a hand on his forearm from the seat next to him and conveyed with a silent facial expression that he should slow down. Adam nodded, but did not want to stop drinking the beautiful liquid. His retrospection as he stared into the bottom of his empty drinking vessel prompted a chuckle, a deep, rumbling sound, to come from the squat man sitting at the head of the long table nearby.

"We make a drink," he said, reading Adam's thoughts, "from the honey of bees," he said simply.

Adam thought for a moment and tried to emulate the formal respect he had heard in Mark's words.

"*It'sverygood,*" he said, stumbling the words into a single, wavering sound as though his lips were numbed from cold. He moved those numb lips around, stretching his mouth through a full range of movement in an attempt to unstick it from itself. The hissing laughter which then erupted louder again made him frown, not only because he didn't like being laughed at, but because he couldn't understand why he could not speak. Mark interjected and rose, bowing towards the King and muttering something in their language, before leaning down to Adam's ear.

"Come with me, boy," he said.

Adam, annoyed as he was at Mark talking to him like a child again, tried to stand and fell back against his carved wooden chair. He stood successfully on the second attempt, helped by Mark's strong grip on his upper arm, and found himself marched from the room where he was bundled along corridors to a small chamber. Mark threw closed the door behind them and turned to face Adam, concern replacing the look of anger that his ward had been expecting.

"Are you okay?" he asked, holding Adam's face in both hands and looking in his eyes.

"*I'mfine*," Adam slurred, then blinked twice with great effort and tried again, "I'm fine," he answered carefully.

"Good," Mark answered, turning to pour water into a cup from a jug on the side table next to them, "drink this."

Adam drank, enjoying the cold water washing down his gullet and the clear-headed sense it brought with it. He drained the cup and held it out for more. Mark poured, watching the young man closely.

"You've never drunk before, have you?" Mark said more as a statement than a question.

Adam's brow knitted again. *Drunk?* he thought, *I've always drunk, ever since I was a baby...* before it dawned on him that the sweet liquid in his cup was not like water and affected his mind and body in a way he had never experienced before.

"Come on," Mark told him as he pulled him to his feet, "let's get you to bed."

"No," Adam responded, shrugging out of the grip and standing unaided, if a little wobbly, "I said I'm fine. No more bee drink for me, though," he added with a smile.

"Good lad," Mark smiled back, jabbing him in the side of his abdomen again like he always did to annoy the boy.

When they regained their seats, Mouse was on his feet with his eyes cast down at his plate. He was regaling their hosts with a great exploit from the time they had used the *Crunch* to knock out a drone tower and escape, hence protecting their true target. He too had clearly enjoyed a few cups of the unusual drink, but that only seemed to remove the painful inhibitions he had when speaking to people who could see him.

The assembled faces sitting around the huge table all watched and listened intently, hanging on every word the awkward outsider said. As Adam entered the large chamber again, he saw their eyes shining out from under their shrouds and their small teeth showing from their parted lips as they smiled at the tale being told.

Mouse's exhibition allowed Adam and Mark to take their seats again without causing a disturbance. As he sat, he glanced to the head of the table where he saw the King and his daughter watching him surreptitiously. Neither looked away when he saw them, which made him feel uncomfortable.

Adam ate the food on his plate and drank the water which was brought after a subtle request to one of the figures flitting around the banquet filling cups from jugs. As he did, he felt his head clearing further after the unexpected effects of the drink. Mouse had finished his story and was now fielding questions from the hooded figures around him until the King clapped his hands together loudly and said something fast and guttural in his own language. As one, the shrouded shapes stood and melted away to leave the four outsiders alone with the King and Dren.

"Lord," said Mark, his voice coming out smaller than he had hoped, so he cleared his throat and began again, "Lord, please accept our thanks again for your hospitality and the refuge you have offered."

The King dismissed this with a small wave of his hand. In truth, sending the signal to the resources inside the Citadel had been done in such a hurry that it bore no small risk of discovery and even greater risk had been taken when his people had travelled above ground in daylight to fake the attack on the convoy to allow for their disappearance.

"And now you have questions?" Dren said, looking directly at Adam.

He hesitated, glancing at Mark, who kept his own face still and expressionless.

"Yes," Adam said simply, then opened his mouth to blurt out the first thing that came to his head before he was cut off.

"Come with me," she said, her accented English less clear than her father's, and stood to sweep away down the length of the table without waiting for him to follow.

Adam, not waiting for any permission, stood and walked after her, stopping at the exit only to offer an awkward and hurried bow in afterthought to the King, who smiled his acknowledgement.

———

Adam's eyes were accustomed to life spent underground, to the low light of a subterranean and nocturnal existence. Any other person, one more comfortable in daylight, would have struggled to follow the small, dark shape moving along the low tunnels but Adam knew how to tell black apart from the darkest greys. Dren was using the poor light to her advantage as she slipped ahead, always just vanishing from sight whenever Adam rounded a corner to see the edge of her heavy cloak flicker from his view. He stalked her, moving low and silently as though he were hunting Party soldiers from the dull, grey rooftops of The Citadel. He smiled. He realised he was enjoying the game that the small woman was obviously playing with him, guessing that she would be enjoying it too.

As he followed her, changing his pace to test his theory, he found that whatever speed he moved at, she was always just ahead and out of his reach. As he moved, he felt his skin reacting to a subtle change in the temperature of the air as it contracted, and the hairs on his arms stood up.

He rounded the next corner and was met with a new aroma; wet grass. He drank in the scent deeply, tasting every part of the new information which had not been available to him until this precise moment in his life. He stopped dead, seeing that she was facing him from the low archway of an entrance to another chamber. He crept forward until she held up a hand and pointed him inside. By the light of a single, rough candle, he saw a small pile set neatly on a chair. His shimmering black suit sat atop two long, wide-bladed knives.

The door shut quietly behind him, and he gratefully pulled the ill-fitting clothes from his body as he snatched up the suit and stepped into it. Fitting the knives into the elasticated folds behind his lower back, he re-emerged into the cool night air and followed his nose towards the exit to the tunnels which he sensed must be nearby.

He found it, the weak moonlight offering a different shade of black and a small silhouette barring the way.

Dren stepped close to him and held a single finger to his lips, simply saying a quiet, "Shhh."

Her skin felt smooth and cold against his warm face, and he found himself leaning into the touch and closing his eyes as she pulled away.

Stepping back and throwing off her heavy cloak, she revealed a petite body beneath, covered in the same shimmering, figure-hugging material as he now wore.

She lifted the hood of the suit up, leaving just the wide eyes visible as they reflected the moonlight back at him, then turned and slipped into the night.

CHAPTER EIGHT

AN ALTERNATIVE HISTORY

Eve had agreed a kind of non-hostility pact with her captors. She reasoned that she was being sensible, that seeming to comply would give her more access to information not to mention food and would make her eventual escape easier. She pretended to comply, willingly submitting to medical assessments and even allowing a woman wearing a white lab coat to pierce her skin with something she called a syringe and take her blood.

"What do you need it for?" she had asked in a small voice, figuring that it was better to act more like a child as this woman had spoken to her like one.

"It's just to check that you are good and healthy," replied the woman, who wore a smile that was as genuine as Eve's own mask. "We test it to make sure there aren't any nasty bugs in there or anything like that."

Eve nodded, racking the depths of her brains for the 'nasty things' she could have meant. "So, you put it back afterwards?" The woman smiled and laughed at her words, so Eve laughed too and pretended that she had made a joke instead of asking what she thought was a sensible question.

Cohen had told her of how the human race had always suffered some form of disease which threatened to wipe them out. It had been the same throughout history, apparently, and every time one disease was cured, or the people inoculated from its lethal effects, then another magically appeared, as though nature itself was trying to cure itself of their presence.

It had been things like smallpox, cholera, typhus, the plague; a vague sounding illness which seemed more of a general term than based on any kind of science. After that had come HIV, AIDS, cancer, Ebola, Zika, then came the wave of parasites which affected the brain function of those infected. Older diseases which people had thought eradicated made virulent reappearances thanks to the flood of refugees from countries with poor healthcare, infecting whole new generations. Then, after the last war, came an illness which killed millions before inexplicably disappearing to leave the survivors in a depopulated, war-ravaged world.

She played dumb to knowing anything of this, instead smiling at the woman as though she were proud of herself for being brave. The scientist left the room, and Eve's mask dropped back into a sullen contempt for the foolish bitch. She let her arm drop, ignoring the bright red spot of blood welling in the crook of her elbow and pulled down her sleeve as she hopped down from the bed without having to use her arms. She padded slowly around the small room, looking into the cabinets containing the medical equipment which had all been painstakingly locked in anticipation of her arrival in there. Whilst they made out that she was now an honoured guest of the Party, she had been kept away from anything which could be used as, or fashioned into, a weapon.

Her mind shot back to the first time they had shown her the sea of food and the feel of the steel in her hands when she picked up the small butter knife. She remembered feeling the weight of it, finding it to lean too heavily back to the fat handle and rendering it too unpredictable to throw with any guarantee of a successful kill. She had looked up to see both men watching her looking at the knife, and had put it down carefully with a smile, acting for all the world as though she were not assessing its potential for use in killing them, but just looking at something shiny. Since then, she had not been left alone anywhere that offered a chance of arming herself, until now.

Glancing back behind herself, she stopped pacing in front of a glass-fronted cabinet, seeing if she had time to break the glass for a shard to use as a blade, when the blinking red light in the corner of the ceiling caught her eye.

Always watching me, she thought with a cold fury that she managed to keep from showing on her face.

Just then the door hissed open again and the smiling woman came back in, having handed off the vial of her blood. The opportunity gone, Eve smiled back, and half skipped, half walked back to the examination couch.

"What now?" she asked in her most childlike voice, excitement projected on her face.

"Now," said the woman as she leaned down and patronised her, "it's time for some lessons."

"Lessons?" Eve answered, screwing up her nose in affected disappointment.

"Yes," exclaimed the woman as she talked down to Eve, making the girl glance at the vein in her neck where she would love to throw a short punch, "the Chairman himself is going to teach you some history. Won't that be nice?"

Eve smiled broadly but kept her mouth tightly shut. Inside she was snarling, and she didn't trust herself to keep those feelings buried.

"Come on now," said the woman as she straightened, "we don't want to keep the Boss waiting, do we?"

Eve walked out of the room with her, the old woman offering her hand to hold, and she swallowed down the urge to take the woman to the ground and snap her leathery, old neck with her thighs. Eve held the hand, trying not to shudder along the entire length of her spine, and allowed herself to be led to a room surrounded by glass and with a table inside. Within the room was just one man, the big man in charge, Nathaniel, now known to Eve as The Chairman of the Party and effectively the head of the snake she had been bred to kill. She smiled as she was deposited in the room, seeing the man turn to her and nod.

He didn't offer a broad, fake smile as so many others did, merely kept things simple and cordial, even if he too spoke to her as though she were still a child.

"Good morning," he said, gesturing her towards a seat at the table. She sat down, helping herself to a glass from the tray and pretending to struggle to lift the heavy jug to pour herself some water. Nathaniel made no offer to help her with the awkward weight, didn't treat her as a child like the others foolishly did, nor did he react when she spilled small puddles on the smooth tabletop.

"That woman said you were giving me lessons today," she said, fixing him with a direct look of expectation.

"Did she now?" he answered, his eyes flickering up at the now empty doorway as though he was annoyed that someone else saw fit to dictate his business. "Well, I suppose that's accurate."

He sat, pouring himself some water and picking up a tablet to tap at the screen. Eve looked around, trying to map the surroundings in her head, as this was a part of the underground facility that she had not visited before. As her eyes drank in the layout to memorise it, the glass suddenly frosted into a haze that she could not see through, and she looked back at Nathaniel, who was still tapping at the tablet, and she realised that he must have made the windows change colour. The lights then dimmed and the blank wall at the end of the long table flickered into life as he swept a finger up the tablet towards it.

"Okay," he said distractedly as he still tapped, "let's start with the early twenty-first century."

The two shimmering, black shapes flowed over the rolling ground like shadows until the smaller one stopped and lay down flat in a shallow depression.

"Our people are called *Tarosvannow*," she whispered. "In your tongue this means the Ghosts."

Adam said nothing, waiting, willing her to go on and shed some metaphorical light on his life.

"Before the Great War," she continued, "we stop the soldiers coming here and taking our people away. When the war begin we go underground, so planes do not see us and drop bombs. We live that way for many years, coming up to the world only to fight." Adam watched her as she spoke, seeing how her big eyes scanned the ground ahead like a huntress before she turned them back on him.

"We break roads, and we use our *teknegieth* to stop

them coming," she paused, frowning and looking down as she searched her brain for a translation, "we use the... sciences?"

"Technology?" Adam offered, seeing a fleeting flash of her white teeth as she smiled at him.

"Yes, this. They do not try for many years to hurt us, apart from the bombs, and eventually they stop trying to come further. My father says this is because they fight other people, easier people to kill, so they leave us alone. When they come back again, they have new weapons, but we do too. *Come.*" She hissed the final word before springing to her feet and bursting from cover in eerie silence. Adam scrambled up and followed, losing her momentarily until a hint of movement to his right tickled his peripheral vision. He followed, seeing her small shape in the moonlight drop into a hole. This one seemed man-made, with straight edges as though the ground had been cut, although it had overgrown and fallen down in places. She stalked along, low and silent, speaking back over her shoulder as she moved.

"They make these, called *trenches,* and try to make advance, but we hold them back. We hold them back since before my father's father and his father's father before. When my great grandfather was King, we go across the dark water and find others who fight the soldiers." With that startling revelation, she crouched and leapt up and out of the trench. Adam followed, scissoring his legs upwards and landing in a low crouch where his ears first detected her direction this time. He set off after her, his eyes wide as he tried not to focus on any of the harsh lights now visible in the far distance and lose his acquired night-sight. Focusing instead on the ground, he avoided the humps of tall, stiff grasses which threatened to trip him, until he caught up with her. She stopped behind a mound of moss-covered rock protruding at an angle from the boggy earth and rested her back against it. Adam was breathing hard with the effort of keeping pace with her, whereas she seemed not to notice the physical exertion at all.

"These others, like us but different, offered to help. We move all our people there, except our family, which rules here. We are like the tip of a knife?"

"The spearhead," Adam said, translating her words.

"If you say," she answered, sounding distant as her head poked around the edge of the stone to look ahead. "We are the warriors of our people, and for generations we mix with the people over the dark water so that we become like one people together.

"We have people come over the dark sea, and we send things back to them. We send soldier prisoners and their guns, and they send us food. This is only part of next war," she said ominously before rising to her feet effortlessly and sprinting off into the darkness again.

Adam followed, matching her pace, slower than that she had previously employed, as she scanned the dark ground ahead. Slipping down into another trench, this one better kept and seemingly newer than the last, she crept forwards before dropping to one knee and drawing two wickedly curved blades from the sheaths on her small thighs. Turning to look at him, he saw that flash of a toothy smile again before she was up and over the earth wall to disappear once more.

He followed and ran, stumbling to hit the ground once where he rolled back to his feet and tried to relocate her. He slowed his pace but could not see or hear her. Suddenly feeling the first hint of fear but not daring to call out her name, he dropped into the next trench.

And saw the reflection of moonlight in the black visor directly before him.

There was a second of incomprehension causing them both to freeze, then the soldier stiffened and began to raise the rifle in its hands. Adam reacted faster, turning his body sideways as he slapped down the barrel with his left hand as it rose, and striking upwards with his right hand hard into the wrist holding the pistol grip of the weapon.

As the gun fell away from the hands now unable to keep hold of it, Adam turned back to face the soldier and shot his left hand out to strike the soft part beneath helmet and body armour, as his right hand reached behind him for a blade. The curious, wet sound it made as the sharp point slipped in and out of the sinewy throat sounded impossibly loud in the darkness, making him hold on to the dying body as it slumped against him. Lowering it slowly to the ground, he heard a whisper from twenty paces away.

"Collins," it hissed desperately, "Collins, was that you?"

Adam said nothing, merely rested the now dead body of Collins on the wet dirt of the trench floor.

"Collins, for fuck's sake…" came the now more insistent call, "don't piss about!"

Rounding on the source of the call, he crept forwards until he could make out the distinctive sheen of the black visor switching wildly left and right in fear. The visor stopped as it pointed directly at him. Adam bunched the muscles of his legs, readying himself to leap forwards and end this next foe, but instead came gargling and ripping noises from ahead. Two bright flashes reflected the low light of the moon as Dren used the hooked knives to half sever the head of the soldier before he could reach him. Rising to her full, if diminutive, height over the twitching and gargling corpse like an animal defending its kill, she stalked slowly towards him, never taking her eyes off his own.

Leaning her face close to his and wearing a triumphant smile of wicked delight, she spoke softly.

"You are *tarosvan* now, Adam," she hissed intently, "you are ghost like me," and with that she pressed her lips to his hungrily before breaking away and springing out of the trench once more.

CHAPTER NINE

PERSPECTIVE

Eve sat back and blew her held breath upwards, sending the wisp of hair which had fallen into her eyes upwards and away. Her behaviour wasn't merely an act to satisfy her captors that she was learning their version of events but was genuine in shock at the destructive nature of her species.

Before the Party had nationalised all of the country's resources, taking unilateral control over both civilian and military as one entity, the outside influences on what had once been their homeland were overwhelming.

Some aspects of her own lessons, given whilst growing up under the tutelage of Cohen as she fidgeted impatiently in her boredom, were mirrored confusingly by Nathaniel's version of events.

The Party, or at least their initial incarnation as political leadership, had viewed the deluge of foreign nationals flooding onto their island as a grave threat to national security. They had taken steps, admittedly drastic ones, to make it safe to live there. They had fought against terrorism, and she had quailed at the images of bombings and the footage of what was marked on the screen as an 'active shooter', as one man laid senseless waste to hundreds of people in a crowded city street, before men and women in uniform arrived to shoot him dead at massive cost to human life. She was upset at the carnage she witnessed, which surprised her, and that empathetic response opened the door for Nathaniel to keep going with her full attention. She asked questions often, ignoring the noises of annoyance and discontent coming from the man who was clearly not accustomed to being interrupted.

"Why did he do that?" she asked in a flat monotone as her eyes stayed fixed on the screen in front of her.

"Who?" Nathaniel responded, unsure which piece of information she was questioning, as her mind seemed to hold on to facts until she had assimilated them, meaning that she could be asking about the active shooter footage or about something he had moved past minutes before.

"The man with the gun," she said, pointing at the screen even though the image had moved on.

"Religious ideology," Nathaniel said disdainfully, "or a political agenda, or more likely that someone with a religious or political purpose had twisted his mind and taken advantage of him. They did that; made innocents fight their war by proxy and made the vulnerable people appear as terrorists," he finished, keeping his eyes clearly on the girl as he conveyed his message without words. She met his gaze and understood his unspoken sentiment loud and clear.

Just like they did to you, his eyes said, *you are the innocent used by the terrorists.*

"But regardless," he went on, snapping both of them out of their silent moment, "the country wasn't equipped to deal with this new type of war. We had fought it in other countries; insurgency, or guerrilla warfare where the armies didn't know who their enemy was, but we hadn't faced it on our own soil. We had a civilian police force back then, like the soldiers who patrol the Citadel for everyone's safety, and only a few of those carried guns. When facing people with knives and guns who were fully prepared to die during the acts they committed, the country was brought to its knees as every day saw two, three, four new attacks. That footage," he told her, tapping the tablet and bringing the still frame of it back to life on the big screen, "happened in what used to be the capital city. It's destroyed now."

"Where is it?" Eve interrupted, seeing his face twitch as he controlled the urge to snap at her. He seemed to think about answering, before responding simply with, "south east. About four hours by convoy. Now, after that…"

"Have you been there?" she interrupted, clearly not letting the subject go. Nathaniel held his breath before sighing and answering.

"Yes. A long time ago. But everything there is gone. Worthless. That's why we built the Citadel, as a new capital because the old one wasn't worth repairing."

"So, the terrorists," she asked, changing the subject as her mouth fell in line with her illogical thought patterns, "what did they want?"

She watched as Nathaniel had to reboot quickly and come up with an answer. She was intentionally hopping between subjects, asking questions out of logical sequence and returning to things she pretended not to have understood. She was doing this to solidify her cover, her projected illusion that she was younger than she appeared, but also because she enjoyed seeing the man in charge of everything force himself to be patient. She could tell that he wanted to lose his temper at times, to throw down the tablet and rage at her for not paying attention, and she wanted to keep prodding that animal to see when it would bite.

"Who knows?" Nathaniel said after controlling himself, "I believe that they just wanted the government to fall, which is eventually what happened after about a year. The crime rate grew unfathomably, and…"

"Crime rate?" she interrupted again, leaning forward on the desk.

"People stealing from each other. Hurting each other," he explained patiently, "and the police couldn't keep order, so the military was brought in. They kept the country safe they still do today if you think about it and the Party took everything under its control to make sure that the people had everything they needed." Eve's quizzical look could have been interpreted as anything, even something unrelated to what he was currently saying, but he believed that he was beginning to understand the chaotic way her mind worked, so he hazarded a guess at what it meant.

"There used to be companies, private corporations, in charge of things like fuel and power. They controlled transport and food rations for their own profit." Seeing her eyebrows rise and her mouth open, he moved on quickly to prevent her next interruption. "People used to have jobs in return for something called money. They used this money to buy residences, and food, as well as other things. The Party stopped all of that by taking the companies under their control and making sure that everyone got food and shelter."

Eve sat back, seemingly deep in thought.

So they took everything, she mused internally, *gave a little bit out so that everyone had a little, and kept everything else for themselves?*

"Okay," she said, accepting his version of events when

she saw it as power seizures by military force, "then there was a war?"

Nathaniel's eyebrows lowered.

"Yes, how did you know that?" he asked her casually. She knew when he was interested in her answers, as he couldn't help but keep his eyes away from hers, in case she saw the intensity behind them. Cohen had called that a 'tell' and had said that hers was when she fidgeted and glanced away to her left. Cohen had always known when she was lying, so she had fought down those involuntary signs until she could lie to her face and maintain eye contact.

"Someone said so," she said in a bored tone, "can't remember really."

Her blatantly vague answer annoyed him, as she intended it to, and despite what he believed, he could not hide that from showing slightly on his face.

"Yes," he said stiffly, "there was a war between other countries, which dragged in almost everyone else on the planet…"

"But not us?" Eve said, half in question and half betraying that she knew a version of events which contained more than a little fact.

"Not us," Nathaniel confirmed. "Actually, we were too busy trying to keep peace on the streets and fight the daily terrorist attacks. Our police force was gone, our military was totally committed to protecting our island. We had a navy keeping ships away from our coastline, our army was patrolling every city and town, and we had enough to worry about without deciding which side to take. We no longer had the infrastructure to invade another country, so we kept our heads down and stayed cut off from the world."

"Are we still cut off?" she asked innocently.

Nathaniel paused before responding. "Yes, by choice. We don't need the problems of others infecting our island again."

Eve said nothing, waiting for him to raise the next subject in his chronological version of history. Nathaniel composed himself, tapped at his handheld screen once more to raise the next subject.

"The Civil War," he said solemnly, waiting for her concentration to catch up with the subject change, "happened when the other countries which make up our Republic did not want to nationalise with us. We obviously couldn't allow these other countries to be a risk to us, so there was, inevitably, a war," he explained slowly, leaving out the facts that the Party needed the resources in and under those countries to flourish. War had been an inevitability as soon as nationalisation had been declared and the refusals of Wales, Ireland and Scotland to willingly submit to this.

"We were attacked by Wales and Scotland over land and we defended ourselves," he went on.

Not the way I heard it, she thought to herself as she kept her face neutral and interested.

"And after that we were forced to bomb Ireland," he said, seeing her face and giving a brief explanation of what he meant by bombing.

"So," he said in a tone which indicated that he was wrapping up to the conclusion of his propaganda, "the Party took control when everything looked lost, and they saved everyone so that they can enjoy a life of safety today."

Eve smiled thinly, hoping that he wanted that response as she found him hard to read in general. Inside, she thought, *he really believes this.*

———

Dren and Adam sat on the rough ground with their backs to the earth, their chests rising and falling fast as they sucked in the air after a long, lung-bursting sprint over rough ground in the still air of the pre-dawn. The hint of light on the horizon indicated that they had stayed too long, had played in the dark charnel-house playground to the point where they had been reckless.

But they had both enjoyed it. They were drunk on it. They tore through four sections of the Frontier, dropping in and out of the darkness like vengeful, furious shadows to cut and butcher the terrified soldiers. Both had lost count of the number they had killed, and both were now satis-fied, their thirst for death and retribution finally slaked.

Dren had seen the glow of light and called him to her, running fast for a tunnel entrance that she seemed to navi-gate to by some supernatural ability. He followed, using his superior height and long legs to match her tireless, powerful energy until she finally switched direction to lead them both below ground. They had strayed out over a mile into enemy territory and slipped through the lines back and forth, attacking unaware soldiers in positions they thought relatively safe. Working their way down the trenches like that had consumed all the hours of darkness they had left, leaving them disappointed to have to return below ground.

She chuckled as though reading his thoughts and turned her head towards him.

"I would like to see the sun," she said wistfully, "but it is not to be. We must wear dark…" she mimed glasses or goggles with her tired hands in place of trying to search her exhausted brain for the right word, which in turn

Adam was too tired to offer, "…our eyes. They only work in the dark."

Adam accepted this information silently, feeling his breathing begin to slow after the effect of their desperate dash over the rough terrain was beginning to fade away. He had learned so much about her that night, not from what she said but from how she moved; how she killed with a grace and a beauty the likes of which he had never seen before.

He had seen something like it, in Eve, but that thought sobered his elation and lowered his mood.

"Do you know what my name means?" she asked him suddenly, breaking the grip of his gathering dark mood.

"No," he relied simply after a pause of thought, "Princess? Is it like a title?"

She hissed her strange laugh again. "No, it means Thorn in your tongue. Like the *thorn in your side?*"

Adam had heard the saying used, and he felt it an inadequate metaphor for the unreal woman beside him.

"But you *are* a Princess?" he questioned, making her laugh some more.

"What is this word?" she asked him, "I don't know what it means."

"Your father is the King," Adam explained logically, "so you are a Princess."

"King is the word in your tongue," she said, "in ours it means more like 'leader'. When my father is too old to be *Myghtern,* then we will have a problem that our people have never had before. My father has no sons, and I am his first and only child. Some believe that I can be the *Myghternes*, but others do not."

"How old are you?" he asked her impulsively, making her move to regard his face with curiosity.

"I have seen twenty-two winters," she answered finally,

smiling at him with her face close to his, "and your next question is what? Do I have a favourite colour?" she teased, making him frown.

"No, my next question was…" he trailed off as his courage escaped him.

Dren's face grew more serious as she regarded him closely. Brushing back the errant strands of hair from her face she leaned close and kissed him again. She lingered there for a long time, just as their hands moved to each other's bodies, before pulling away.

"Was that your question?" she asked playfully.

"It was one of them, *Myghternes*," he answered, before kissing her again.

CHAPTER TEN

BEYOND THE SCOPE

Acting Captain Jasmin Blake was enjoying the last of the days off on her shift rotation with a pre-breakfast run. She had worked the two long days, followed by the two night-duties, and had rotated onto her two days of leisure. During these two days she was free to do as she pleased, as long as whatever she chose was within the confines of the sealed compound.

She had been running outside and lapping the interior of the perimeter fence, regardless of the weather, since the day after she had arrived. She was under no illusion that one of her greatest personal weapons was how she looked and keeping her body weaponised took more exercise than anyone could have expected.

She had obtained permission to run outside first, which had been readily given, and she enjoyed the looks on the faces of the soldiers guarding the fence line as she ran past in small shorts and a sleeveless top, returning them a sketch of a salute as she went. Her gym gear bore no rank, but word had soon spread about the enticing young officer newly posted to their station.

She arrived back at the main entrance, chest heaving and a film of sweat already beginning to dry on her skin. She nodded greetings to people she passed, exchanging a few words here and there as she pretended not to notice people trying to make out the parts of her that they couldn't see. She rounded one corner and half collided with the adjutant Major, who was reading from a sheaf of papers as he walked.

"Sir," she said as she knelt to retrieve the paperwork, "my apologies."

"My fault, Blake," the Major said as he tried not to look down the sweaty cleavage of her top and failing utterly, "I, er, I wasn't looking where I was going,"

The Major, Paul Bentley, was a kindly man who exuded an air of fatherly pride or disappointment, depending on the reasons he had for speaking to the soldiers and officers under his command. Removing his glasses and rubbing the very top of his nose he successfully averted his guilty eyes as she stood and offered him back the pages.

"It's this, you see," he said as he held out the very top sheet for her inspection, "got the Colonel in a bit of a fluster if I'm honest and now we're an entire platoon down after the additional escort to The Citadel."

Blake looked at the brief report, taken from that morning's drone coverage. It detailed an anomaly of debris on the shoreline eighteen kilometres to their north east. Nothing more, nothing less.

"The thing is," Major Bentley went on judging that she had had sufficient time to take in the information, "that I'll have to recall the off-duty troops to check this *anomaly* and their commander is rather against the idea. They're already working an additional rotation to cover the detached platoon..." he trailed off again, a subtle, unspoken plea for assistance evident in his expectant smile. Blake smiled back, broadly like she was pleased for any opportunity to be useful and turned her body to walk alongside the Major with a hand on his shoulder.

"Major," she said in her velvet voice, "why don't you let me see if there are any volunteers in the canteen, and let me get back to you to see if we can help?" She turned her best conspiratorial smile on him, melting him like soft snow on a fire, "Will a squad of eight suffice, do you think?"

Major Bentley did think that sounded sufficient, not that he understood the precise number she suggested, and thanked her profusely through his reddening face.

"Don't thank me yet, Sir," she said, smiling at him again, "I might not get any volunteers!"

She stood before him, sweat-glistened pale brown skin shimmering beneath the most beautiful face he had ever seen.

My dear girl, he thought to himself, *you could ask for volunteers to assault The Citadel itself and men would climb over each other to get to your side.*

Jasmin Blake put on her game face as she walked into the canteen. It was a little early for breakfast but seeing that food was one of the main events for those soldiers and officers not on duty, the room was already filling up in anticipation of the day's offerings. She scanned the room, her eyes resting on young Toby Baxter with other junior officers crowded around him as the unlikely centre of popularity. Rolling her shoulders and faking it every step of the way, she cleared her throat and pulled a chair out from under a long table.

The chair made an awful noise as it dragged backwards, gaining the premature attention of almost everyone in the room. She judged whether to stand on the chair or not, hesitating for a brief moment before she stepped up and cleared her throat again, this time theatrically.

"As you know," she began, "we're currently short staffed." Nobody responded, as they waited for the reason she was standing on a chair wearing a small top and shorts, "I need volunteers to undertake a scouting mission to the coast under my command." At the mention of 'volunteers' and 'my command' she fancied that she could already see a half-dozen young men beaming at the prospect.

"But only those who are not rostered for duty tonight or tomorrow morning can come. We don't want to cause Major Bentley any more worry than he rightly needs…" She trailed away to allow the chuckles to subside. "I need seven volunteers, all up to date on weapon qualifications, ready to go in an hour." She paused, scanning the room and wondering if she had just embarrassed herself. Deciding to add some propaganda to her short speech, she raised her right hand to salute the room.

"For the Party!" she declared loudly, seeing everyone present snap to attention and return the salute as they chorused her words back to her. She stepped down, and almost landed on the feet of Second Lieutenant Baxter.

"Toby," she said in mild reproof, "if I get killed, then who is going to run our team?"

The look of abject horror on his face made her throw her long hair back and laugh. He soon caught up with the joke and chuckled along with her. The crowd around them tightened, and she could hear quiet shouts of her name from would-be volunteers. Turning, she saw far more than twenty men and women jostling for position.

"Oh," she said to herself with a frown, "Toby, dear?" Baxter looked at her like a puppy expecting food. "Have you got a pen and paper to hand?"

Baxter produced a notebook and pen, an eager look of childish delight on his face.

"Lovely, would you be a darling and take names and the rest? Two sergeants or corporals and the rest can be whoever," she asked with a smile.

Baxter suddenly became the eager young officer she knew he was and put on his big boy voice to call for order. Blake took a few steps back and watched as close to twenty people mobbed the young man. She listened to the names and ranks as they tried to get to Baxter before others, and mentally picked her team as she went.

She wanted people she hadn't had the opportunity to interact with as yet. She wanted to speak to people who she would never get to work with ordinarily; people who could be converted to her cause by the short mission.

In the end, she had to relent and allow Baxter to come as she couldn't bear to see his disappointment. Her original plan to take just two fire teams was drowned out by the sheer number of volunteers. She selected three fire teams of four, each led by a sergeant and comprised a corporal and two privates. Better to stick with convention as an excuse to pick who she wanted to come along. The only exception to this was a senior Lieutenant from one of the troop battalions, who had been granted two days leave after a nine-day stretch of twelve-hour guard shifts.

"Oakley," he said, introducing himself with an outstretched hand.

"Blake," she responded, before dazzling him with a smile and offering her first name.

"Andy," he said, mirroring her personal touch.

"I suspect, Andy," she said in a low tone which dripped with conspiracy, "that you technically outrank me…"

Oakley smiled back. "Technically, *Captain*, I don't," he said with a smile. "If you'd pulled this stunt last week I would have, but not now. I'm happy to be one of your grunts today, if you'll have me?"

Blake regarded him subtly. He was taller than her by an inch, but his chest seemed like two solid plates of meat under his black shirt, and the power in his shoulders was evident. Clearly, she thought, Lieutenant Oakley liked to play with weights. His face was rough, with a short beard that doubtless would be regarded as being outside of regulations in The Citadel, and his easy manner made him instantly attractive to her.

"Fine," she relented, "but at least lead a fire team for me?"

Oakley agreed, leading one team of four along with the two sergeants who made the final cut. One, a ludicrously tall and spare man who had to spend his entire life unable to find uniform to fit, and the other was a short, blonde woman with her hair tied back severely and a resting face of pure malice that actually turned out to disguise an easy mannered woman who was quick to laugh.

"Okay," she said aloud after reading out the names of the three fire teams she intended to take, "armoury in…" she checked her watch for some unknown reason, as though seeing what the time was then would change how long she needed to shower and get dressed in combat gear, "…forty minutes. Thank you."

Trying to ignore the sounds of disappointment from the unlucky crowd members, she saw her selected team be granted access to the front of the food line as the others shuffled their brave volunteers forward. She snapped out of her trance as she watched men and women throwing hastily constructed sandwiches quickly into their mouths and rounded on Baxter with a winning smile.

"Toby, would you be a dear and give our personnel list to Major Bentley?" she asked.

Baxter straightened up, as though having a reason to report to a Major was the best part of his life to date and saluted her before running off to his assigned task. She watched him go, hearing a snigger behind her. Turning, she saw that Oakley was still standing there.

"What's so funny?" she asked.

"Nothing," Oakley laughed in an obvious lie, "…okay, maybe Baxter being in love with you isn't at all funny," he offered with a disarming smile.

"He's a sweet boy," she said dismissively as she walked away, turning once to fire a smile of wicked delight back at Oakley.

Showered and dressed in combat gear minus her helmet and visor, Jasmin Blake jogged to the armoury to arrive with a minute left before her allocated forty.

"Squad, atteeeen*shun*!" bawled the female sergeant who laid eyes on her first. She nodded her thanks and walked in confidently.

Taking a pistol, loading it and slotting it into the holster on her right thigh, then checking the action of an assault rifle with practised ease and fitting it to the magnetic holder on the back of her body armour, she turned to face her volunteer crew. Baxter, looking like a boy playing dress-up, handed her a slip of paper. It bore their frequency and callsign, which she knew was her responsibility to give out before a mission.

The main problem, she now realised, with her impetuous plan, was that she had never commanded a mission. She wasn't even a trained officer, let alone an experienced acting Captain, and she had no right at all leading troops anywhere.

She also had no right to have tampered with the Citadel mainframe, to have changed her identity and allow terrorists to escape, but she had. She put on her serious face and stepped on top of an ammunition crate to scan her eyes over her volunteer squad.

Her serious face cracked as she smiled and announced, "That's better. I can see you all now!" The squad chuckled and she turned to Baxter.

"Stand them at ease, Lieutenant," she asked softly.

"Squad," Baxter called out as he drew out the word with more authority than Blake knew he possessed, "stand at, *ease.*" He paused a heartbeat for the assembly to relax their body positions from attention before ordering, "Stand easy," and watched as their collective shoulders relaxed again.

Blake called out the frequency of their squad net and also for command at the base, watching as the members of her three fire teams keyed them into the control panels on their right forearms.

"Our callsign is Foxtrot-Three-Three," she announced before folding the piece of paper into a pouch on her assault suit. The combat gear they wore in the north differed from the usual patrol uniform seen in The Citadel, in that it was more geared towards the harsher climate with its lower temperatures and propensity towards sudden, unpleasant weather fronts. It was a vestigial tradition, she knew, harking back from the days when their posting was first a forward operating base for the war against the Scottish. Despite it supposedly now being an easy duty, it still bore some feeling of being a frontier outpost.

"Right," she declared with a smile, "eighteen Ks on foot then. Let's go, shall we?"

"Squad, atteen*shun!*" bawled Baxter, ruining his small authority with a squeak in his voice. "To your duties, dismissed," he said in a slightly quieter voice, covering his embarrassment.

The female sergeant, whose name tape she saw now read 'WILLIAMS', led her fire team under Oakley's command on point, with Blake and Baxter behind, followed by Oakley's team and the curiously tall sergeant leading his team of four at the rear. She had learned from talking with the troops as they walked on a heading as the crow flies towards their destination, that the sergeant's men called him Tiny. The simple irony of the nickname made her laugh raucously before she remembered her station and composed herself. Tiny, or Willis as he was actually called, clearly knew his trade. At all times, at least one of his men had their eyes pointing backwards to cover their rear. They advanced in a long, loose line, following the bearing dictated by Baxter, who constantly checked the ruggedized tablet he had taken with them.

"How much further, Lieutenant?" she asked after an hour, prompting Baxter to flick two fingers across the face of the tablet and do some quick calculations in his head before answering.

"We've covered six kilometres," he said, "I'd estimate two to three hours at this pace."

"Shame they couldn't have sent us somewhere with a road," she said with a smile, getting one in return.

All around them were the remnants of a world long dead. The passage of time and neglect had returned the landscape to a natural state, only now the grass-covered humps had once been buildings fallen down in disrepair. Everywhere Jasmin looked, the unseen echoes of the past seemed to haunt her just out of sight and sound. She shrugged off the feeling of being small in a vast landscape and turned to her hastily assembled unit.

"Okay, let's take a break," she announced, "Lieutenant Oakley?" she said expectantly.

Oakley did not respond, merely turned to two of his men and pointed them to the nearest piece of high ground wordlessly. The two men scampered away to maintain a vigil over the squad as they shrugged off their small packs. Blake watched in satisfaction as they all went about their business without the need for her to be constantly giving orders, and marvelled that leadership was basically just making the decisions and looking confident. She sat on a moss-covered rock delicately and opened a bottle of water as Oakley and Baxter joined her.

"A little longer," she said in between sips of water, "and we'll get the wasp up," she declared.

The WASP, or Wilderness Assault Squad Protection drone, was a small, armed drone which ran on replaceable battery packs of which each member of every fire team carried one. The batteries lasted an hour in good weather, far less in practice when the winds picked up and it had to exert more energy to stay on course. It was ruggedized for use in the north after being used on the southern Frontier as a prototype, but as every single unit deployed was lost, they were withdrawn and repurposed years before. The name was apt, as the drone had a sting in the tail in the form of a single-fire, high-calibre rifle, controllable via the tablet it was slaved to, and the ability to drop smokescreen devices. In reality, the smoke was caused by a very volatile substance burning and releasing the cloud of vapour which would allow the squad to exfiltrate under relative cover, but the heat of the burning substance in itself was a weapon. Only their training didn't permit them to use it as a weapon because it was apparently inhumane. But they had been told, if they dropped their smoke device and it happened to land on an enemy, then they weren't directly using it against personnel...

Blake allowed the team five minutes to take on fluids and rest before packing her bottle of water away and shrugging her pack back on. Turning, she saw that everyone had followed her lead and was climbing to their feet to put their gear back on. Oakley had waved his two men back and she saw them jogging down the slope to re-join them.

"Okay," she said over the noise of the growing wind, "twelve K to go, we'll do thirty minutes at fast pace and stop to deploy the wasp. Are we ready?" a chorus of manly noises responded to her light challenge and they set off.

Blake took point, jogging carefully over the rough ground, being careful over every footfall whilst simultaneously keeping her eyes on the terrain ahead. She pushed them hard, glancing behind to see that none of them faltered and clearly, they all took their fitness seriously as their own responsibility. She found that, with non-combat roles and higher ranks, personal fitness was usually avoided unless it was a passion of the individual. For the lower ranks, daily physical training was as natural as waking or eating, but some had let themselves go, in her opinion.

None of those people were in her squad of volunteers, and all seemed to be enjoying the exercise in the harsh countryside.

Reaching an area of higher ground, she called into their squad radio net for a halt and for Baxter to join her at the head of the loose column. He jogged up, his boyish face glowing pink from the exertion, and brought up the map on his tablet for her to view.

"Seven K left?" she asked him, checking her reckoning against a second opinion.

"Just under, I think. Two hours from here unless we keep on fast-pacing for a bit longer?" he responded.

Blake's eyes scanned the horizon ahead as she thought, then answered him, "No, regular patrol march from here, go tactical from two Ks out with the wasp up from four." She turned to Oakley, who had joined them and evidently overheard her assessment. "Agreed?" she asked him, trying to disguise the fact that she was making her tactical decisions based on having read many reports, and mixed with a good deal of bluffing and common sense.

Oakley said nothing, merely nodded his approval before asking Baxter a question.

"How many hours of sunlight left, Toby?" he said in the tone of a big brother, even though he was likely only three or four years the boy's senior. Baxter tapped at his tablet, bringing up another screen beside the window showing their map.

"Six hours," he responded, "give or take, depending on if we get hit by a weather front heading in from the sea," he finished ominously.

"Plenty of time. There in two hours, check out this debris, and back before dark," Blake said with a confident smile. She rested them for ten minutes; long enough for them to regain their breath but not long enough for their muscles to cramp from the sudden cessation of steady exercise.

She rotated the fire teams so that Oakley led in front of her, with Williams at the tail and Tiny's team just behind her.

Within the hour she halted them again, asking a lance-corporal to come forward as he was the designated wasp driver. He took Blake's battery out of kindness, or more likely admiration, and the small, squat drone fired up into life as its twin rotors began to spin.

"Syncing now," said the lance-corporal eagerly as he watched the loading bar on the drone's tablet inch from left to right before it completed with a satisfactory pinging noise.

As the angular craft rose upwards, the sound it emitted soon disappeared into the wind which had risen significantly since they had left base fourteen kilometres previously.

They resumed their march, stopping again as Baxter checked their route and held up a finger and thumb to Blake.

Two kilometres out.

Blake turned to the squad, eyed them all, and pulled on her helmet to obscure her face behind the black visor. Seeing the electronics spin up into life and give her multiple readouts on the head-up display inside the visor, she pressed the transmit button on her radio which was tuned to their squad net.

"Foxtrot-three-three Actual, squad check," she said in clipped professional tones.

"Three-three Alpha," came Oakley's voice.

"Bravo," said Willis.

"Charlie," Baxter responded.

"Wasp, all clear," said the lance-corporal who operated their armed eye in the sky.

Satisfied that they were all in sync on the net, she unfastened the rifle from the magnetic plate on her back, readied it, and nodded to Oakley, now *Alpha* as they were tactical, and he took his team to lead the way.

Although most of the north was open ground, the areas near the coast where the shallow water naturally lay had once attracted population centres to grow outwards through commerce. These areas now offered channels of high ground where old buildings had fallen down and had been reclaimed by nature. These channels offered perfect ambush positions should any enemy still exist out there, but the Party had been nothing if not thorough in training its soldiers.

Squad by squad, they advanced towards their target at a slower rate as they performed a three-squad leapfrog manoeuvre, where one team moved forwards as the other two maintained cover with guns ready. In this scenario, the lance-corporal driving their wasp moved with the unit commander and her second in command, who acted as communications and technical support. They attached themselves to fire teams as they moved, never straying independently, as they bounded their way onwards.

The squad net, which everyone was tuned to with the exception of Baxter and Blake, who had both the squad and the command channels tuned in simultaneously, sounded intermittently with clipped voices. Each fire team leader called their phonetic sub-callsign as they moved, making an almost hypnotic repetition until the routine was broken by Oakley.

"Halting. Target location in sight. Actual, copy?"

Blake waited, forgetting her position until Baxter gave her a nudge.

"Captain," he said through his visor and not transmitted over the radio, "did you copy?"

Cursing herself internally for forgetting that she was actually in charge of the unit, she responded, "Actual, copied. Hold position."

With that, she rose and ran towards the lead team with Baxter and the lance-corporal following her.

Dropping to lie flat on her belly, Blake inched forward to the crest of a low rise which offered a view down to the sandy beach below. It struck her hard at that point that she had never seen the ocean before, had never laid eyes on the edge of her island. In that moment, she temporarily forgot where she was, who she was pretending to be, and just allowed herself a moment to drink it in.

Until the lance-corporal to her left swore loudly.

"Report," she snapped at the man squinting at the tablet showing the live feed from the wasp.

"Captain," he said uncertainly, 'I'm getting some kind of interference... I'm... oh, fuck it!"

"Lance-corporal?" she enquired icily.

"Ma'am," he said, not covering his annoyance, "the wasp is down. Last image I have is this," he said as he turned the tablet to face her.

The anomaly, the unidentified debris, was two small boats run ashore beside one another.

"Sniper?" she called into the squad net, hearing a rough acknowledgment as a woman ran low towards her position from Bravo team.

"Captain?" the private asked when she had dropped to the ground beside Blake.

"Horizon," she said back as she twisted the dial of her own scope to enhance the view as much as possible and scanned the ground ahead, "tell me what you can see," she ordered.

Agonising seconds passed as Jasmin felt the rifle barrel of the bigger gun move millimetres at a time. Millimetres at their end was tens of metres at a mile out, which is about as far as Blake reckoned the weather would allow.

Those agonising seconds ended abruptly with a gasp from the sniper.

"What?" Blake snapped at her, her patience snapping before an answer came as she took the rifle off the younger woman and trained her own eye to the scope. The same seconds ticked by until her own throat emitted a gasp similar to her sniper. She steadied the reticule on the shape, willing the focus to give her a clearer view, until a low cloud passed by between her and her target.

Far out to sea, and very alien to the Republic of Britain, lay a ship.

CHAPTER ELEVEN

WRITTEN BY THE VICTORS

"So, it was the Scottish who started the war?" Eve asked, this time unintentionally annoying Nathaniel, who was suspecting that his patience was beginning to wear thin.

He had been forced to eat his breakfast as he walked that morning, because he'd been delayed leaving his residence after spilling hot coffee down his shirt and having to change.

The catalogue of errors did not begin or end there. He'd intended to rise early and exercise, but he made a mistake setting the usual alarm and missed the opportunity to get to the gym before it filled up with everyone else. He had been intercepted before he reached his office, no doubt due to the delay caused by the scalding liquid he'd decided to pour on himself, and had found himself diverting to the large briefing room with an array of senior officers who had been summoned early by the night shift Major in charge of the Citadel control room.

What did Stanley call it, he mused, *dumb luck?*

That early morning briefing, the kind of briefing he would be prepared for, would not normally bother him because he would ordinarily have been awake for almost two hours, would have exercised and eaten breakfast and would by that point be enjoying his second cup of coffee and not a delayed first. The reason for the briefing darkened his mood further still, as he learned that a large-scale attack on four different sections of the Frontier had been carried out during the night.

Casualty reports indicated that close to thirty soldiers were killed at their posts, with no sign of the enemy having been engaged. The report went on to state that every dead soldier still had a fully charged weapon, meaning that, quite literally, none of them had got a shot off, and it ended with the curious news that there were no injuries.

Of course there are no bloody injuries, you insufferable fool, thought Nathaniel as he sipped at his too-hot coffee, *the enemy on the Frontier do not leave survivors.*

The Colonel commanding the Frontier finished his report with an interesting request of the Chairman, asking that he send more troops and make contact at his convenience to discuss plans he had drawn up for a counter-offensive.

Nathaniel had absorbed the information, given orders, and left to take the secure elevator down to the depths of The Citadel itself, to the sub-basement housing Special Projects. He had gone via the nearest canteen and grabbed food to eat as he walked, making him even more annoyed as he had to try on three occasions to wipe the grease from his thumb before the light by the biometric security reader blinked green. Then he rode the vertical journey downwards to keep his appointment with their young guest.

"In a way, yes," Nathaniel answered Eve patiently, "because the Party tried to nationalise everything for the good of the people, but they decided to turn terrorist and rebel."

"And they lost?" she asked, temporarily silencing the Chairman.

"Well," he said hesitantly, unsure if he had understood her question correctly, "yes. Obviously."

"Buuut," she responded as she drew out the word in thought, her eyes focused on a point on the wall where nothing existed, "if *they* had won, wouldn't *you* be the terrorists instead?"

Nathaniel was taken aback by her simplistic logic, because he simply couldn't deny its accuracy.

"I suppose we would have been, logically," he accepted, "but that was a very long time ago," he added hurriedly as he tried to divert her attention away from a subject which he might not be able to defend logically. "Now, when Ireland launched attacks at us, we responded with an aerial bombardment," he paused, seeing her mouth open to interrupt him and speaking quickly to cut her off, "which is a lot of bombing runs from aircraft, that bombar…"

"Like the drones?" she asked, deflating the air from his lungs and chipping a significant chunk from his willpower with her perfect timing.

"No," he said into his hands which now held his face to cover the exasperated expression, "bigger. Much bigger. They were all abandoned years ago because we ran out of the fuel they needed to work, and no," he said quickly to interrupt her forming interruption, "there isn't any more because it has to be refined from another substance called oil, which needs to be pumped out from very deep underground." He dropped his hands and looked directly at her. "There's no more oil and we couldn't refine it even if we had it, so don't ask."

"Why did they start wars with us, though?" she asked, switching the subject again and making Nathaniel pause before answering her tiredly.

"I believe the tipping point," he said quietly, "was the dissolution of the Monarchy." He paused to wait for the inevitable interrupting questions, waiting longer than usual and imagining her brain working hard to catch up. But when she didn't ask, he looked at her, her face staring back at his own, expressionless and neutral.

"Ironic," she said, "didn't you say that Scotland and Ireland fought against us once to get rid of our Kings and Queens?"

He said nothing but looked at his watch and decided that the three hours he had spent bringing their prisoner up to speed with recent history had felt significantly longer, and he rose to pull on his jacket and search for caffeine.

"Can I learn more tomorrow?" she asked him, making him pause midway through putting on the jacket.

"I might not be able to," he told her with what surprised him as being genuine regret, despite how intentionally annoying he knew she was trying to be, "but I will try."

A soldier, albeit one dressed in simple clothing and a white lab coat, was waiting outside the door to escort Eve back to her cell. She could tell instantly what he was, as none of the scientists held themselves so squarely and upright. None moved in such a way that they betrayed their strength and poise, and none had obvious protrusions in the small of their back where a weapon was so obviously hidden.

That was her next objective, she decided, to not have to be put back in a hole in the ground, no matter how fancy it was, every time they tried to brainwash her. She said nothing on the return journey, merely peered at things she saw like they were interesting, instead of overtly looking at door locks, signs and notices, as well as mentally mapping every inch of the floor she was held on. She smiled and waved as the floor of her cell descended to carry her back down, finding that clean sheets had been added as well as a platter of snacks for her enjoyment. She smiled again. For the purpose of the cameras no doubt hidden in the cell, she aimed that smile at the food. For herself, secretly deep inside, she smiled as she recalled Nathaniel fighting with himself for hours to control his temper. She guessed that by now he had raged at the first Party member to have annoyed him even the slightest bit and unleashed all the morning of pent-up anger as she had persistently, incessantly interrupted him. She knew now that the man had better self-control than just about anyone she had ever met, and although her intentional behaviour had clearly got under his skin, he had held himself together.

Taking a snack and reclining on her cot, she thought over the history lesson she had been given. Her concentration had not been absolute in many parts, mainly as she was waiting for the perfect opportunity to change the subject or to make Nathaniel go back or forward to pictures he had shown her, but she reflected then on what she had learned.

Much of the early parts were the same as Cohen had taught her, but the differences in perspective intrigued her. How the same factual incident could be explained from another point of view made her mind race with the endless possible outcomes for right and wrong. How simply arguing the case *for* instead of *against*, using precisely the same information but starting with a different opening view, could produce such drastically different theoretical outcomes.

For the first time in her life, she began to question whether she was on the side of good, or the side of evil.

———

Adam had spent the night with Dren. More accurately, he had spent the entire morning with her as their night had been spent running riot through the enemy lines, cutting down soldiers at will. Neither of them knew, but before they washed the blood from their clothing and bodies, before their weapons had been cleaned and oiled, a message had already been sent to The Citadel from the commander of the Frontier himself, claiming that an attack of 'at least half-battalion strength' signified an esca-lation of hostilities and was likely a pre-cursor to outright invasion.

They would both have laughed at the dramatic tone of the message, even more so at the idea that two people carrying nothing but sharpened metal could cause suffi-cient panic as to be mistaken for a hundred soldiers. By the time each section had understood that they were under attack and had activated the painfully bright floodlights in front of their sections, their shadowy assaulters had moved on to wreak silent havoc in the next unit.

When they regained the sanctuary of the tunnel complex, Adam helped Dren pull the entrance cover back into place and obscure any sign that there was an open doorway to an underground world. The temperature and the air pressure changed as they descended, weaving their way through the twists and turns of the illogical labyrinth until they reached a chamber where Dren peeled off her blood-drenched suit and stepped under a stream of hot water running from the pipe in the low ceiling. Adam watched in awe of her openness, how unashamed she was of her body, and felt empowered to be like her. She beck-oned him towards the water, watching as he too peeled off his black outfit to reveal crusted, darkening blood all over his hands and body, then laughed as he ruined the moment by being a head too tall for the chamber, and making a dull thud echo around the room when he hit his head again.

Lying in her comfortable bed, Adam played with strands of her dark hair as they drifted in between sleep and talking. Only hunger eventually drove them to seek anything outside of her chamber, and because he could hardly walk around naked or wear the blood-encrusted suit, she left him in her bed as she ventured out for provisions. As she slipped back through the entrance and secured the door, she shrugged out of the cloak she wore to reveal that she had put nothing else on when she'd left. She set down a tray of food; meats, bread and fruit, and took long, thirsty pulls from a bottle which she handed to him wordlessly.

Climbing back into the bed, she smiled at him, making him marvel at her neat features and mesmerising eyes.

"I'm glad I like you, Adam," she said seriously, "it would have been…" her eyes flickered away as she sought the right word, "…pain? No. Awkward?"

Adam chuckled at her, brushing a strand of hair away from her forehead in the dim light, "Awkward why?" he asked.

She looked at him seriously, as though she couldn't be certain if he were joking with her or not.

"Awkward, because I would not like to be promised to a man if I did not like him," she explained.

Adam's face tightened, thinning his lips as he spoke his next words tensely.

"Promised to me?" he asked, trying to keep the anger from his voice and not totally succeeding.

"Yes," she responded quietly, all mirth gone, "you did not know this?" she asked as she gathered up the sheets to cover herself, suddenly very self-conscious.

Adam put a hand on her bare shoulder, sensing her recoil slightly at his touch, before he tipped her chin to his. He was happy, but at the same time he was livid and the only thing keeping him from storming through the tunnels to find Mark it could only have been Mark and ask him why he was trading him like livestock, was her beauty.

"Dren," he said solemnly, "this was what I wanted. I wanted you. If people have made a deal using us, then we still get what we wanted anyway, don't we?"

She smiled at him, relieved that he did not reject her as an offering he did not want. She was upset that her father had made this deal with the city people, and that was the reason for his polite imprisonment when they had first arrived as she argued day and night with her King about being used as a bargaining tool; like the men and women who traded animals in the land over the dark sea and in Ireland. She was upset to have lost the power of choice, as much choice as she had anyway, being the only daughter of the King, but on meeting him she had been happy. Happy despite him being a head and shoulders taller than her, but now she saw that he was unhappy at the knowledge that he had been traded as she had been.

"So what does your side get in exchange for you?" he asked aloud as he lay back on the bed with his arm around her. She laughed, that hissing, chuckling noise going through his head as though he was imagining instead of hearing it.

"Not me, *Tarosvan*," she said with amusement, "it is *you* they traded to *my* people."

———

As Helen had little to do, given their enforced state of inactivity, she decided that to be useful in any way was to be knowledgeable. She reviewed everything she knew of their history, using the censored, official version taken from the Citadel archives and studied in tandem with Fly as they spent their long evenings underground. The other members of the new command were present, although not usually all at once for there were no decisions to make, as they too sought some useful purpose.

They had been activated, bringing with that activation all of the excitement and trepidation that the feeling of being at war brought, and now they had been side-lined; ordered by their superiors to do nothing.

Until that order had been passed on to them, only Helen had even known about any outside influence carefully pulling the strings of their revolution.

The discussion that news had invoked was carried on at length, loudly, as she and Fly took turns explaining that the Resistance had always, for as long as their records existed, cooperated with the people on the other side of the Frontier. Their technology, their intelligence, their planned attacks, had all trickled down from their effective masters in the south west. Even their recent and biggest success in many years, the covert information tap giving them access to the Citadel mainframe, was orchestrated and catered for by the Nocturnals.

Fly knew that they must have their own version of the tap, because how else would they know so much about the daily activities of their enemy? How else would they have obtained real-time information and communicated with assets inside the Citadel to get the others out safely?

Further questions scratched at his brain, like whether they could make changes and have their link remain undetected, as their own interference had clearly drawn too much attention. He wondered who and where they were, what their intentions were, whether they knew if this cold, monotonous and permanent hunger he called a life would ever change. These questions, he was sure, would have been answered for Mouse, who he imagined even now enjoying warmth and food and knowledge, and he promised himself that he would make sure Mouse felt guilty about leaving them behind.

Helen continued to be thorough, cross-referencing the Party's facts against their own passed-down history. She, like Eve held in the bowels of the Citadel, found that many differences were down to a perception of whether she chose to believe that the Party was an evil overlord intent on the subjugation and control of the lowly citizens, or a necessity that took power and used it to stabilise their bleeding island and cauterise the wounds.

Deciding that she still disliked the propaganda which preached racial superiority, she chose to keep believing that the power belonged with the majority; with the people.

CHAPTER TWELVE

A MATTER OF DESTINY

Adam, now dressed in fresh clothes which Dren had ordered to be brought to her chambers, stormed through the tunnels, intent on an inevitable confrontation with Mark. He stormed, that is, as best someone can when they are forced to make themselves almost a head shorter than they are.

Making awkward and uncomfortable, yet determined progress, he finally found his mentor in a chamber with Mouse. The two were standing close to one another, discussing something in hushed tones that he could not hear, and both glanced up as he approached. Both recognised the look on his face, and both straightened in readiness for what they assumed would be a verbal onslaught.

Adam surprised them both by swinging his right fist and connecting with Mark's jaw, knocking him backwards onto a low table and sending Mouse tumbling away as the two men collided. Adam, clearly not believing that the punch had made his point sufficiently, threw himself forward to grab the clothing of Mark's chest and haul him back to his feet to face him.

"You *sold* me?" he snarled, releasing the grip of his right hand and drawing it back to ball it into a fist again. Mark saw the blow coming, as could anyone watching, and decided that he didn't want to be punched again. He ducked his head under Adam's left hand and stood up tall as he turned his upper body inwards, hence forcing the left arm straight and removing the target of his face from the reach of Adam's right hand. Breaking away from the weakened grip with a one-handed shove to his left shoulder, Mark took two paces backwards and spoke.

"The first one was free," he said in warning, "but you won't get another."

Adam, now upright and facing the man who had raised him, wore a look of fury and indignation which the older man knew wouldn't calm down any time soon. As he moved forward, Mark dodged the first two attacks, then blocked the third, until the fourth and fifth landed hard on his body. The first blow to connect, a savage low kick which struck him on the outer thigh just above his left knee, forced an involuntary drop in his body weight and left him vulnerable to the elbow which hit him with a glancing blow just above his right ear. The blow was glancing because he was already pushing forwards and upwards from his good leg to drive his shoulder into the abdomen of his angry attacker. He continued the momentum of the initial hit and pushed him, extending his body forwards and upwards, as he used both hands to pick up Adam's legs in the process.

The boy was faster, more flexible, and infinitely more fired up than the man who had taught him how to fight, but despite the obvious advantages of youth there was no escaping the fact that, unarmed at any rate, Adam was outweighed and way behind in terms of dirty tricks.

Mark spun on his right foot as Adam reached the peak

of his upward journey, pirouetting both of them through a hundred and fifty degrees, before contracting his stomach muscles violently to smash Adam's back down onto the table he had been leaning on before the attack. The table gave way, leaving Mark standing over Adam, who lay in the ruins of broken wood as he fought for the breath which had been driven from his chest by the unexpected impact. His eyes locked onto Mark's, fire still burning behind them to indicate that though he might be temporarily defeated, he was not yet finished.

"Don't," Mark threatened him, pointing a finger at his chest, "if you just calm dow…"

His words were cut off as Adam coiled himself up and leapt to his feet, flicking his legs up, then forward, forcing Mark to retreat and defend against the next flurry of blows. He dodged and deflected just as he had before, only now he wasn't merely training a boy or allowing him to vent his anger and frustration about the slither of truth he had learned.

Now he was fighting.

Adam had long since gained sufficient size and ability to be considered an equal or, in many ways due to his youth, superior to Mark in many aspects. So he felt no remorse, nor did he feel abusive or a bully when he traded blows with him now. Each of them fought with an intensity and a realism as they both strived to end the fight quickly by preventing the other from fighting on. The fastest way either of them knew to do that was by killing the other but seeing as that was never an option for them, they simply made it their business to try and bludgeon the other into unconsciousness as quickly as possible.

Adam drove a knee into Mark's ribcage, forcing him down where he could deliver a top-down elbow strike to his skull. That second blow failed to connect as Adam's body unwillingly doubled over from the brutal uppercut which Mark had launched between his legs. The blow did not connect fully but being spared the blinding nausea was no real reward as the pain still threatened to bring tears to his eyes. Staggering backwards, angrier than he had been before at the cheap shot, he started to use his superior reach and sent kick after kick at Mark, who was struggling to regain his feet under the onslaught.

Mouse, standing back out of reach so that he didn't get caught up in the melee, sighed aloud in disappointment. He was hardly rushing to tell Adam that he too knew about the source of their disagreement, but he didn't think that letting the two of them tear each other apart was going to solve anything.

Reaching under the edge of his jacket into the small of his back, he pulled the electrified baton from the sheath he had fashioned for it and hesitated before lazily flicking his wrist and extending the single section into three. He hoped that the sudden hum of the power coursing through it would cut through their fog of combat and encourage both men to stop fighting, but he was prepared to use it if necessary.

It was clear from the fact that neither noticed or responded to his unspoken threat that he would have to use it, and he took solace in the time he had spent adapting the weapon to suit his own tastes. His main addition, on top of a better battery, was a capacitor which allowed him to regulate the strength of the voltage that sought a fleshy conductor to run through. Dialling it down to a sedate thirty-five thousand, Mouse lightly touched the tip of the baton to Mark's right arm.

The two had closed on each other again and were now grappling in a race to secure an unbreakable hold on the other's neck and force an end to their bout. The thirty-five thousand volts, uncaring and indiscriminate, coursed through Mark's body and into Adam's, making both men convulse momentarily. The fighting stopped immediately as both went rigid in tonic pain, and when Mouse removed the weapon and stepped smartly back, they collapsed into a roiling, swearing, cursing and gasping pile of limbs. Both of them trained their eyes on Mouse. Having solved the problem of them fighting each other, he then faced the unwelcome prospect of having united them in their hatred against him.

Maintaining his distance and making a show of dialling the capacitor up to its maximum of seventy thousand, he allowed the fizzing hum of the current to fill the room and focus their attention.

Adam and Mark, both breathing heavily, glanced at one another before Adam climbed to his feet and shot a last, menacing look at Mouse before turning and offering his hand to pull Mark to his feet. Mark look at the hand, then up at Adam, and raised his own hand to accept being hauled up. As they straightened themselves, the cease-fire obvious to all, Mouse deactivated the baton and stowed it away behind his back again.

Mark, still breathing hard, turned to Adam.

"I didn't sell you," he said simply, "but I did know that you were promised to the Nocturnals as a kind of payment," he finished, letting the cold facts hang heavy in the air.

"It was part of a deal made before you were even born," Mouse said, earning a wide-eyed look of horror from Adam, who was only just beginning to understand how much he didn't know about pretty much everything in the world, "by the previous Command in exchange for our best male fighter to strengthen the bloodline. The King wanted a strong mate for his daughter…" he trailed off on seeing the look in Adam's eyes grow darker still.

Adam looked back to Mark, his eyes questioning why he had kept so many secrets from him his entire life. His eyes asked if his mother had known what was planned for him all along, and if he had ever even been going to tell him about the Nocturnals, let alone that he was destined to be given to them for breeding. Only dumb luck had dictated that the curious woman he was promised to had captured his adoration and interest from the moment he first saw her, and that he found her alluring and not frightening or repulsive.

"It's not the first time," Mark said quietly, earning a dangerously questioning look from Adam, "the genetics of the Nocturnals have changed over the last few hundred years, because they mixed their bloodlines with the *Dearmad* after crossing the sea and wa…"

"Whoa, wait," said Adam lifting a hand and taking a step backwards, "the *what?*"

"The *Dearmad*," Mouse said simply. "It means *'the forgotten'* or something similar, I think."

Adam just stared at him, switched his glance back to Mark, then back to Mouse again.

"Would it have killed either of you," he said in a voice of icy acceptance, "to have told me *any* of this in the last ten years?"

Mouse and Mark exchanged looks. Mouse's expression said that he agreed with Adam, whereas Mark's resigned look told the younger man not to judge him.

"I'm sorry," Mouse said simply before moving on. "Anyway, the Dearmad and the Nocturnals have made some alterations to themselves, but their breeding pool needs an injection of outside influence every generation. You're it," he finished bluntly with an unapologetic shrug.

"Great," Adam said, shooting one final malevolent look at Mark for keeping him in the dark about so many things, "so what now? I stay here?"

"No, actually," Mark responded as he dabbed the fingertips of his right hand to his nose and pulled them away to check for blood, "we're all going to the forgotten land, apparently."

Adam went to lean back against the table, only realising at the last moment that it was flat on the ground in pieces. The growing feeling of soreness which was beginning to creep into his consciousness told him that the brief fight with Mark was going to cost him more dearly than spending half the night running through enemy lines had.

Just how much bigger, he thought to himself, *is the world going to get?*

CHAPTER THIRTEEN

CONTACT

"Control, Foxtrot-Three-Three Actual, urgent, over," Acting Captain Jasmin Blake hissed into the inside of her visor where the microphone picked up her voice to transmit it via the command net to their base eighteen kilometres of rough ground away to their south west.

No answer came.

"Control, this is Foxtrot-Three-Three," she said more insistently as the lance-corporal beside her slapped the side of the drone control tablet twice, "urgent message, are you receiving, over?"

Still no answer came.

"Atmospherics," came Oakley's voice in her ear, as he too was tuned to both the squad and the command nets like Blake and Baxter were. "We have high ground between us and the base."

Blake's black, reflective visor turned towards Oakley's, both seeing a distorted view of their own featureless heads looking back at them, and she nodded once to accept his assessment before turning to the junior officer.

"Baxter, take your team back and keep trying," she

ordered as she turned again to pick up the sniper's weapon to use the enhanced optic to view the strange boats beached ahead of them down the long, gentle slope of sand and shale. "Hopefully, you can bridge the gap and still keep us on the squad net."

Baxter acknowledged her orders. "The message?" Toby Baxter asked her, his voice muffled by the helmet as he did not transmit his words over the net. Blake thought for a few seconds, then responded to him.

"Tell them we have encountered evidence of non-Party activity. Tell them there is a boat at sea and two landing craft on the shore. Ask for a drone squadron and rein-forcements."

Baxter nodded, then turned to his duties. Within half a minute, Blake and Oakley watched the young officer jogging into the distance with the four members of his fire team leapfrogging each other in simple fire and manoeuvre drills.

"Perimeter?" Oakley said aloud to her, only just audible enough to be heard and without looking at her. The junior man, a lieutenant who, before her brevet field promotion to Captain, had outranked her. His experience outranked her too, being a troop leader whose only field craft was precisely what they were doing at that moment. He was helping her but making it obvious that he was not after taking her command away. She didn't thank him, as to acknowledge the prompt would put the emphasis on him to keep making her decisions; instead she acted as though the reminder was unheard, as he'd intended.

"Bravo?" she said into the squad net.

"Send," came Willis' response immediately.

"Split your team, three hundred metres north and south," she instructed, getting an instant affirmation and glanced towards the tall man to see him organising his team with hand signals.

She looked at Oakley again and said, "two soldiers to our rear, please."

Oakley nodded and gave hand signals to the two closest to him to run at a crouch in the direction that Baxter's team had taken. Now, with Willis moving further up the coastline to give them fair warning of anything coming from there, and the remaining two of his squad doing the same further down the coast, she looked at the remaining soldiers she had at her disposal. She saw Oakley and his remaining soldier to accompany her and the sniper from Bravo, as well as the lance-corporal who was still trying in vain to make the drone tablet work by the practical application of mild violence.

Three whole fire teams and three commanders, fifteen armed troops, had left their base and were now spread too thinly to protect themselves, should the unexpected visitors have hostile intentions. She worried that she should have sent just two soldiers back with Baxter instead of an entire team, but that decision was made and there was little point in recalling troops now. Putting her eye to the scope again, she tried to make out any detail of the ship she could, marvelling at it with equal measures of fear and excitement. It sat heavily in the water, not appearing to rise or fall with the ocean's undulating movement.

She thought for a long moment, before making a decision.

"Lieutenant?" she asked off the radio.

"Captain?" Oakley responded smoothly from beside her as he too squinted through his rifle's optic to make out any detail on the beached boats.

"Would you be so kind as to conduct a recce of the landing craft? You'll have overwatch from here," she said as she passed the big rifle back to the redundant sniper, and saw how her face lit up as though she were being handed back her only child, "and drone coverage as soon as the lance-corporal has bullied his control module back to life," she finished as she took up her own rifle to scan the beach.

"Roger," Oakley said as he nodded to his remaining fire team member before moving out. Blake called on the squad net to warn the others that Alpha was moving forward as a pair, then watched as they moved forwards down the gentle slope, staying low and moving carefully as Oakley covered the soldier moving, then moved as the soldier covered him in turn. Blake caught her breath as she saw them sprint in turn over the long distances between areas of cover, until they disappeared in a patch of lower ground.

"Actual, Alpha," came Oakley's voice. Just as she began to react and answer him, the command channel stuttered in and out of life, giving her intermittent bursts of static.

"Actual, Alpha," Oakley's said again in the same calm, measured tone.

"Wait one," Blake said, her own voice clipped in contrast.

"Charlie from Three-Three, Actual," she called into the squad net to try and raise Baxter. He came back straight away, now telling her to stand by. Her annoyance was covered by another soldier speaking on the radio.

"On to Command now," he said simply.

Satisfied that at least something was going right, Blake returned her attention to the Lieutenant she could no longer see.

"Alpha, go ahead," she called smoothly.

"Eyes on the drone," he said quietly, "still active and on a search pattern," he reported, meaning that the drone was flying up and down in a grid pattern as part of a pre-programmed setting. Blake looked to the lance-corporal, who hit his tablet again and shrugged at her.

"Received," she said into the radio, "still no data link our end."

"Roger, moving to target," he replied, just as the lance-corporal made a triumphant noise beside her. Turning, she saw that the screen had returned to life and was now showing fast-moving sand and rock as the drone's camera was pointed at the ground. The triumphant noise had now become a growl of frustration as the lance-corporal jabbed his fingers at the controls to try and resume manual operation of the drone.

"Bloody thing…" he muttered, just as the image on the screen resolved into a wavering shot of Lieutenant Oakley looking at her, confusion evident in his body language even though she couldn't see his face.

"Actual, the wasp is here an…" he said, before a gasp from the operator cut through her hearing. He had gasped, she could see, because the weapons system of the wasp had activated, indicated by a red border flashing on the control tablet.

"Take cover! Get out of the…" she shrieked into the radio, instinctively knowing that something was horribly wrong, but her words were snatched away by a single gunshot heard in stereo, both from the low ground ahead and the speaker built into the tablet.

———

Adam had sullenly complained that he didn't want to travel, especially not to somewhere ominously called the Forgotten Land.

"Why?" Mark asked him, expecting a childish response and getting one.

"Because it sounds shit," Adam spat back.

Only the influence of Dren rescued his attitude, and Mark laughed out loud at him as the boy seemingly became a man as soon as she entered the room. He stood taller, held himself more confidently, and spoke with an authority that mere moments before had escaped him entirely in his puerile, argumentative state.

Now, suddenly, when Dren had explained how much she was anticipating the trip, Adam too said how he was looking forward to meeting new people and discussing how to take the fight to the Party. Dren's eyes met Mark's, or more accurately her bright eyes burned into him from within the hood of her cloak and conveyed a question which Mark answered simply with a very subtle shake of his head.

Adam noticed this interaction and shot a warning glance at Mark, knowing that neither of them had forgiven the other for their brief but brutal fight, yet Dren interjected and asked Adam to go with her. He followed her, keeping his eyes lingering in Mark's direction until he joined his shorter companion in the tunnel outside. It was darker there, allowing her to fold back the hood and not need to protect her highly light-sensitive eyes.

"You must not blame Mark," she chided him, "he told you what he felt was best for you to know," she went on gently, betraying the fact that she had spoken with Mark about their fight.

"He told me nothing," Adam snapped back, earning a backwards glance from her as they walked, which he took as a warning to change his tone, "he didn't even tell me your people existed, let alone that I was already sold to you…" he finished lamely, regressing visibly as he spoke.

"Stop with the same... *krodvolhas,*" she snapped as she turned on him, her sudden annoyance flaring brightly in the confined tunnel. He didn't know what the word meant, but he got the general message. Dren clearly didn't think that she had made her point sufficiently and stepped close to stand on tiptoes and look him closely in the face. Her elliptical eyes seemed to glow brighter as she spoke angrily.

"I am more man than you, and I am a woman," she said with a derogatory sneer, "you want the truth?" she asked rhetorically, silencing him with a sudden, "*Shh,*" as he opened his mouth to answer.

"The truth is that we all work for others," she went on, laying the truth out for him in such brutal simplicity that his mouth stayed open. "You thought you were special? Well you are not. You work for your masters. Your masters work for us just as I work for the *Myghtern*, my father, and he works for the *Dearmad*. Who the *Dearmad* answer to is not my place to say, and I would suggest that you do not ask them when we go there," she finished on a crescendo of angry words as her eyes stayed locked onto his.

Adam swallowed, maintaining eye contact with her more from fear than anything else. He may have been promised to her, may have shared a mutual infatuation, but the small woman before him was a killer. She was a warrior *Myghternes*. He said nothing and stayed still as she calmed and seemed to withdraw slightly, and she drew up the hood of her cloak. That action seemed to signify a retreat, that she had finished showing her steel and was now the supplicant once more as she turned and walked into an antechamber of the main hall where he had first seen the king.

"You will be prepared here," she told him before leaving abruptly, pausing only to reach a small hand out of the folds of her cloak and brush her fingers against his.

"Prepared for what...?" he asked in a small voice to her retreating back.

"For our marriage ceremony," she shot back over her shoulder.

————

Lieutenant Andrew Oakley watched with uncomprehending annoyance as the wasp moved closer to him than it was supposed to. He had seen it going up and down the beach, combing the sand in a quadrant pattern on some pre-programmed course where it travelled so many metres before turning a right angle and moving again. Only now it made straight for him, the buffeting of the wind making it fight to stay level as it seemed to look directly at him. He heard Jasmin's sweet voice in his ear, only this time it wasn't sweet and he heard the panic in her screamed words just before the small rifled barrel just under the shiny sensor and camera array on the nose of the drone blossomed in a sudden yellowy-white plume of explosion.

He didn't see the high-velocity round leave the end of the barrel at a little over eight hundred and fifty metres per second, as the distance between him and the hovering threat wasn't sufficient to even register that the drone's on-board sniper system had activated before the bullet hit him.

Four hundred metres behind him, up the slope and out of view in the dead ground, Jasmin Blake screamed as she watched the scene from a first-person perspective. She couldn't see the second member of fire team Alpha break cover and line up their own rifle on the errant drone. If she had kept her eyes trained on the screen of the useless tablet which was supposed to be controlling it, she would have known their fate; instead she put her eye to the scope of her rifle as she broke cover and stood tall, sky-lining herself on the ridge above the beach as she sought the drone in her crosshairs.

"No shot, no shot," she said to herself as she concentrated hard, searching for a target. Other things snatched at her concentration and threatened to draw her focus away. She heard screaming over the squad net as the other soldier deployed with Oakley received a second bullet from the drone at savagely close range, smashing through his visor and taking his right eye with it along with a section of skull. That screaming ended abruptly, even before the echoing report of the single round faded away. She heard the lance-corporal barking into the squad net as he reported the loss of control over the wasp, which was now attacking them. She heard Baxter's voice clearly now, the weather which had previously obstructed their communication with their base now gone, as he called in the second-hand details of the attack on their team.

"Got it," she heard from the ground near her feet from the female sniper, her tone as cool as ice given her role, briefly before her large rifle cracked a single, echoingly loud report which was answered with a distant smashing in reply.

"Drone down," the lance-corporal reported to the sniper, confirming her kill.

CHAPTER FOURTEEN

THE FARCE

Adam stood, blessedly to his full height in one of the few chambers that could accommodate him, in a semi-trance as the attending warriors prepared him for the upcoming ritual.

The time frame between finding out that he had been subject to some form of arranged marriage and actually going through with the ceremony had been brutally short. He was adorned with a dark cloak similar to Dren's, only much longer, and he stood awkwardly still as his hair was wetted and arranged. A thin singlet of unrefined metal, rough and hand-crafted, was rested on his thick hair making him wonder if he were being made into a member of Nocturnal royalty and dismissing the whiff of vanity immediately.

"This is for *semlans*," Dren had told him, "for how it looks to others? It is for three reasons; one is that the *Dearmad* will not speak to outsiders."

So, he was going through this for the sake of appearances. A show for others. A way to legitimise his standing with this other race whose existence he'd been unaware of.

"And the other reasons?' he had asked her.

She smiled before responding, "One other reason is to silence those who whisper in secret about change. Those who do not think that a *Myghternes* will be strong enough to lead, so the strong bloodline will make them quiet again..." She paused, thinking, or at least thinking of the right words to say what she meant, "... and also because my father thinks I will have a son from you before he is too old to rule, and the legacy can pass down to him," she finished, evidently annoyed.

Everyone answers to someone else, he thought in frustration. *We thought we were special, but we are just puppets of someone else and they are just puppets to another isolated people. How much does the Party really know about what is happening underground?*

When his attendees decided that the fall of the cloak was right and covered his body and the simple black cloth beneath, this time thankfully extending the full length of his legs, a slab of polished black stone was carried forward. On the stone were two hooked knives, similar to his own and the pair which Dren had used during their night running through the trenches, only these were ornately etched with chasing, swirling lines along the two blades. The handles were waxed over slithers of rough-cut metal embedded into the smooth, polished wood before culminating at the blunt end in a metal circle large enough for a finger to slide through. The eddying patterns on the blades ran to the very tip and covered each part of the exposed metal, save only for the edges which shimmered almost blue in the dull glow. He reached out his hand to touch one and received a hiss of warning from the warrior holding the stone tray.

"No," he said in a voice more heavily accented than Dren's, "no touch. Too sharp for *kowr-den.*"

Adam frowned, not knowing if he was being insulted or whether the man was showing concern and deference, snatched his hand out quickly and looped his right index finger into the metal ring of the hilt. With a strong gesture of his right hand the knife came alive in his grip and spun smoothly in response to his gestures as he turned his hand over and back to show a skill borne of a lifetime of practice. He stopped the spinning action suddenly, snatching it into an overhand grip and held the blade up to the light. The blade's edge had been honed like nothing he had ever seen before, and the straight line of the sharpness spoke volumes to him.

"See?" said the shape before him, "very sharp. You give this to Dren when *Myghtern* say so," it finished, then disappeared through an archway, taking the stone tray and the ornate blades.

Adam was called to follow only seconds later, and walked through a short, low tunnel to emerge into the large chamber where he had first met the king. The room was packed with cloaked figures, and closer towards the raised dais where the king sat resplendently on his carved throne were the three other *outsiders* as they were called, made conspicuous by their height, and each wearing a look of confused amusement. Adam was shoved lightly in the small of his back, beginning his slow procession towards the centre of the room as the cloaks melted away and made space for him.

He could see the king clearly on his raised stone seat and saw that he wore a suit of armour of shining black plate, obviously more ceremonial than functional and likely as old as the glittering sword which lay across his lap. He wore a more regal look than Adam's companions, although evidently the situation also gave him cause to grin and make Adam feel even more foolish than he already did.

Those feelings washed away when he laid eyes on his intended.

On the *Myghternes*.

On Dren; his thorn.

In contrast to him in the heavy cloak that the Nocturnals favoured, she was resplendent in a hooded, light, flowing gown of chalky white material. Dull gold clasps adorned the dress, pinning it at both shoulders, and her slim wrists were encased in the same precious metal fashioned into greaves. As he approached in a daze, wearing a nervous smile at being surrounded by so many people all looking at him, his brain took a few steps to fathom the difference. Two paces away from her, he now saw that she was almost his height and glanced at the foot of her graceful gown to figure it out. She was standing on a carved wooden stool to reduce the almost one and half feet disparity in height. He smiled at her as he looked back to her face, seeing the bright eyes and wide smile under the white translucent cowl covering her head. Standing next to her, as he turned to face the king standing above them, he leaned close to her and whispered in her ear.

"What does *kowr-den* mean?" he asked, prompting a rapidly stifled giggle to burst from her lips to earn her a reproving look from her father. Leaning her mouth close to his ear, she chuckled again as she whispered the translation to him.

"Giant-man," she whispered with barely disguised mirth.

Adam turned away, fixing the shadow obscuring the face of the Nocturnal bearing the stone platter of knives and scowling meaningfully.

The king's booming voice echoed out above him, making his head snap back to the front. The words intoned were full of passionate meaning, rich with tradition and powerful significance. Adam didn't understand a single word of it. At the crescendo of the short speech the king raised his sword aloft and lowered it to point at Dren and Adam in turn.

Dren, on hearing the words, turned behind her and reached for an identical stone platter that he had seen in his own preparations. She picked up two wide, long-bladed knives, their bright steel glinting in the warm glow of the low light. At Dren's expression urging him to take them, he found that the hilts were bound in soft, grippy leather. The balance of the blades was incredible; perfectly weighted to his height and strength. He marvelled at them hungrily, anticipating how the beautiful steel would perform, before remembering where he was and taking the knives to swap them with the two hooked blades behind him.

Dren's eyes widened, something that he didn't even know was possible, as she saw the ornate beauty of the razor-sharp claws he presented to her.

Lowering the sword to rest it, point down, at the foot of the throne, the king looked out at the chamber and announced a single, guttural word which prompted the most curious sound Adam had ever heard. As one, each hooded, diminutive member of the bizarre congregation emitted a low whistle. The sound grew, the tones melting together to become one single force of sound and vibration that seemed to make the chamber hum and vibrate as the harmonised whistles connected and grew in power and intensity.

Just as suddenly as it had started, the noise stopped, leaving Adam's brain still vibrating to the frequency left resonating inside his skull. Glancing to his side, he saw that the others who had travelled from the Citadel with him were similarly affected by the alien sensation. Looking back at the smiling woman stepping down from the stool beside him, Adam's face panned the room in confusion as the assembly began to melt away.

"What's happening?" he asked her.

"They're going," she answered simply, returning his look of bewilderment, "it's done."

"What?" Adam asked incredulously. "What's done?"

"We are bound, you and I," she said with a smile.

"We…" Adam stuttered, "we're *bound?*"

"Yes," Dren answered with hint of worry in her voice, "that is what you said you wanted…" she finished, trailing away to silence.

"Yes, yes of course!" Adam answered hurriedly as he took her hands in his own and looked into her big eyes, "Yes, it's just… I have no idea what just happened…"

"Oh!" Dren exclaimed as her worried expression split into a wide smile. "My father said," she coughed and composed herself in readiness to impersonate her king. "People, we are here to see my daughter be bound to this man. I say that they are now bound, and my word is law. So it is."

Transforming her face back to its more familiar, beautiful visage and discarding the grumpy frown of the mimicry, she looked up at him expectantly.

"Okay!" Adam said, returning her infectious smile before allowing himself to be pulled from the chamber by the hand and out through tunnels to a chamber adorned with flickering candles and knotted wreaths of wiry-stemmed flowers, containing nothing but a bed.

———

Eve had stood still on the rising platform, her muscles tensing and contracting in tiny movements as she maintained her upright stance with seemingly effortless ease.

She never took her eyes off the tall man who had been giving her lessons on the history of their country; most days anyway. Nathaniel explained, by way of apology for his absence, that he had many other duties which he could not delegate to anyone else. He intended to make up for the amount of time she had to sit and wait with nothing to do by agreeing to move her to a new room.

He called it a room, but she knew she would still be in a cell.

"This way, please," he said to her smoothly as he led the way. Unusually for time spent out of her cell, the walkways and offices she passed were busy and populated by people in shirts and lab coats and soldiers without the anonymous black, reflective visors they normally wore.

That small fact alone had disturbed her. She had always seen the Party soldiers as her enemy; faceless, androgynous, anonymous things. Things that could be killed, that *had* to be killed, but things didn't feel fear or pain like people with faces did.

Shrugging off that unwelcome feeling, she followed Nathaniel as he led the way ahead, explaining what had kept him so busy in the world above.

"We've had a bit of a shortage of personnel, you might say," he explained as he half-turned back to her. "The mining colonies to the north have needed extra workers and that has meant more soldiers to escort them safely. It's the same with the farming colonies to the west," he told her, giving her the alternative version of the truth that he had obliterated the residence block and forcibly relocated almost every man, woman and child living there to other work allocations.

Three more turns brought her to a private room with a solid door and a single, horizontal window high up in the wall facing the corridor.

"Here we are," he said as he opened the door and walked in. Eve followed, eyes bulging widely at the interior of what she was expecting to be a slight upgrade to her previous cell. She found herself facing a larger, infinitely more comfortable room than her first prison.

More comfortable, she found as she sat on the edge of the mattress, than anywhere she had ever slept in her entire life. The blanket was thicker than anything she'd experienced before, stuffed with a spongy substance which promised warmth and softness the likes of which she had never known.

"This," Nathaniel said to attract her attention before reaching for a small control panel by the door, "controls the light," he finished as he demonstrated by dimming the light to almost nothing before raising it back up halfway. He saw Eve's eyes light up in her face, which had melted into an expression of relief and sorrowful gratitude. It was enough to get through to him on an emotional level and force him to change the subject before he became affected.

"Intercom here," he said, pointing to a small device on the desk near the doorway, "use that to ask for food or anything else you need. Bathroom," he said, casting his eyes up, and he walked three confident strides to the door on the far side of her room. Opening it automatically activated the light inside the room and a low hum sounded from within. He saw her expression and explained.

"Extraction," he told her, "for the steam. The showers in these rooms have quite hot water."

Eve peered around the door, poking her head under Nathaniel's arm resting on the door frame. Her close proximity, the absence of deference and evident lack of fear of him made him smile down at her as she marvelled at the bathroom.

"Whoa…" she hissed, drawing out the word and slipping under him to pick up the bottles of different coloured liquids bearing single-word labels.

"For your hair," he said, lining up first a bottle bearing the label 'shampoo' and then a second marked 'conditioner'. "And for the rest of you," he continued, lining up another bottle beside the first two called 'body wash'. Turning and walking back into the main room, he pointed out the plush sofa and then picked up a black, reflective slab from the arm of it.

"This," he told her, "is yours too. It has films, books, and you can also contact me if I'm not here." He handed it over and watched her undisguised look of glee as she dabbed uncertain fingertips on the screen.

"I can't promise I'll be able to answer," he warned her, "I'm usually busy, but I'll answer when I can." He watched the top of her head as she squinted over the unfamiliar screen. She didn't answer him, and he realised with surprise that this lack of response annoyed him. It stung not just of ingratitude, but something on a deeper level that he couldn't quite articulate.

"And these are your size," he said, opening a cupboard on the wall and indicating a neatly folded stack of clothing, black instead of the clinical white she had been forced to wear since her arrival. Eve jumped up to look, smiling at him in genuine gratitude and making him feel uncomfortable.

"Right," he said, composing himself, "I've got things to get on with. I hope you enjoy the room and I'll see you tomorrow." Then he shut the door, listening to the automatic electronic lock engage to trap his erratic young prisoner inside. Holding his thumb on the reader on the wall beside the door, he saw the light flicker and flash green twice.

Walking away, he tried to convince himself that he was

tired and overworked, not that he was saddened by what he saw as personal ingratitude towards him.

Inside her new cell, Eve beamed. She was very pleased with the accommodation and was already stripping to stand under the hot jets of water, where she used up every ounce of the bathroom lotions, squeezing out the bottles for their final, reluctant drops. Stepping out of the bathroom wrapped in a towel that was thicker than the blanket she'd been forced to wrap around herself to keep warm when she lived underground, she pulled out fresh, warm clothing to try on.

Okay, when I lived in a different type of underground, she thought as she forced herself to remember that she was still a prisoner.

Pulling on clean underwear and comfortable jogging bottoms, Eve wrestled with the straps of a bra to try and get the fit right before giving up and throwing it back into the cupboard to cover herself with a plain t-shirt and a warm top of the same materials as her bottoms. Dropping onto the couch, she picked up a tablet and tapped the screen to bring it to life, flicking through the film options until she found something about sword fighting.

Her mind wandered as she watched the unimaginative reproduction of battles, seeing the scenes for what they were and applying the knowledge of a true fighter to remove the appeal and realism. Her fingers danced over the screen until she found the icon of an envelope. Following the step-by-step process, she composed a message to the only contact in the list.

"I'm lonely," it said simply.

Sending the message, Eve sat back and smiled wickedly to herself.

CHAPTER FIFTEEN

THE ARROGANT BELIEF

Nathaniel slumped into a chair, his eyes wide with incredulous, horrified disbelief and accepted the glass wordlessly offered by Major Stanley. They had spent a far longer than expected day in the main control room, going from briefings to tasking meetings to intelligence reports. Urgent communications had been sent and received, and Nathaniel and Stanley had personally debriefed a desperately young and nervous second lieutenant, along with a severe looking female sergeant about the unexpected contact they had experienced in the north.

Of all the senior Party members present, only about half a dozen knew of the previous interactions with the outside world. None of them had known about it personally, as the last recorded contact was over six generations prior. The accords signed and agreed then were to prevent hostilities by way of independence. The Party leadership wanted no repeats of history and maintained that their borders were closed for both migration and commerce. They were an island nation, they needed no outside help, and they would not open their borders a second time for the rest of the world to overrun them. These accords were buried now, deep in the stand-alone archives, and no living person knew of their existence. The Party had been careful to eradicate the potential of that news escaping through soldiers' gossip, and a number of deaths were arranged to maintain the secret.

Nathaniel's arrogant belief that their people could exist in a vacuum, could live independently of all other life, had been rocked, dealing a crushing blow to his self-confidence. He sipped his drink as his logical mind wandered back to the sealed debriefing by video link.

"Lieutenant... Baxter, is it?" Stanley had asked as he sought the correct information on his tablet.

"Yes, Sir," Baxter snapped crisply in return whilst the woman beside him remained stony-faced in a neutrality that bordered on hostility. The boy's face was pink and round, made worse by the palpable fear of his audience being who they were. From his end, all he could see were two men so senior that they wore no uniform, and yet everyone knew who they were. There was no door they could not open, no information classified above their level, and in a world where a person's security clearance dictated their position in any hierarchy, they were the epitome of intimidating.

"Tell us," Nathaniel said carefully, not bothering to raise his eyes from the report in front of him, "what happened."

Baxter swallowed visibly, starting from the beginning and almost reciting his words, which were presented on the screen facing the Chairman. He listed their planning and progress towards the target, explaining that the only knowledge he had of this was that it was described as an 'anomaly of debris' almost twenty kilometres from their station. The way he gave the facts made Nathaniel feel that the boy was, at every turn, justifying what his commander had ordered, through fear of some kind of reprisal. The Chairman bit down his annoyance at the manner in which the questions were being answered, and the sigh he emitted told Stanley precisely why he was growing irritated. Stanley interpreted the sigh correctly, interrupting Baxter's next reply with, "Just the facts please, Lieutenant, save your feelings and recommendations for your full report."

Baxter looked as though he might cry at any second but steadied himself and continued.

"Approximately three kilometres back from the target location," he said in a voice which betrayed his youth by the blatant attempt to sound older, "I had made contact on the command net when the contact happened. I heard parts via the squad net…" he wavered, going paler still and swallowing again, "I heard… screams and…"

"Yes, Lieutenant," Stanley interrupted before the boy's eyes began to leak, "and you were ordered to stand by and not return, is that correct?"

"Yes, Sir," Baxter answered miserably.

"And yet you chose to disobey that order and return with the entire fire team deployed to protect you and the information you carried?" Stanley enquired with deliberate neutrality, his eyes cast down to the tablet to prevent any unintended intimidation affecting the young officer's response. With only the smallest of hesitations, Baxter fixed them with his glistening eyes and responded.

"Yes, Sir," he said, with something indicating courage entering his voice, "I believed, as the senior Party member in the field, that the order was given without knowledge of the full facts. The commander would not listen to further justification, so I made the decision to return to the area."

Nathaniel looked up at the boy now, seeing the total conviction in his face supporting his words. He agreed with him, not that he would stoop so low as to reassure an officer with less experience than his breakfast had possessed, and made a mental note to re-educate the captain who had issued that order about the importance of protecting the soldiers of the Party.

Perhaps some front-line experience in the south would do him good, he thought acidly.

"Anyway," Stanley said picking up control of the conversation once more and conveying the small hint of doubt that Baxter was wrong, "describe what you found," he instructed.

"It took us twenty-one minutes to return," he said with the unnecessary precision of a youth among superiors, "and we advanced tactically," he said, falling back on a professional manner which bored Nathaniel sufficiently to rouse himself.

"Yes, thank you, Lieutenant," he snapped before consulting his tablet for the name belonging to the other face on the screen "Sergeant Williams?" He looked up to see Williams start at the sound of her name, then continued as she opened her mouth to respond.

"Describe the target location on your arrival," he instructed, then cast his eyes down once more to follow the written report.

"Sir," Williams answered woodenly, her eyes focusing on the screen in front of her and on a spot of far wall between the heads of the two officers, "we found blood at the point where we left the Captain. There was a smashed drone control unit which tallied with what we heard on the squad net which…"

"We have listened to the communications recordings," Nathaniel interrupted in a quiet voice. Williams, unfazed, carried on.

"I deployed my team and we found the defensive

perimeter set by Captain Blake. Sergeant Willis and his fireteam were dead or missing. We left nine people there and found three bodies. Six MIA," she added for gravity. "We deployed ready for a search pattern when the relief drone squadron arrived and took over. We were then ordered to return to base."

Nathaniel and Stanley offered each other a single glance, knowing that Williams had said a great deal of things between the lines. She had said that they were ready to search for survivors but were ordered again to stand down. Both senior men knew that the captain had threatened them with a charge of desertion and treachery if they did not comply, solidifying Nathaniel's intention to redeploy the officer somewhere more uncomfortable.

"Thank you, both," the Chairman said as he rose abruptly and left the briefing room. Stanley faced the two people in screen sitting hundreds of miles to his north and bone-tired from an exhausting and emotional day. He nodded once, then severed the digital connection and followed Nathaniel. Catching up with him, he asked the question he knew would elicit a gleefully evil response.

"So, Captain… Roberts," he said after glancing at the tablet again, "is going to the Frontier?"

"Yes," Nathaniel snarled, "spineless shit. And he can walk there for all I care, but until then, he does *not* command troops. In fact, strip him of his commission. Hopefully, some officer can make the decision not to reinforce *him* when the time comes."

Stanley nodded his acceptance and approval, tapping out the order on his tablet as they walked back to the control room for further intelligence reports. Glancing down at his own tablet, the Chairman glanced at the flashing icon indicating that he had received a message.

Opening it, his pace faltered. The message was only

two words, but it hit him in the chest with the sudden sensations of guilt and responsibility.

———

"Where could they be?" Major Bentley asked with desperate concern on his face. Baxter could not answer him, because he did not know.

He and Williams had found three dead soldiers, their weapons and equipment ransacked, and their bodies riddled with bullets. Baxter, livid at their orders of cowardice, had disconnected himself from both radio networks and raised his voice for Williams to hear him. He had suggested that they ignore their orders, that they go and find the rest of their team, but Williams pointed out what the Party did to those who did not follow orders.

"The Frontier?" he snapped at the Sergeant, "Who cares? We need to find Jasmin!"

In that moment, Williams knew that to follow Baxter would be to take her orders directly from his infatuation with the charismatic and beautiful officer who was now missing in action along with five others.

"I'm sorry, Sir," Baxter said genuinely, the tears finally pricking his eyes at the look of devastating concern on the old Major's face, "I tried, we tried, but…"

"Not your fault, son," Bentley told him as he placed a fatherly hand on his shoulder, "we must have faith that she, that all of them, will be alright."

Baxter sniffed as he walked away, unable to trust himself to speak without losing the remaining composure he possessed.

The station Colonel, roused to having to interact with those under his command, did so with an aggressiveness that did nothing to foster an air of cooperation. He asked his senior officers for answers, and because of his demeanour, nobody wanted to offer a theory and face ridicule or punishment for being wrong. He raged internally at the collection of terrified faces staring mutely back at him, exasperated that he had no answers to give the Chairman.

And the Chairman would be calling inside ten minutes.

He was in possession of some facts, but the assimilation of those facts into a logical report where all the dots connected to paint a picture that was both plausible and possible was a task that had, so far, eluded him. He knew that the anomaly, the debris that hadn't been properly assessed by the drone sweep that morning, had been picked up on review. He knew that, despite his reduced troop numbers, a detachment of volunteers was deployed under the command of the eager young captain he had just temporarily promoted until a replacement could be brought up from the Citadel. He'd had no intention of allowing a field rank to stand, precisely because of the potential for just such a catastrophe; junior officers growing too big for their boots acted rashly, and idiots willingly followed them. He was certain that an experienced troop commander would not have blundered, which Blake must have done, and for that he blamed Bentley, who still seemed more concerned with the welfare of the missing troops than his own career.

He had seen the footage of the anomaly and had heard the reports of the troops who had gone with Blake, so he knew it to be landing craft from a ship out to sea. He dismissed this information as a mistake, as eager young troops being overexcited, but the persistent confirmation of the information forced him to believe that it must be true.

A ship? he asked himself. *How is that possible? We don't have a navy.*

His arrogance blinded him to the very real danger presented by the evidential facts. They had been attacked by a foreign invader, which was everything the Party had feared since its inception.

"Sir," said an operator from behind him, confidently interrupting the display of power in the main control room, "incoming communication from The Citadel," he said.

"I'll take it in my office," he responded, and left the room.

———

Nathaniel stared at the terminal in his office for so long that the power-saving mode kicked in to darken the display and force him to tap a key and bring it back to life. He had long since dismissed Major Stanley, having given him a long list of tasks he wanted achieved the following day and recommending he get some sleep to tackle the problems fully refreshed.

Something about the report from the north troubled him deeply, only he couldn't quite put his finger on it. The appearance of an external force, one with the capability to cross the seas, had been concerning enough but he always suspected that day would come when outsiders tried to brave their homeland again. He had reviewed the reports before calling up the control room and asking for the radio transcripts to be forwarded to his personal terminal. Moments later, his screen flashed up a link to follow which took him through automated authentication processes to confirm he had the clearance to listen to them, now that they had been reclassified as top secret.

As there was no higher authority than him, the process was simply an exercise in protocol.

"Control, Foxtrot-Three-Three Actual, urgent, over," the female captain leading the mission hissed through the speakers of his terminal. He stopped, hitting the key to pause the recording and rewinding it.

"Foxtrot-Three-Three Actual, urgent, over," the voice repeated. He replayed it twice more, hearing the subtle change in the voice of the woman, which started a small fire in his mind. As he replayed it over and over, that fire took hold, crackling into flames that rose and finally warmed his brain enough for the recording and his memory to connect two distant and obscured dots.

He played it again to be sure that he wasn't imagining it, before killing the audio replay file and accessing the personnel records of the dead or missing. Who had been involved in the mission was of no consequence to him before, but if he was right now, then he had no idea how it all fit together.

He skipped over the files of the soldiers with red stencils over their service records declaring them deceased and settled on the one that was marked MIA.

Blake, Jasmin. Lieutenant.

Acting Captain Blake.

"Corporal Samaira Nadeem," Nathaniel said out loud to himself as he picked up the phone and ordered an entire division of soldiers to head north without delay.

CHAPTER SIXTEEN

BEYOND THE DARK SEA

Adam, having never even laid eyes on the ocean before, was utterly terrified. The stories he had been told as a child made him believe that the sea was a calm, reflective place prone to making people think happy thoughts as they watched the waves roll gently onto smooth beaches.

In stark contrast, he had scrambled down razor-sharp rocks to a rocky cover where a small craft rose and fell violently beneath his uncertain feet. He watched Dren time her leap perfectly, seeing her step lightly away from the rock face to hover motionless in mid-air for the briefest of moments before gravity took her light frame downwards to meet the deck of the boat swelling upwards.

Adam refused to let go of the rocks, screwing his eyes shut as the foul, stinging rain lashed his face relentlessly and forced him to shout to her as she stood with annoying ease on the moving deck.

"Come on, *kowr*-den!" she mocked him.

"Piss off!" he yelled back, before the pain of appearing weak overcame his healthy respect for death and serious injury. Jumping away from the rocks, he gave the leap too much upward momentum, flailing his arms as he found himself falling with gravity at a rate insufficient to catch the deck of the ship, which moved away from his feet with the motion of the water. As soon as his toes caught up with the wooden deck, so did it reverse its course and travel directly upwards, folding his body at every joint like a concertina until his impetus was rendered neutral.

That neutrality embodied the shape of a tall male in a heap on the soaking wet deck of a boat in rough water, cursing with fear and embarrassment.

"You'll get used to it," Dren laughed at him as she helped him to his feet unsteadily.

"I doubt it," he said, stomach already threatening to empty itself as his world moved in a way he had never thought possible.

Mark hadn't fared much better, but he at least retained his footing as he stepped aboard, even if he stumbled to the rail and had to be held back from pitching back overboard. He too had laughed at Adam, at least until he was also rendered violently ill by the sickness from the alien motion of their transport. They both lay on the deck inside a small cabin, both sliding feebly as the boat rocked, and both with their heads in buckets to catch the remnants of their stomach contents as they retched intermittently in turns.

They had been at sea for a little over an hour, and the journey had rendered both outsiders utterly useless. Dren knew that it was not a failing; they simply hadn't ever been aboard a boat before, let alone in typical weather such as they were experiencing. She had deposited them below decks, set two men to watch them and to find her if there were any problems, then she wrapped her cloak around her petite frame and stepped onto the deck, where her legs moved with the boat to keep her steady.

There was no light visible, either on the slightly darker landfall behind them or anywhere else in the black expanse they were in. The weather was too bad to make out land ahead of them, but she knew there would be no lights there anyway. As far as the Party knew, nothing had lived on that island for centuries, and they had never been back to make sure. The shipmaster, a man of her own age, had spent his entire life aboard the small fleet of boats they ran between the west coast of Ireland or *Talamh dearmadta*, the forgotten land, and their home peninsula. He was born aboard a boat, lived his whole life at sea or in port, and knew the waters as he knew his own mind. No charts existed, no maps to their home or their destination, and without the stars to navigate by, as they were that night because of the bad weather, they navigated by pure feel. By instinct and memory.

Dren had made this journey two dozen times, often being invited by the rulers of the Dearmad to offer her a new suitor and a means to cement the bond between the ruling houses. Dren saw it as an attempt to seize control of the foothold on the mainland, and treated such offers with the polite, disinterested, dissidence she felt they deserved.

Adam's arrival had been the final straw in her belief of the story she had been told her whole life. It had been told to her as a prophecy, that the warrior from another people would arrive to unite the people and bring on the age of the next war, but as she grew older she knew it had been more of a political advantage between people who wanted something from each other.

The people in the city, who called themselves the Resistance, largely believed themselves to be alone in their fight against the soldiers on the mainland. Adam had not known of the existence of the Nocturnals, but some of his people had, and he was evidently angered by the subterfuge. He had not known that *he* was the warrior from another people who was destined to be her mate and would bring on the next war, nor had he even known there were other people to unite, and she was cautioned by her father to take his education slowly so as not to overwhelm him.

"It is a fragile thing, a person's mind," he had told her enigmatically whilst holding a hand aloft as though he cradled the imaginary brain in his palm. "Too much flowing in will break it, like electricity."

She had no intention of overloading Adam's brain, having only just managed to keep him calm by giving him a better, more accurate account of history than Mark had taught him. Now she struggled to decide how best to tell him that the people who'd fought the Party for the longest, those who'd held out and forced the soldiers to eradicate their entire people, still lived and thrived, just as her own people and the Dearmad.

Going below and hearing a gut-churning dry-retching coming from the cabin where her new partner was lying on the floor gave her pause.

Maybe I'll wait, she thought to herself. *Yes, much better to wait,* as her own stomach fluttered in sympathy for the noises and forced her back on deck where it was safer. And smelt better.

CHAPTER SEVENTEEN

CAPTURED

Jasmin Blake opened her eyes and gasped in a panicked breath as she sat up fast and hit her head again. Slumping back down to the lumpy mattress under her back, she groaned in stunned pain and rolled to her side instead of sitting upright.

Flopping onto a cold, metal floor she stayed on hands and knees and tried to steady herself but found that she couldn't stop the swaying motion from taking over her body. Taking a long time to fathom why, she finally fell on the assumption that it wasn't *she* that was moving, but the room itself.

A groaning, metallic sound vibrated dully through the floor and up her arms until the horrifying realisation of where she was dawned on her.

Gasping again and staggering to her feet, she looked around the sparse interior, seeing nothing but an empty, fixed desk and stool and bunk beds beside a wooden cabinet stretching from floor to ceiling.

She aimed herself at what looked like a door and took three paces towards it, confused that she was heading to her left instead of moving forwards, until she collided with the metal wall to ring out a hollow thud. Slumped against the wall and fighting to take long, deep breaths without vomiting, she heard a clanging noise from the door and recoiled to the corner as it opened and admitted two men.

She stared at them, seeing sharp, shrewd eyes beneath scruffy hair and wild beards as they stared straight back at her. She was under no illusion, no false modesty about how she looked, and she recognised something in their eyes that she had seen in men throughout her entire life ever since she hit her teenage years.

Her ability to control, to manipulate people men especially had been borne of knowing how she looked and using that to affect the situation and bend people to her will. Even now, feeling dishevelled and in pain, she was aware of what at least one of them must be thinking deep in the back of his mind.

"Please," she said in a small voice, deciding instantly on playing the terrified innocent, "please don't hurt me."

The man at the front, streaks of red running through his muddy brown hair and beard, gave a snort of a laugh and chuckled lightly before turning to the other man and saying something in a language she didn't understand.

Jasmin, her mind running an assault course behind the frightened image she projected, sought any logical way to establish a connection with either man that she could exploit.

"I don't understand," she said, sounding more frightened than before, "are you from the Frontier?" At the mention of the last word, the one who had spoken turned back to face her. He took two efficient steps in her direction, seeming not to even notice the movement of the room, and crouched down before her.

"We're not from the Frontier," he said in English that

bore an accent so melodic that he almost sang the words softly to her, "and we're not from your army either." He stared hard at her for a few seconds, making her wonder if he would reach out a hand to touch or grab her but instead, he issued the same short huff of a laugh and stood.

"You need our *leighis* to take a look at your head," he said in his low, calm voice, "he won't hurt you, so don't try anything, you understand?"

Jasmin nodded quickly, still acting more frightened than she was as the world began to make more sense to her with each passing second. She stood hesitantly, as though she feared he would still lash out to grab at her and stayed in the corner until he backed off and beckoned her to walk towards him.

She followed, legs wobbling uncertainly until she caught her balance and reached out to place a steadying hand on the bunks. She smiled a small, self-effacing smile, catching the eye of the man who just returned her look with amusement but not unkindness. She followed, conscious of the heavy footfalls directly behind her as she walked down a narrow metal corridor with no windows. She kept her hand on the wall for balance as the floor beneath her feet heaved again and she gasped. The man she was following turned to look at her, suspecting an injury causing her pain or to see her doubling over, but instead he locked his green eyes onto her big brown ones and saw in that moment that the gasp was one of realisation and not pain.

"We're..." she said, stopping to swallow down a mouthful of saliva that threatened to invite the contents of her stomach up to join it, "I'm on that ship?"

"We're at sea," he answered simply.

"My pe..." she stopped, unsure if her captors knew

her position among the Party soldiers and deciding not to reveal her officer status just yet, "my friends," she tried again, "did you take them too?" The man's eyes flickered almost nervously past her head to the one behind her before returning to meet her pleading look.

"Only one survived," he said without emotion, "and he's in a bad way, so he is." Without offering any more explanation, he turned on his heel again and moved off, forcing her to either stay there and be pushed along or follow.

Her path continued on until natural light began to penetrate the depth of the ship, and a glance to her right showed her a circular glimpse of a dark grey sea with no land in sight. The sight made her feel so alone it ran cold throughout her entire body until she was distracted by the man in front of her stopping to direct her inside another room.

She climbed inside, stepping high over the raised lower section of the door as though it was designed intentionally to strip the skin from her shins. Inside the room was a man leaning over a supine body strapped to a flat bed with strips of black clothing hanging down where it had been cut away. She stifled the next gasp with a hand over her mouth as he turned away to reveal the face of the man being treated.

Blood sheeted his pale torso, which was almost as white as the thick bandage that covered his right shoulder. She took three quick steps towards him before rough hands grabbed her arms and held her back.

"He was your commander, was he not?" asked the man with the shining green eyes.

"He..." Jasmin started to say before her brain kicked into gear and woke up her higher-functioning self-preservation instincts. "Is he going to live?" She hated herself in that moment, unable to cut away her caring instinct but not wanting to be caught in a lie if he regained consciousness and betrayed her unknowingly.

"No way to say for certain," the man treating him said casually, "best we can do now is let him sleep it off and hope he hasn't lost too much blood."

"So, he's your boss man, is he?" a man asked from behind her. Jasmin was unable to conjure a believable lie quickly enough so feigned her knees giving out. As she'd hoped they would, the same hands holding her prevented her from hitting the metal floor hard. She was lifted easily and carried to another flatbed where a wide strap was stretched over her torso.

"It's to stop you falling off," the healer reassured her, feeling her tense against the restraint, "you've had a hard knock to the head, and you need to rest."

The pain in her head was real enough but the stress and uncertainty of the situation overcame her more than she knew. She lay back, turning her head to the side so she could watch the gentle rising and falling of lieutenant Oakley's chest as he breathed weakly.

"Questions later," the man who seemed to be in charge said, "rest for now."

CHAPTER EIGHTEEN

THE DEARMAD

They lived much in the same way as the people of the Frontier did. Vast underground caverns filled with a mash of technology both new and ancient ran in great interwoven complexes that connected over huge tracts of land that was destroyed and scorched from the centuries-old destruction of the Party bombing.

Caverns leading from the rough seas had been excavated long ago, allowing access to their strongholds by boat, which was how they travelled to and from the mainland.

When the boat from the Frontier arrived, guided into one of the sea caverns and into the belly of the land by the expertise of the crew as though they navigated by instinct and relied on no technology, the city dwellers had only just begun to recover from the ordeal of their first journey by boat.

"Sip," Dren said gently as she cradled Adam's head softly and held out a cup of fresh water to him, "do not drink fast, or you will be sick more."

Adam grunted an acceptance of her words as he

sipped thirstily at the water, feeling the acidic coating on the inside of his mouth fade away. As he drank, his senses returned to him marginally and he felt the change in their movement.

"We're here?" he asked.

They weren't a fully united people as the Nocturnals were, however, and a century before, a group had split away from the old ways to occupy new territory on the west coast of their island, far from the prying eyes of their own kind and way beyond the reach of the Party and their drones. These people had sought a return to the old ways, living above ground, although careful to avoid attracting any attention to themselves, and had become a sea-faring sub-race with eyes on the horizon instead of their own existence underground, waiting for change and prophecies.

As well as fishing, they had rebuilt and constructed a small fleet of ships capable of crossing the ocean to the burned lands on the other side of the Atlantic. There they had discovered more people; colonists living in a huddle of fortified towns and seeming to be in a constant state of conflict with others like themselves.

The early days of trade with these people had been fraught with risk and confusion until a common language could be established, reverting to the speech of the mainland to communicate with them. From these people they traded goods from their home for weapons, which were more plentiful there than any of them had seen before. Armed with those weapons, the Dearmad known as the *Cine nua*, or new breed, began to raid the vast emptiness of what had once been their Gaelic cousins of Scotland.

The confidence built by these raids led them to move further south and to sail around the tip of the island to the fishing grounds and undisturbed land on the other side of Party territory. It was there, while scouting for resources and hidden treasures of the old world, they learned from their scouts of a war party dressed in black heading their way. The ambush was a simple one to create, but the real finesse came in the form of wirelessly connecting to the drone they flew ahead of them. It took their man designated as the technology specialist only seconds to override control and use it to attack the soldiers, and when that drone had been blasted from the sky, the rest of the crew ashore had subdued the survivors quickly, capturing the few who had been brought down safely or who else had the good sense to surrender.

The Nua, bold and adventurous, were always seeking ways to show their superiority to the old-fashioned Dearmad. Bringing back prisoners from the Party made little difference to them, but they knew that the old ones would pay and pay very well for live prisoners to interrogate.

———

Adam found it best to stand tall and look resolute as the Nocturnals and the Dearmad went through their greeting rituals. They were quick and seemingly routine, but as with all things he didn't understand, Adam found himself wondering what the point of them was.

"Why don't they just say hello and get on with it?" he muttered to Mark not quite under his breath, earning a hiss of warning from the older man.

"Because it's their custom," he said, "don't be disrespectful." Adam kept his face rigid but seethed at the admonishment. He wasn't intentionally being disrespectful, only curious about the answer and his manner made him sound too blunt.

"You know," he whispered to Mark who was still unsteady on his feet even after half an hour back on dry

land, "*you* should be more respectful. I'm a prince now."
Mark laughed openly, earning a few pointed looks of
disdain from Nocturnal and Dearmad alike, before bowing
his head as a sign of respect.

Dren, evidently leading their group as envoy, spoke in
low tones with the biggest of the other people for a while
longer before they were asked to follow. Feeling as though
the series of underground tunnels of his life would never
end, Adam spent an awkward twenty minutes walking with
an enforced stoop to his step, until the series of winding
walkways opened out into an underground city far bigger
than he had seen on the Frontier.

The end of their journey was almost a repeat of their
first group meeting with the myghtern of the Nocturnals,
as they were ordered into a large chamber where a man of
almost square proportions sat on a raised level looking
uncomfortable in the ornately carved chair he occupied.

Long speeches were delivered in a language so alien to
Adam that he couldn't even decipher a few words, and he
was beckoned forward by Dren, who stood beside him and
spoke loudly and confidently to the leader of the
Dearmad.

After she had finished speaking and retreated to his
side with a deep bow, a warrior from the flanks of the
throne stepped forward to speak with intensity and fire in
his eyes which he directed at Adam. He spoke briefly,
turned and bowed to his leader, who returned the respect
with a nod before leaving the chamber and not showing his
face again the rest of the day.

Dren told him later what had been said. After the feast
and the fiery liquid that he tasted once and politely
declined to touch a second time. After they had been
shown to their guest quarters and washed the sea journey

from their skin under hot water and fell into bed beside each other.

"They know you and I are bound," she said, "and at first they weren't happy at this, but I have told them about your life and where you came from." His eyebrows rose questioningly as she spoke, earning a calming pat of her slender hand on his broad chest. "I told them what they needed to know," she explained. "It is important that they know you are the one to strengthen the bloodline." Adam smiled to himself, oddly pleased with his status but not yet fully considering the mechanics of how that would happen. "Also," she said in a more cautious tone, "their *ceannaire*, their leader, he gave permission for his best warrior to challenge you for me."

"Wait, what?" Adam said as he sat up and stared at her in stunned silence.

"It is their custom," she explained as though a challenge from a warrior was of little concern. "They have offered me husbands for the last five summers and I have said no to every one of them. Now that I am bound, there is to be allowed one challenge to show that I picked the best fighter."

"I've got to fight one of them?" Adam said, sounding a little younger than he intended to, "Who? Why?"

"Because you do. And for the who, it is the second son of their leader." He stared at her, unable to comprehend why she was so casual about it all. She saw his hurt look and pouted at him teasingly. "You will be fine," she said with a dismissive shrug, "I have seen you fight."

CHAPTER NINETEEN

ACTIVATION

Corporal Rebecca Howard tidied her desk three times while she waited for the end of her duty shift. She didn't like her posting for obvious reasons and found herself wondering every hour of every day if she could go through with it.

Her activation had come in the form of a handwritten note on a scrap of paper in her laundry when her uniform was pressed and returned to her quarters in the Citadel's headquarters. She had sat on the bed for so long that it had started to go dark outside her window as she held the note and read it over and over again.

Of course, she knew that the previous command of the resistance had been purged; she'd read the reports on most of them as the correspondence came through the office of the Chairman and she was left alone there for hours at a time. She had suspected that she would be called on to help the Resistance soon, but her loyalty to that shady underground organisation was as weak as her belief in Party politics.

It was blackmail, there was no other word for it. Her

mistakes during her first posting would have led to significant punishment, but she found those mistakes covered up with a falsified claim of equipment malfunction and the incompetence of the workforce. When she arrived back at her post to find all evidence of her error erased, she faced the difficult choice of owning up to her supervising officer and inviting punishment or else keeping her head down and going along with the cover-up, even as she watched the workers punished with reduced meal allowances and more strict oversight.

After a week of this she suspected that she might have got away with it, even managed to convince herself that the screw-up was actually the fault of other people and not her lack of concentration, but that bubble was burst when the notes began to arrive.

It started with the original, unfalsified logs of the activity which laid the blame squarely on her. Moreover, it made it look as though she had doctored the record to lay blame on the people and not herself. The log bore a scribbled note, telling her that she owed the people who'd saved her career and that the payment would come in the form of information.

She felt as though she had no choice, because to admit her fault now well after the fact would make things worse and to admit that she had been protected by what she suspected to be members of the resistance would put such a spotlight on her life that she couldn't bear the thought.

So she agreed, and had only given them information twice since she had capitulated. Not once in almost two years had she met any of them face to face, as every transfer of information had been done under the strict instructions of what they called a dead drop. A note would find its way to her through one of the three places she had to check each day when she left or returned to her small residence. When she finally found the note that told her she was now required to actively report, she shivered as though she were cold despite the warmth inside her residence.

Standing abruptly and running the water in her sink until it turned hot enough to steam up the simple mirror above it, she wiped away the condensation and stared hard at herself as she considered her choice.

The choice, she knew, was compliance or potential execution. She had collaborated with the Resistance for two years, failing to provide information to the Party that could have led to the capture of their members when they checked the dead drops she had used. There was no way to hide her involvement and no way to explain the delay in reporting it, so she knew she was trapped with only one viable option. Still, she wasn't prepared to be infiltrated so close to the nerve centre of the Party.

Tidying her desk again, opening and closing the drawers for want of anything better to do, she rose and checked the time on her wristwatch against that of the clock on the wall. The larger timepiece, she knew as her own watch was accurate, was running four minutes slow.

Hitching up the uniform skirt, which was cut to an uncomfortably tight fit, she raised her right leg to get her knee onto the side next to the coffee machine, which she had already washed and set up ready for the following morning. Rising onto her knees to reach the clock, she was forced to stick her backside out into the air for counterbalance. She leaned up to wind the control with her index finger just as the outer door to the office burst open.

"As you were, Corporal," Major Stanley said in a tone that made her feel naked and somehow as if she'd been caught doing something vulgar. She climbed down as Stanley and the Chairman walked into the office, hurrying her movements so that she could recover her poise, but scraping her shin painfully on the edge of the wood of the furniture.

Hissing sharply before clamping her lips shut, she stood before both men, who just stared back at her. For one horrified, terrifying moment she thought they knew. Thought they must have found out about the lie that was her life after making just one mistake and finding herself embroiled in a secret war far bigger than her life and ambitions had ever been.

"S…Sirs?" she stammered nervously. They both just stared at her, Rebecca expecting the worst but praying for her release from their presence.

"My office, Corporal," the Chairman said as he stepped around her and out of sight, leaving her alone in the outer office with Major Stanley. She hesitated for a moment before turning and walking inside. Stanley followed, stopping in the doorway to listen as Nathaniel started speaking.

"Your clearance is high enough to work here," he told the young woman, "so I'm assuming that you are up to speed with our progress relating to the girl we captured?" She nodded, hoping that she was right and too frightened of the situation to respond verbally in case her voice betrayed her somehow.

"I feel that she is in need of… how can I put this? *Female* company," Nathaniel said. "I'd like you to spend some time with her and answer her questions; gauge her responses and understanding and report back."

Rebecca didn't know why she of all people should be chosen for this, but her greatest concern was that a closer proximity to anyone or anything relating to the Resistance would expose her complicity.

"Why?" she began, coughing to clear her throat and

try again in a stronger sounding voice. "Why me, Sir? Surely there are more qualified people for that? Maybe someone trained in intelligence work or interrogation?"

"Of course there are," Nathaniel said, "but I rather suspect that's the point. I firmly believe that our *guest* would see through any attempt to plant an intelligence operative close to her and she'd be quite likely to game that system to manipulate us in some way. No, I want *you* to do it. I don't think you could fake it enough to arouse her suspicions, and I believe that a more personal approach would break down her barriers. I don't think she's had much in the way of contact with a girl close to her own age."

"I…" she began, unsure of what to say before he spoke over her again.

"I'll have your duties here covered by another adjutant," he went on as though her acceptance of the task was an irrelevance, because it was. "I'll have the necessary clearances authorised for you to access special projects." He leaned back and opened a drawer in his desk to pull out a paper-jacketed file which he slid over the polished wood towards her. "Some light reading to catch you up on the history you might not be aware of. Report to Special Projects at zero-eight-hundred tomorrow." He glanced at his wristwatch and looked back up to her.

"May as well get away a few minutes early," he said. "Dismissed."

———

Conflicting thoughts ran through her mind as she walked fast back to her residence. The frightened part of her said that she should report her contact with the Resistance to her superiors immediately and suffer the consequences of her actions. The truly terrified part of her toyed with the idea of reporting her new assignment to those rebels, those terrorists, and see what they wanted her to do about it.

It all came down to who she thought would win, she decided. She scrubbed that thought from her head and instead asked herself who she *wanted* to win. Did she enjoy Party rule and the permanent surveillance and lack of freedom? Did she enjoy having all her decisions made for her or did she want to live in a world where her path and her future wasn't dictated by senior officers who always acted for the good of the Party and never for the individual?

The lessons of her youth came back to her with a resounding echo in her mind. The selfishness and greed of people led the world into war and famine, and only the power of the Party made their survival possible by acting for the good of the people. She had asked one of the state-appointed educators once why the people couldn't choose their own leaders, why they couldn't make decisions and opt to live outside of Party rule. That inquisitive nature had earned her a month of individual education where the Party vitriol was force-fed to her until she could recite it with enough passion and fervour in her voice that they believed *she* believed it.

She knew she had never believed it. She had always just flowed along with the system, allowing her looks to excuse her apparent lack of passion in support of the Party ideals, allowing people to think her pretty and vapid instead of being what she truly was: a disbeliever.

Clutching the scrap of paper tightly in her right hand as she walked, she made her decision. *Her* decision; not anyone else's. Not one made for her for the good of the people or for the glory of the Party, but hers and hers alone.

Looking down at her feet for appearances' sake, she

pulled a face of exasperation and steered her course towards a statue of a former Chairman on a raised stone dais. Hitching her tight skirt up a little, she bent down and raised her foot to place it on the stone where she untied and re-tied her shoelace so that anyone watching her progress would see nothing amiss with her actions. Standing and straightening her skirt, she continued her journey and didn't slow her pace or deviate from her path until she had closed the door of her small residence behind her and let out a long breath to relax.

CHAPTER TWENTY

THE GREY MESSENGER

Nobody saw those citizens assigned to janitorial work allocations. They saw them, true enough, but they never noticed them. Never really *saw* them.

Doing the final sweep of the day, the man pushed his cart as he made his slow progress along the concrete promenade and stopped in the shade of the statue honouring some military man his grandfather would have known, but he couldn't recall any tales of the man's exploits.

Perhaps he was the one who'd destroyed their neighbouring countries or annexed some pocket of rebellion. Perhaps he had ordered the deaths of thousands of people whose only crime was standing up for their belief in their right to elect their own government or to live peacefully under their own rule. Perhaps he was the one who had ordered the construction of the high-rises that housed all the lesser people like the simple street cleaner now looking up at his likeness.

Lesser people, he thought and allowed a small huff of mirth to escape his mouth. *Aren't we all equal in the Party?*

He dropped the rhetorical question into his mind and

left the subject where it was, not needing to answer it because he knew all too well what the Party's idea of equality was. He'd pushed that cart, or others similar to it before, for near on twenty years up and down the same stretch on the same route each and every day of the week, with only every other Sunday to himself.

The walkways of the Citadel were to be kept pristine each and every day, and he longed for the onset of winter proper when the fallen leaves wouldn't mess up his stretch of hard, grey concrete and provide him with an unreasonable amount of seasonal work to do. Although winter was no better, as he had to replace the broom and dustpan for a shovel to clear the paths of any snow that might fall. At least in bad weather the uniformed members of the Party wouldn't spend their break outside and deposit their wrappers and their waste on the ground for him to clear up. That was his job, after all, so why should one of those equal members of the Party do any more than their allocated part?

Only one piece of rubbish was there to be picked up as he swept off the lower sections of the statue to keep it clean and clear and prevent any marks appearing on his permanent work record, which was far from blemish-free through no fault of his own.

He picked up the scrap of paper wedged in a crack between the big blocks of stone where the mortar had been worn away over the years by alternating sunshine, rain and frosts, slipping it into his other hand as he mimed throwing the scrap into the open bag hanging on the cart.

He replaced his brush and dustpan in the cart and resumed his slow progress, limping on his right side and twisting his hip and back to alleviate the pain in that leg which had caused more discomfort in his pelvis and back over the years. He continued his journey then back to the unmarked door in the service area of the fortress.

He pushed his cart back to the place where it sat when it wasn't roaming with him, unhooked the bag and emptied it into the chute where all of the waste would be taken away for incineration. He struggled out of his coveralls and hung them back on the clothes peg allocated to him when he was still a young man so many years ago.

He replaced the coveralls with a heavy, plain, civilian jacket and pressed his thumb onto the glass reader to clock out as he had done so many times before. Then he continued his sedate walking pace towards the tall tower of residence block two, where he treated himself to a ride in the elevator to the third floor, having been on his feet for most of another day spent picking up after the occupants of the Citadel.

Not once did he take out the scrap of paper from his pocket. He knew he would be watched every step of the way until he got back inside his residence, and only then could he be sure that no cameras were turning and zooming in on him to focus on whatever piece of information he held in his possession.

Reaching his door, he fished inside his jacket pocket to come out with a key and fit it into the lock on the door. Only in the tower blocks did their security deserve such low standards, and before he closed it behind him, he left a thin band of red elastic taken from the keyring hanging over the handle of his door.

Almost forty minutes later, after a change of clothes and a meagre meal placed into the microwave to satisfy his dietary requirement, a knock sounded hollow against the door. It came in a rhythmic pattern, short but easily identifiable, and it prompted him to press his face to the small fisheye set high in the door. The check was simply to ensure it wasn't a snatch squad in Party paramilitary uniform waiting there, not that he ever dreamed they would identify him, and he took the scrap of paper from his pocket where it had remained unread, and slipped it under the doorframe. He stood there, waiting for the soft footsteps to melt away towards the stairwell where the lights were dim and the cameras mostly unserviceable, before heading back for his meal and a night spent in front of Party television. He'd eat, clean up the small amount of mess he'd made in the tiny residence, then sleep before doing it all over again the following day.

———

The boy who roamed the landings of the tower block saw the thin red band hanging from the handle of the apartment door. He didn't know what it meant in terms of the bigger picture, but he knew that to him it meant running back to the first sub-level and giving the floor and residence number to the old man who sat there every day. The boy went, returning to his duties that earned him extra food, not giving another thought to what it all meant.

The residence number was whispered through a door crack and someone else climbed the stairs to rap out the agreed signal on the door. When the slip of paper appeared under the frame it was picked up, stuffed safely into another pocket without being read, and transported down the stairs to where it passed through two other sets of hands before coming to rest under poor light on the desk of a woman.

Helen Randall, the newest leader of Command and nominal head of the Resistance, set down the large book, the handwritten notes of which she'd been reading, after carefully marking her place with another piece of paper.

She picked it up, unfurled it to smooth it out after the collection of sweaty hands it had been passed through had crumpled it, and read the words.

"Fly?" she called out as she read the note a second and third time. Footsteps in the room beside hers echoed in the underground confines until the young man appeared in the doorway. "Get the code book," she instructed him, "I want to know who asset six-eight-six is."

Fly left, returning a few moments later as he leafed through a book to the back pages and ran a finger down the column of words.

"Rebecca Howard," he said, "adjutant to…"

"To whom?" Helen asked, not liking the delay one bit.

"…adjutant to the Chairman," Fly finished. Helen's eyes widened as she hadn't even known they had an asset that close to the Party leadership.

"Why?" Fly asked her.

"Because she's been assigned to befriend and educate a certain girl you know."

CHAPTER TWENTY-ONE

FEAR

Jasmin had healed from the blow to her head enough that she was no longer suffering from long bouts of nausea and dizziness. Of those symptoms, she wasn't entirely sure how much was due to the concussion and how much of it was courtesy of the rising and falling of the deck beneath her feet.

The boat never ceased to move, and no matter how hard she tried to anticipate the unnatural movement of their transport, she always found herself off balance and bouncing off metal walls. One of the biggest problems with her ever-adapting balance and the movement of the sea was that nothing on the entire ship seemed designed to cushion any kind of impact; quite the opposite, in that everything she banged into was hard enough to leave a new bruise on her body every time. Her only respite from this came when she was lying down and groaning to try and stop her empty stomach from roiling.

She had been shown back to her room, given food and water, and told to bang on the door should she need anything. They treated her like a guest, but she and they knew that she was a prisoner.

Even if she could escape her cell and overpower the guard or guards who she was certain were posted outside her door day and night, then where could she possibly go? If her intention was to commit suicide by drowning in the freezing waters off the northern coast of Scotland, which was her best guess as to their location and direction, she could probably manage that. If she intended to escape and survive, however, she saw little point in doing anything other than what she was told to do.

The fate of Lieutenant Oakley weighed heavily on her mind. She felt a responsibility for him mixed with more than her fair share of guilt. He was injured, terribly, following the orders of a traitor. A corporal of the Party, masquerading as an acting captain under a false identity, who had no right to be there at all, let alone commanding troops.

Her arrogance, her avarice, had got people killed.

She was a member of the Resistance and wanted the Party overthrown from power as her ultimate goal, but that didn't prevent her from having feelings about the men and women she lived and worked with every day. The presence of a higher objective, of an ultimate goal, didn't help to reconcile her to the truth that her day-to-day life was spent in the company of so many Party soldiers who, with the exception of plenty, were good, decent people.

To some the Party was totalitarian. It was their true calling and they would follow orders with an almost fanatical obedience, but to many it was simply a job. A means to an end and a way to be housed and fed well, instead of suffering back-breaking manual labour through mining or construction or agricultural work. To know that she had put people like that in harm's way and got them killed in the pursuit of her own foolish ambition stung her more painfully than the knowledge that her false identity would doubtless have been discovered already.

She lay on the moving bed, intermittently holding her breath to prevent the small amount of water in her stomach from reappearing with each upward swell of the boat. She tried to recall each and every move she had made from joining the adjutant core in the Citadel right up to faking her own orders and creating the personnel record which she had travelled north under, and using which she had assumed the new role, while drawing a little too much attention to herself.

None of the moves she'd made could lead back to anyone or anywhere in Command or the Resistance. She was sure of it. She would stake her life on it, which was a curious thing to imagine, given that her life was held in the balance by people she had never seen before and of whose existence she'd had no knowledge until now.

The movement of the boat changed, not that she could decipher how, and seemed to slow as the movement became less violent.

Someone banged on the metal door twice with a heavy hand before it was pulled open with a metallic protest and the man with the fiery red streaks in his beard stepped smartly inside, as if the deck wasn't moving for him as it was for her.

"I'll need you to be dressed and ready to leave now," he said, the friendly tone of his voice gone since their last conversation.

"Where are we?" Jasmin shot back. "What are you going to do with me?" She tried to think as she sat up, this time avoiding hitting her head, because she had learned from painful experience not to move too fast. She thought that they hadn't been at sea for long, then recalled that she

had no way of gauging how long she had been unconscious and no way of knowing how fast they were moving,
so she abandoned any attempt to figure out the distance
they had travelled.

"We have reached the home of my ancestors," the man
said cryptically, "and you will be traded to the Dearmad."

CHAPTER TWENTY-TWO

THE CHALLENGE

Adam was swept up in the confusion of high activity and the languages he didn't understand. He caught words here and there that sounded like English, mixed with the few words the Nocturnals used that he understood, but apart from that, he found himself at the centre of a beehive he felt he had no part in.

He had been taken to a bare chamber where he was asked to remove his clothing. He resisted at first until the insistence of the few short warriors brought from across the water with them won through and the skin of his bare chest tightened in the chill, underground air.

"Do you know the challenger?" he asked one of them, seeing large eyes looking back up in response to his question with evident amusement.

"You do not need to know about him, *kowr-den,*" he said, "only need to know yourself." Adam didn't know if the broken English the man used translated properly, because what he said went against everything the young man had ever learned about fighting an enemy. He had always been taught to know the strengths and weaknesses of anyone he fought; in the Citadel it had been the many faceless soldiers who had strength in their numbers and their weapons and technology but a weakness in their ability to see him coming. They were no match for him at close quarters, but if his experience of the Nocturnals, of Dren's fighting abilities, was anything to rate the Dearman on, then he feared the challenge.

The two warriors gathered up his clothes and shoes, leaving him wearing only the tight trousers he was permitted to keep, and left the chamber without another word to him. They spoke to one another, the tone of their muted conversation leaving him with a worrying sense that they both had a gleeful anticipation of the fight to come. Adam clapped both hands to his face, leaving them there while he took two long, deep breaths to calm himself. He wanted to know the rules. Wanted to know more about the man who was challenging him for his new bride and wanted to know what weapons he would be given, to reassure himself that he was proficient in their use.

He wanted to know, more than anything, if he was going to be forced to kill his opponent. That thought left a cold feeling in his chest, because following that train of logic forced him to face the very real prospect of being killed himself.

The door to the chamber opened to admit the hustle and bustle noises from outside before those sounds were muted by the door closing again. He turned, expecting to see more Nocturnals bringing him unfamiliar weapons and no more answers, but instead found him looking directly into the concerned face of Mark.

"What the hell is going on? What do I have to do? Is this a fight to the death?" the questions tumbled from his mouth like rain from the sky to saturate his mentor and force him to hold his hands up to stem the flow.

"I've been trying to find everything out," he said, stress sharpening his words more than he probably intended, "I've tried to get to Dren but she's been taken away to the king to watch."

Adam stared at him, waiting for more facts in the hope that one of them might be useful to his situation.

"The man's name is Conor," he said, as though just giving a name would benefit him. Adam's hands shot out to his sides before slapping back down against his thighs as he turned away in frustration.

"Great," he snapped, "what good is that?"

"The man's name is Conor," Mark said again, allowing a hint of annoyance to creep into his words, "and he's the heir to the Dearmad throne." Adam fixed him with a silent look for a few heartbeats before deflating.

"So he's what? Their prince?"

"Something like that," Mark admitted, "and as far as I can tell, the challenge is a series of tasks that you'll compete against him in."

"Tasks?" Adam asked, suddenly hopeful that he wouldn't be fighting for his life against royalty in their own kingdom.

"From what I can gather, yes…"

Adam widened his eyes at Mark, exasperation radiating from him. "And?"

"And if you keep up," he admitted, "then you'll have to fight him." Adam gave up and sat heavily on the packed earth of the chamber's floor.

"What tasks," he asked in a resigned voice, "and what are the rules of the fight?"

"I haven't got that far yet," Mark said, "but I'm working on it."

Noises from outside rose in intensity to leak a sense of excitement through the door to them as it creaked open.

Adam looked up to see two of the Dearmad warriors, also bare-chested, with their faces adorned in bright streaks of white and blue which were caked and cracking where their skin moved.

"It is time," one of them intoned solemnly as neither appeared willing to cross the threshold into the chamber. Adam rose, unfolding vertically as he exerted downward pressure through his crossed legs without touching the floor with his hands. It was a simple enough thing to do for someone who had been raised as he had, but the unwitting demonstration of his strength and control did not go unnoticed by the Dearmad.

"You hear that?" he asked Mark, wearing an emotionless mask, "it's time."

He went to walk past the man who had raised him, who had trained him and who he loved and hated in equal measure, depending on the situation. As he went to walk past, a strong hand shot out and gripped the sinewy meat of his right bicep. Mark leaned close to his head, pressing their skulls together as he muttered what he hoped wouldn't be their last words to one another.

"Trust yourself," he ordered simply. "Know your own strengths and *think*."

Adam pulled away, meeting his intense gaze for one last time before he stood tall and followed the warriors out of the chamber and through a few short tunnels to the large open area.

The huge underground dome had been transformed since he had last been through it, leaving room for hundreds of the locals arrayed around the edges to see the cleared central area. Alone in that area, underneath a raised platform bearing chairs made of twisted tree roots, stood the barrel-like king beside the slight, dark figure of Adam's own wife. He couldn't see her face but thought that he knew her well enough that her features would be an unreadable mask. A third person was there, dressed the same as Adam but with swirling patterns of blue and white paint tracing the outlines of his muscles, and that man looked up in the dim light of the flickering flame torches lighting the dome to stare directly at him.

"It's time," Adam said to himself, and walked tall and proud towards his challenger.

He was expecting some kind of deathmatch, some kind of gladiatorial contest between himself and the challenger, Conor. So when the central ring cleared to leave only the two young men, he was surprised to see that his challenger showed no signs of readying himself for a fight.

Adam, in contrast, rolled his neck on his shoulders and moved his arms through their full range of movement to stretch out the muscles, ready to do combat. The king said something, loud and rumbling which was met by a muted wave of agreement from the gathered crowd.

Just as he was beginning to suspect that the contest was not in the format he was expecting, Conor launched himself with three fast, powerful paces to leap into the air and aim a devastating punch at Adam's face. Despite his surprise at the suddenness of it, he avoided the blow easily, his mind bursting in elation that his opponent would be rash and predictable. But no sooner had that arrogance flooded his body than he found that the bold opener from Conor was merely a test to see how Adam would react. Had he taken the threat seriously, had he reacted with less nonchalance and more urgency, he would've told his attacker something very different about his capabilities.

Instead of staggering to recover and be more cautious, the Dearmad prince dropped low to the ground and swept a savage kick out to take Adam's feet out from under him. He saw it coming, stepping over the unexpected blow and retreat a pace out of reach of the shorter man's limbs, which he began to suspect were just as lethal as his own.

Conor stood, not relenting or wasting time in testing him, just advancing on him to close the gap and take away the superior height and reach of the man he thought soft and unworthy of fulfilling the prophecy. Adam blocked and ducked and avoided desperately, retreating all the way until he stepped backwards over a ring of painted stones and a loud shout pierced the air. Conor stopped attacking, relaxing at once and wandering casually back towards the centre of the circle. The crowd muttered, sounding like a distant cheer heard through a wall, and Adam looked around for an explanation to see one of the painted warriors who had escorted him there marking a flat stone under the raised dais with a blue mark.

Thinking that he had gained some clue as to the rules of the contest, Adam straightened himself and walked back towards the middle of the ring, angry that he was being forced to fight at a disadvantage.

"What is it?" he asked Conor as they squared off for the second round. "Best of three?" Conor smirked in answer, seeming to relish the prospect of humiliating the tall man, and that smirk was his undoing.

Adam didn't wait patiently for the next round in their contest. As soon as they readied themselves, he launched an attack that might to the untrained eye have appeared a desperate attempt to remove his opponent's head inside twenty seconds.

Conor blocked and dodged as Adam had done in the first round, sidestepping as much as he retreated and wary of the boundary that would cost him the bout. Adam made noises as he attacked, sounding every bit as desperate as his attack appeared, and when he began to slow his movements as though tiring, he saw the look on his opponent's face crack into a cruel smile of triumph before he came back at him.

That was when he launched his real assault.

Lulled into a false sense of easy victory, Conor landed one blow hard into his abdomen as he turned to spin away but stayed close to unleash the punch. Adam staggered, hearing the muted sounds of the crowd show appreciation for their champion in readiness for the end of the spectacle to come too soon for their bloodthirsty liking.

Adam stayed bent over as though winded by the shot, turning to see Conor with his hands up to the crowd in premature celebration. He heard the sounds of the crowd hush in an instant as he stood tall, no longer appearing damaged, and advanced on the other man who had yet to add up the crowd's reaction and understand what it meant.

Flying through the air after a series of powerful bounds to spin and line up a brutal kick, Adam watched with satisfaction as Conor turned just enough to see the kick coming and twisted frantically to avoid it. He moved too slowly and reacted too late, as the kick slammed into his back between the shoulder blades to pitch him face first into the packed dirt to skid to a stop only inches from the boundary line that represented a failure he wasn't expecting. Scrambling back to his feet, he stayed low and rolled backwards to narrowly avoid the spinning heel strike that would have connected hard with the back of his skull, had he not been so wiry and fast.

Adam anticipated the dodge and indeed counted on it, as he maintained his spinning momentum and bent his head low to the ground while his foot kept moving in an upwards arc that would have connected the flying limb with his challenger's jaw if he had not put both hands up to defend himself.

The force of the kick was too strong for the weak block

and Adam's foot slammed both of Conor's hands into his face hard enough to knock him back down to his back. Adam stayed intentionally close to the boundary line where he treated him to his best smile and allowed the other man time to regain his feet,

That smile had the intended effect, and Conor rushed him, enraged, hoping to drive him out of the ring and end the contest.

Adam closed the distance between them before any real attack could be launched, ducking under his outstretched hands to deliver an elbow strike to his abdomen just under the ribcage to send the man's diaphragm into spasm. Conor's hands dropped in response to the blow as Adam carried on spinning away to drive his elbow hard into the back of the skull he knew instinctively would be within reach, to send him stunned and sprawling out of the ring.

A cheer sounded over the hushed noises of the crowd, belonging to one man who quickly lowered his voice to the sound of the hissing laughter of the few Nocturnals who had accompanied them over the water.

A white mark was daubed beside the existing blue one, making the contest equal in score as Conor angrily brushed off the help of another Dearmad warrior who ran to his side. He turned and fixed Adam with a look, only this time it wasn't hatred or derision but one of cold analysis. Adam guessed that he knew he had been duped, knew that his advantage of home ground and his knowledge of the rules of their engagement was wasted, and now that he had the measure of the speed and savagery of his opponent, the freeborn man steadied his breathing in readiness for the final battle.

Instead of resuming their positions to fight hand to hand, low shouts in a language Adam neither spoke nor understood rang out and echoed. Two sticks of dark, polished wood were thrown to Conor, who whipped them through the air with practised hands. Two more were tossed at Adam's feet, forcing him to stoop to collect them.

He had been fighting with a weapon in both hands from the time he could walk, but he picked them up uncertainly to sell the ruse that he was unfamiliar with the concept. The wood felt much heavier than it appeared, making him suspect that the cores of the short staffs had been drilled out and weighted down with soft metal to add the heft he felt in both hands. He tried to mimic Conor and spun the weapons hesitantly, hitting himself in the shoulder to the great amusement of the crowd.

Adam thought that their final round would be difficult now that both men felt they understood the capabilities of the other, but the addition of weapons made it easier for his skills to be underestimated. Underestimating an enemy, he knew to his own very negative experiences, led directly to failure.

At no discernible signal, Conor began his approach with both sticks twirling in his hands incessantly. Adam backpedalled a few paces, showing caution in the face of this new attack which seemed to enthuse the crowd with a desire to see blood drawn from this man; this foreigner to their soil.

Conor leapt towards him, both hands held together and both thin clubs arcing downwards towards his collar bone, which would have left him broken and disabled if the blows had landed. He dropped and rolled away, avoiding the attack and spurring the crowd onwards to mistake his avoidance for cowardice. Conor didn't seem so convinced. He had learnt only moments before not to underestimate his treacherous foe and advanced on him more cautiously this time.

He threw blow after blow at Adam, testing him with feints and following up with hard reversals with both weapons, which Adam blocked while trying to appear panicked. All the time he defended himself, his mind was analysing his opponent's skill and attacks for signs of repetitive weakness or opportunity to counter. Conor stepped back only to come fast towards him again and sweep upwards with his left hand in a move that Mark would have dubbed as 'ungentlemanly'.

Adam saw it coming and knew that the instinctive reaction was to protect the vulnerable part of his body.

He also saw the right hand of his attacker drop to fall behind him. Saw the tensing in his shoulder muscle in slow-motion as the signal was sent from his brain to his arm to bring his right hand down hard on what he anticipated would be Adam's unprotected skull.

Adam made as though he was going to put everything he had into the block with both weapons, before twisting aside and spinning to sweep both hands up and aim blindly at where he calculated Conor's leg would be. As his momentum took him hard in a tight circle Adam lowered his body weight. Just as he hoped, the savage downward blow sailed into empty space.

It was that extended right leg that took the full force of both of Adam's staves directly to the meat of his hamstring just above the knee.

With a scream of agony, Conor's leg gave out and he toppled hard to the ground to lose his grip of both weapons and clutch at his temporarily crippled leg.

Adam stood tall, staying intentionally out of Conor's reach in case he recovered enough to launch a desperate counterattack from the dirt. He didn't hear any sounds from the crowd, not knowing if that was his brain blocking out the irrelevance or whether they were truly silent. He watched as Conor went rigid, drawing in an exaggerated breath to bellow a roaring scream of anger and pain.

Had Adam been carrying his customary knives, the Dearmad prince would currently be minus one leg at worst, and at best be clutching cuts so deep that his survival would be more a matter of luck or divine intervention than any medical help available nearby.

He turned and looked up to the raised dais, seeing a flash of large eyes over a wide and unashamed smile on Dren's face and an impassive look on the features of the king.

He turned, looking to see the second white mark painted on the stones and seeing those men with the pots of colour standing still in anticipation. Sound returned to him as Mark's voice pierced the veil of his concentration.

"The ring, boy!" he yelled. "Get him out of the bloody ring!"

Adam spun back in time to see Conor dragging himself upright to hop on one leg and swing both weapons at his skull. Adam leaned back just in time to avoid a glancing blow and dropped his weapons to clasp Conor hard on either side of his head to pull him towards his body and tip him off balance. Rolling backwards and bringing his right foot up to rest hard against the flat stomach of the wounded man, he rolled backwards and down to the dirt to pull hard on the man's head and time the release of his powerfully long leg to extend it and launch his burden high through the air.

Conor left the ring still in full flight, sailing clear over the stones to topple half a dozen spectators as his limp form slammed into them. Adam had continued his roll, rising to his feet effortlessly and turning in time to see a small swathe of the crowd go down under the weight of Conor's body.

Movement caught his eye, making him turn his head to see one of the other Dearmad moving, only this one wasn't attacking him but reluctantly wiping a second white stripe on the stone before turning to face the king and kneeling. Slowly at first, then in a sudden rush that left nobody but Adam still on his feet, they all knelt to the king.

Adam looked up at him, still standing defiantly with his chest heaving from the effort of combat. The squat man intoned something loud and rumbling, evidently speaking for the benefit of everyone present before turning to say a few unheard words to Dren and nodding his head in mild deference to her. She bowed in response as the king left the stage without turning back and turned her big eyes towards her man. She beckoned him, and needing no second invitation, Adam stepped out of the ring to leap up and climb easily to gain the height of the raised platform. Dren took his face in her slender hands and crooned soft words he didn't understand as she took in the minor damage to him.

"What did he say to you?" he asked her.

"I am not so sure as how the words change to your tongue," she told him, still stroking his skin almost mischievously, "but he told me that he hoped we could get on with the business of war now that his son's foolish pride has been put in its place."

"Sure," Adam said, looking into her large eyes and forgetting all that he had just been through the second she smiled at him, "I just need a little rest first."

CHAPTER TWENTY-THREE

FEMALE COMPANY

Rebecca Howard was fearful at accessing a new area of the Citadel and worrying that her new credentials wouldn't admit her to the bowels of the facility where the ambiguously named Special Projects was housed. She expected to be seized by guards at any point, to be detained and hooded to be whisked away for questioning and to be tortured until she gave up everything she knew.

She didn't know much, but what she did know was enough to justify her execution three times over for treason. Refusing the assignment was just as dangerous, as that would be to defy an order given by the Chairman himself who, to most people who didn't find themselves working in close proximity to the man and his very small inner circle, was some vaunted and mythical being only seen in terrifying glimpses.

Working close to him every day made him no less terrifying, not to her at least, and the fact that Major Stanley seemed connected to him by an umbilical cord made it so much worse.

She felt strange walking through the clean corridors of the Citadel wearing a pair of jeans and a relaxed-fit sweat top. Being her, the jeans were tight and even the loose fit of the sweat top accentuated her phenomenal figure, but she hoped that she would seem less formal to the girl she was about to meet. She felt less protected somehow, not being in her fitted uniform, and that accentuated her fear of being accosted by soldiers. She was afraid that she wouldn't be able to react accordingly if anyone asked her for ID, worrying that she'd just blurt out her confession there and then, but her face stayed unreadable and her pace remained strong and confident.

Reaching the elevator that would take her down to the depths of things she'd never even dreamed of seeing, she scanned her ID and waited for the red light to turn green, or else sound an alarm if her credentials weren't accepted.

The light switched to green and the digital display requested her retinal identification. Leaning forwards, she brushed the loose waves of her hair behind her ear, her hair worn down inside the Citadel for the first time in her life, and she held her right eye wide open to be scanned. The digital display flashed twice before going blank. Rebecca stood, unsure of what would happen next, but the door to the elevator hissed open to admit her. She hesitated, forcing herself to step inside and scan the vertical buttons for the lowest level and pressed it, seeing the green ring illuminate around the deepest sub-basement. As the fleeting sense of weightlessness threatened to flip her stomach, she took a deep breath and readied herself.

———

Eve paced inside her room. It had begun to feel small and restrictive not long after she had been first locked in, and no amount of enjoying long, hot showers and watching the repetitive diatribe on the tablet she had been given kept her occupied for long.

She was desperate to be outside, to be free from the confines of one room, as though the taste of freedom she had experienced was burning inside her like an insatiable thirst. She had sent more messages to Nathaniel, to *The Chairman*; the very head of the snake that was her born enemy, and some of them had been responded to. The last one read simply, "I'm sending someone to keep you company tomorrow. Be nice to her."

Eve didn't know what he meant by that. She wasn't unkind to anyone, apart from the few guards she had made to feel more than a little threatened, as well as the strange, silent creature whose nose she had broken.

She woke long before the time they usually came to give her food, feeling restless and as if she had slept too much and was becoming soft and slow, and decided to pass the time reading an account of battles against the last resistance in the far north, recorded in a language so stilted and alien at times that she struggled to make sense of it. She scanned the words, careful not to drop the tablet in the soapy water she lay in, and when she had been still for too long and her attention span was exhausted, she wrapped herself in a towel and stepped back into her room.

"Hello," a woman said, startling her so that she almost dropped the towel covering her slender body.

"What the hell?!" Eve erupted, standing still and closing her eyes for a moment, which the woman might have interpreted as fright, when in truth it was Eve's display of self-discipline in not attacking her.

"Sorry," the woman said as she stood and stepped nervously from foot to foot. "I'm Rebecca," she said, offering out a hand to cross half of the gap between them.

Eve froze still, opening her eyes to bore them in to the woman's and convey her feelings. She hitched up her towel and let out a strained breath, unhappy at herself for being startled, and greeted her with a simple hello before going back into the bathroom.

A minute later she reappeared, wearing the simple sweat top and loose bottoms to match. She poured herself a glass of clear water and carried it to the bed where she sat to sip the cool drink and regard the woman.

She saw a young woman. Very attractive and with a body that spoke of a disciplined approach to her diet and exercise regime. She appeared to be wearing makeup a concept new to Eve and more than a little confusing but it had been applied with such subtlety that she appeared to be wearing none at all to anyone who didn't regard her closely. Eve guessed, though, that most people *did* regard her closely, because she detected something intoxicating about Rebecca, and just knew that if she were a man, that air would be magnified. Deeper than that, below the enchanting surface and the radiating sense of innocence, Eve intuited a fear far greater than her own.

"I'm Eve," she said finally, turning off the unreadable expression and softening her features. "But you already know that." Rebecca smiled.

"I do, and I'm guessing you knew I was coming."

"He said someone was coming," Eve replied with a mischievous smirk, "but I was expecting another one of the old crones with a clipboard." Rebecca smiled back at her and opened her hands to show the obvious lack of pen and paper to take notes.

"Want some breakfast?" she asked. Eve nodded and stood, following her out of the room and forcing herself not to mimic the way her hips swung as she walked.

———

"What I really want," Eve said through a mouthful of runny eggs and toast, "is to go outside." Rebecca put down the coffee she was drinking and used her finger and thumb to toy with the single slice of toast she had allowed herself.

"I'm not sure I can make that happen," she admitted, "I'm only a Corporal."

"What's that?"

"It's a very low rank. I'm not even an officer."

"The white coats down here aren't officers," Eve challenged her, "they use their first names or call each other Doctor or whatever. They can make decisions."

"I don't make *any* decisions," Rebecca admitted, opting for almost complete honesty in dealing with the girl from the moment she met her shrewd eyes and realised that lying to her was pointless.

"But you've been sent here by people who do, haven't you?"

"I have," Rebecca admitted, "so I'll have to take it up with them."

"Him," Eve said.

"Sorry?"

"You'll have to take it up with *him*. We both know that." Eve swallowed her mouthful, leaning back and wiping her lips with a crisp, white napkin. She allowed the subject to drop, having sewn the seed she wanted to, and set about bending the young woman to her will, which was a task she didn't think would be as easy as it purported to be. Something about Corporal Rebecca Howard didn't add up, not to Eve's mind anyway, and she had to force herself to tread carefully until she found the weakness to exploit.

"How about some exercise, at least?" Eve asked her,

seeing the relief on Rebecca's face as the subject of stepping outside their underground prison vault was temporarily forgotten. She left the half slice of toast uneaten and stood to drain her coffee cup as Eve chugged a third glass of sweet, sharp orange juice and rushed to follow.

They walked the sterile corridors of the sub-floor they were on, with Eve running the guided tour for Rebecca, who had clearly not been there before.

"Down there is where they first kept me," she explained, "in a glass cell under the floor with the lights on all day and all night. I guess that was to disorientate me... down that way is where they took me for lots of tests and gave me injections."

"What kind of injections?" Rebecca cut in, seeming to speak before she'd thought it through.

Eve narrowed her eyes, almost closing them, as she recalled. "Pneumococcal vaccine, meningitis A, B and C, measles, diphtheria, tetanus, polio and flu." Rebecca almost stopped walking in shock and stared at the girl with her mouth open.

"What?" Eve asked her innocently.

"How long ago was this?" Eve's eyes narrowed again as she accessed the information stored in her brain.

"Four weeks and three days ago," Eve said, "in the morning."

Rebecca resumed her pace and thought, asking another question to test the girl. "Who was in the canteen just now when we had breakfast?"

"Not counting the person in the back putting the food out?"

"Not counting them," Rebecca said, chiding herself internally for not even noticing there was a person putting food out.

"Six," Eve said, anticipating the next question and continuing, "two white coats; one I know is called Gillian and the other one is a medical person. There was you and me, obviously, and the two men dressed in coveralls trying badly to conceal their stun batons and pretending not to be guards following us." Rebecca spun on her heel, seeing a fair-haired man in dark coveralls duck into a doorway about twenty paces behind them as though that was his destination all along.

"It was the blonde one," Eve said without looking, "I'm guessing the one with the shaved head will be working around the next corner."

"How do you…"

"When you spend your whole life looking over your shoulder, you learn to pay attention," Eve told her. "Plus, the one with the shaved hair uses something that smells like soap on his head. Can't you smell it?"

Rebecca's mouth opened to answer that she couldn't before she realised she hadn't even tried. She sucked in a long breath through her nose, holding it at the back of her mouth, waiting for her mind to decipher the code. She let it out and admitted that she couldn't. They reached the next junction in the corridor and saw a man in dark blue coveralls gazing into a maintenance panel as though he knew what he was looking at. Rebecca laughed and bumped her shoulder into Eve's as they walked, seeing the younger girl recoil slightly from the gentle impact of their bodies and shot a curious glance at her. The confusion lasted only a heartbeat before she smiled lightly and stepped closer, bumping her back to connect their hips and shoulders in such perfect timing that Rebecca was thrown off her course and almost stumbled against the wall.

"And here," Eve said as they rounded a corner to look

out over a triple height space, "is where they tested me against the monsters they grew down here."

———

"The Chairman will see you now," Rebecca's replacement said to her, smiling falsely up from her desk as she replaced the phone receiver. She smiled her thanks and walked through the door to Nathaniel's office, feeling more vulnerable without the uniform to hide her individuality behind.

"Take a seat, Corporal," he said, eyes still down at his terminal. He looked angry, she thought, or at least annoyed about something. She waited in silence as she tried to control her breathing until he finally looked up and regarded her.

"Well?"

"Well, she's certainly something else," Rebecca answered, adding a hasty, "Sir," after her words that sounded dangerously informal.

"She is that, Corporal. Any other, more useful, observations?"

Rebecca sat forward in her chair, scared out of her informality by his tone. "She has exceptional observational skills. She knew without even really looking at my security detail that they were following her. She could even *smell* one of them, or at least a skincare product he used, when he wasn't in sight."

"Go on," Nathaniel said, clasping his hands together and leaning towards her. It was late in the day and her body clock was telling her that she should be on the way back to her residence already. She fought against the tiredness in case she betrayed her duplicity to the intuitive man in front of her.

"I saw her glancing up at the corners," she went on,

"I'd be amazed if she doesn't have a map in her head of the entire facility and know where all of the cameras are situated. She recalled word perfect, I imagine what immunisations she was given a month ago. I'd say she has a photographic memory."

"I've noticed that," the Chairman said, his eyes the only part of his body not to be perfectly still. "I rather suspect she plays dumb for my benefit, so putting you in today has already been of value. Report back tomorrow and do the same. Dismi…"

"Sir, if I may?" she interrupted, seeing a flash of amusement instead of anger on his face. He nodded once. "Eve, I mean the subject, wants very much to go outside." She hesitated, knowing that the suggestion was a wild one. "I think that would really help break through to her."

Nathaniel sat back, fingers of both hands steepled under his nose as he considered the suggestion.

"I'll give it some thought," he said. "Thank you, Corporal, please submit written notes in your own time. A formal report can wait for now. Dismissed."

———

Rebecca Howard walked out of the offices of the Chairman without giving her replacement a second look. She felt somehow superior to that role already after just a day out of uniform, and her duplicity amplified that sense of excitement. She walked fast back to her residence and kicked off her shoes as soon as she closed the front door. Peeling off the tight jeans, she padded around her rooms in her sweat top and underwear to pour herself a drink and sit at her terminal. She recorded her notes and observations on Eve, waiting to save the file until she had copied the typed text in tightly packed handwriting onto the only real writing material available.

Once finished, before clicking the terminal's keyboard to submit her notes, she rolled the secret copy tightly and slipped it inside a clear plastic wrapper from one of her state-provided feminine hygiene products. Slipping the tool of her treachery under her pillow, she turned on her shower to wash the stress off her skin.

CHAPTER TWENTY-FOUR

SIDES

Adam drank three cups of the icy cold water they served underground in the Dearmad kingdom as he slaked his sudden thirst. He was grateful to be given back his shirt as the women were beginning to stare now that they were congregating up close to him and his sweat-sheened pale skin.

Mark had no words for him, only a wide smile and an enthusiastic slap to his back harder that Conor had managed to hit him. Pride radiated from him and it dawned on Adam that Mark had never seen him fight anyone other than himself and evidently took great delight in seeing how his creation through training and mentoring had evolved into a weapon in his own right.

Noises of excitement from up ahead of them in the king's chambers made their feet move faster to find out the source of the disturbance, and when they entered the grand cavern, Adam's eyes rested on something he didn't expect to see.

He saw a dishevelled woman wearing the uniform of the Party soldiers on her knees before the king.

Men and women were shouting, from what Adam could gather imploring the king to make a decision, until the king called for quiet with raised hands.

"What are they saying?" Adam whispered as he bent down to Dren's ear.

"They are the Nua," she explained, "from the other side of the Dearmad lands on the wide ocean. They have captured some of the enemy from the mainland…"

"What else?"

"Shh," she hissed. "I try to hear but you talk too much." Adam waited as patiently as he could manage, standing tall to see the conversation he couldn't understand, to try and read their body language instead.

"The king wants to execute them," she said, "the Nua want payment for delivering them and others want to interrogate them for information." As Adam watched, one brave warrior stepped forwards to brandish a blade of dark metal that sang in a sharp whisper as it was drawn from the leather sheath.

"Wait!" screamed a female voice in English, "I'm with the resistance! I'm not your enemy, I swear it!"

Adam needed no translation. He stepped fast through the crowd and forced the shorter forms of the natives aside with ease. He reached the prisoners in time to shoot out his right hand and stay the blade of the would-be executioner, who rounded on him with savage murder in his eyes.

"*Stad*!" the king barked, rising to his feet and making himself only slightly taller than when he sat in his throne. The warrior relented, lowering his blade and stepping backwards. Adam looked down at the woman who had screamed the words that had ultimately saved her life. She was stunning, even if her hair was a mess of tangles and her face dirty and travel stained. She looked up at him, surprised to see a face that she seemed to recognise.

She opened her mouth to speak but was interrupted by the groggy voice of a man beside her.

"You… you're one of *them*?" he spat. "You're a traitor?"

"Oakley, it's more than that, I swear it," she pleaded but the man with the heavily bandaged head kneeling beside her roared and launched himself in a wild attempt to attack her.

A blade hissed, whispering through the air on a short arc that sparked a gagging, choking noise and spilled hot, sticky blood onto the packed earth at Adam's feet. As he lay between Adam and the woman, choking out his last drops of blood to soak the ground, she sobbed and wailed her apologies to the dying man before looking up at Adam in desperation.

"My name is Jas…" she shook her head as though she forgot something and tried hard to remember it. "My name is Samaira, and I've been with the Resistance for years."

CHAPTER TWENTY-FIVE

UNEXPECTED PROGRESS

Nathaniel remained in his office late that night, watching the live mirror feed of Corporal Howard's personal terminal in her residence as she tapped out the words with a speed and efficiency rarely seen outside of the Party's adjutant corps. His face remained impassive as he sipped brandy from the coffee cup that still retained the smell of its usual contents to mix with the harsh liquid. He found it was to his liking, providing a short distraction as he stared at Howard's unmoving screen for minutes.

He imagined her reading over her words meticulously, checking each line for spelling and grammatical errors, but when he spotted minor errors that she didn't correct, his brow furrowed in thought. After a long pause when he guiltily imagined her undressing, the notes were submitted to the main server and the screen was shut down. He sipped his drink again as he thought and sat forward to click on the other reports sent to him.

Scrolling through the long list of standard information that he should have dealt with during the day, he found one from a special projects data miner which piqued his interest. It was a response to his personal request to look deeper into the case of corporal Nadeem's request for transfer and showed the origin of the data.

It had come from his personal terminal.

———

He was back at his desk long before the next working day began. He'd visited his father in the evening, only to find him asleep, so he hadn't disturbed him. He had returned home and lain in bed for a few hours, unable to find sleep. Giving up, he'd decided to get up and exercise before showering and returning to his duties.

He pored over the report again, trying to analyse the information and connect the hidden dots surrounding the disappearance and reported death of the woman who had miraculously reappeared with a new name and rank in the north, and he sent further requests to analyse the origin of Acting Captain Jasmin Blake's personnel record.

He planned to set major Stanley to the task of interrogating the commanding officers of her previous postings, only the last few to be certain, but he was sure that none of them would be able to recall the striking young female officer, as he was convinced she didn't exist; Blake was Nadeem and Nadeem was Blake.

He tapped into the surveillance monitoring system, taking direct control of a drone and tasking it to monitor the exit doors of a particular residence, with programmed orders to identify and follow one single person.

He didn't have to wait long. The door of the residence, shown in high-definition colour, opened to show corporal Howard leaving and walking with her head down towards the centre of the Citadel. She stopped only once, making a face of annoyance and placing her bag down at the feet of the statue of the third Chairman of the Party to rummage through it and appear satisfied that she hadn't forgotten an item she needed.

She resumed her journey, not stopping or talking to anyone until she reached the entrance to the gymnasium. He released the drone back to its automated pattern and brought up the screens showing the inside of the gym as he waited for her to change and begin exercising, fighting the urge to use his override codes and access the restricted hidden cameras inside the female changing area. She appeared, filling a bottle with water and starting a walk on a treadmill which increased in pace until she hit running speed and maintained that fast pace for a little over nine minutes.

By his reckoning, that was her ensuring her combat fitness test scores were well within the limits of a pass. She continued with a routine of squats and lunges to maintain that particular part of her physique that drew so many surreptitious glances from the men, not to mention some women he'd noticed observing her.

She exercised for forty minutes until sweat glistened on her bare arms and shoulders, making his mind wander, until a knock at the door of his office startled him back to the present.

"Morning, Sir," Howard's replacement greeted him, "coffee?" In response Nathaniel merely indicated the pot already half emptied which he had brewed himself. She nodded, apparently annoyed that he had already conducted one of her morning duties, as if it spoiled her routine somehow, and she retreated to her desk in the outer office.

When he looked back to the screen Howard had gone. He typed the commands to select the camera he had decided not to view before, his index finger hovering over the key to connect to it, when Stanley walked in.

"Morning, Sir," he said, heading straight for the coffee pot to pour himself a cup.

"Morning, Major," Nathaniel replied, exiting the camera menu and convincing his paranoia that Corporal Howard was not the traitor that her predecessor evidently had been. "You'd better sit down and take a look at this."

Major Stanley sat. He checked the reports and agreed with the Chairman's assessment that Nadeem must have been somehow colluding with the terrorists and unconvincingly faked her own death. Nathaniel tasked the junior officer with some background intelligence, specifying that he only needed to corroborate their beliefs with two officers before their assumption could be fully relied upon.

"This stays between us for now," he told the major, "although I'd like you to bring Colonel Barclay up to speed as soon as we're done here." Stanley nodded his assent. "This obviously brings into question the events in the north, because this may be an attempt by the terrorists to destabilise the Party's territory."

"Agreed, Sir," Stanley said, "we also have the issue on the Frontier to consider…"

"I've checked the overnight reports," Nathaniel told him, "and there have been no further attacks since the last major offensive. That, obviously, doesn't mean there won't be soon."

"So we need to reinforce the north and the Frontier?" Stanley asked him.

"I'm afraid so, but that means leaving the Citadel less protected than I'd like."

"I'll have shift rotations extended and keep a standby force ready to deploy," the major responded. "Drone surveillance is already running at close to maximum but still, there hasn't been any activity since the holding facility was attacked."

Nathaniel sat back and pursed his lips tight as the thought in his head forged into words, and Stanley knew him well enough to wait in silence.

"I don't like it," the Chairman said eventually, "reinforce the north and the Frontier, extend rotations everywhere across the board, because I think this period of quiet will end soon."

"A coordinated attack?"

"Possibly," Nathaniel answered. "While we're at it, upgrade the communications checks for all outposts to hourly signals with a rotating security algorithm." Stanley nodded, finishing his coffee and standing before asking a question on a different subject.

"And Corporal Howard's tasking?" he asked, trying to sound nonchalant. "Anything of interest?"

"She wants to take the girl outside at her request," Nathaniel answered without emotion, "and I'm inclined to allow it."

Stanley, his eyebrows finally lowering after the Chairman detailed his security measures for such a risky event, left the office without giving the replacement adjutant a second glance and went directly to special projects, where he spoke with colonel Barclay.

Nathaniel watched him travel down in the elevator, seeing him walk out into the underground complex tapping at a mobile terminal in his hand on his way to the colonel's office. Another screen showed the main above ground access to that same elevator, and the figure who appeared there to scan her ID card and thumbprint before sweeping her damp hair behind her right ear, combined with a practised flick of her head to scan her retina and access the elevator.

He watched her descend also, seeing the look of apprehension on her face mixed with impatience, despite the speed of her travel downwards. When the doors opened, she walked fast, as was her manner, along the corridor towards the comfortable cell Eve was secured in. He watched how the tight civilian jeans she wore, black instead of blue this time, clung to her hips under the simple white shirt and jacket she wore. She looked incredible in her uniform, but somehow seeing her again in civilian clothing was more of a lure to him, as though the sight of her out of uniform offered something more personal; an invitation into her personality.

He chided himself for imagining that. Not because he recognised the misogyny in his thought process but because it would be improper for him to pursue a junior non-commissioned officer under his direct chain of command. It would be a breach of regulations, not that regulations had mattered to any Chairman before him, but he drew a mental line and refused to consider crossing it.

He watched as she knocked at the door of Eve's room, her cell, and waited before using her ID card to open the lock. Eve came out, dressed in sports clothing that somehow made her appear dangerous, like the suit she'd been wearing when she was captured, and the two of them chatted with smiling faces as they walked towards the canteen for breakfast.

He leaned away from the screen as he watched them, pushing the open window on his terminal displaying them and typing out a series of orders directly on a communication to Stanley and Barclay to prepare for Eve's visitation above ground.

He sent it, bringing up another communication to type some redacted orders for Howard to follow.

———

He didn't go back and check the route corporal Howard had taken that morning. Wasn't thorough enough to have her followed covertly by a female operator who would be able to search the woman's locker as she exercised.

He didn't see the cleaner begin his morning routine by walking his route to assess the work he had been caused overnight, didn't see that cleaner stoop to pick up a tightly wrapped bundle of paper as though it was a simple piece of detritus to be removed and discarded.

It went into his pocket, and eventually wound its way to the Resistance leaders who waited with anticipation for more information.

CHAPTER TWENTY-SIX

THE TRUTH BEHIND THE FACES

"Seriously?" Eve asked. "I get to actually go outside?"

"That's what the man says," Rebecca told her, checking the message on her handheld for a second time. "Tomorrow after breakfast."

"Will they be coming?" Eve asked, lifting her chin to nod backwards over her right shoulder to a pair of innocent-looking diners trying their hardest to mind their own business. Rebecca leaned around the girl, learning from her observational powers and detecting the hidden weapons inside their clothing.

"Most likely," she replied honestly. "I don't think the Chairman would let just us wander around on our own. You might take me hostage to try and escape or something," she joked.

"Nah," Eve replied through a mouthful of sticky pastry, "not high value enough. They'd probably just shoot you to remove my leverage." Rebecca laughed lightly, expecting Eve to join in with her and stopping when she realised the girl was deadly serious. Clearing her throat to cover her anxiety, Rebecca tidied the cutlery on the plate she had barely eaten from and fidgeted as Eve's eyes bored into her.

"Anyway," she said finally, unable to bear the scrutiny any longer, "what shall we do today?"

"You had any combat training?" Eve asked lightly. Rebecca sensed a trap. She'd read the reports and even seen some footage of the girl in action. She was a killer, and Corporal Howard had only received the basic combat training that all Party soldiers got, regardless of their role. She was relatively fit and could defend herself, but against this girl she knew she didn't stand a chance.

"I, erm," she tried, covering the silence with nothing meaningful.

"Relax," Eve told her, "I just want some exercise. I might be able to teach you a few things while I'm at it."

Rebecca agreed, telling her that she'd have to go back upstairs to collect her gym gear before Eve waved that excuse away.

"I've got loads of clothes in my... *room*," she said. "You're not that much bigger than me. Come on." Rebecca found herself swept up with the girl's excitement, not entirely sure whether she believed the enthusiasm or that she was being used as part of some other play. They returned to Eve's cell where the girl threw open the cupboard to show neat stacks of the same clothes she was wearing. Rebecca eyed her up and down, thinking that she was much fuller in the hips and chest but would have to make it work. She ended up opting to keep a more loose-fitting sweat top over the tank top underneath, as she was showing a little more cleavage than the Party's dress code allowed.

They went back to the gymnasium area, Eve waving and smiling at someone apparently inspecting a light fitting as they approached. She told the man where they were going, seeing him feign confusion and failing badly. Rebecca actually laughed out loud at the girl's audacity. The guards had been rotated again so that the same pair weren't following them, but Eve seemed to have the ability, quite literally, to sniff out those who didn't belong there.

The route Eve led them on went past another room with glass walls and a uniformed guard posted outside. Eve held Rebecca back at the corner, peeking around to see the room before ducking back when the guard looked in her direction.

"Who's that woman?" she asked. "Do you know why she's here?"

Rebecca took her turn to peek, ducking back and squealing lightly as the guard saw her, and giggling with the girl who seemed to genuinely be having great fun playing with someone even remotely close to her own age.

"She's…" Rebecca said, looking around theatrically before she spoke, "… she's one of the Resistance leaders. Don't you know her?" Eve frowned in confusion, ducking her head back around again and coming back to look Rebecca in the eye and treat her to a sad-eyed expression.

"I was kept on my own most of the time," she said in a small voice, "I didn't get to see many people unless they were there to teach me things."

Rebecca's heart melted a little and she wanted to wrap the girl up in a hug like she was the little sister she didn't have. Rebecca was younger than her brother, and would never be a big sister, given the Party's cap on the number of children Citizens could have. Eve returned her look, giving off vibes of hope and appearing almost happy to be where she was. Rebecca felt sorry for her. Protective of her and wanted above all else in the world to make her happy.

"Come on," Eve said, grasping her hand and dragging her away towards the gym, "I'll show you the monsters they keep down here," and pulled her along by the hand to where the two subjects lay motionless, at rest on their plain beds. Rebecca pulled back from the thick glass of the cell walls, unsure if she should be seeing what the girl was showing her.

"It's okay, silly," Eve said, pulling her close by the hand again, "they can't get out. Watch this: *Shadow, report!*" she barked in an imitation of a deep, male voice.

One of the still forms leapt up from the bed, stepping fast and light towards them and stopping short of the glass to cant his head sideways a fraction and regard her with cold eyes. Rebecca shuddered, feeling the cold malevolence of the young man radiating through the glass with such force that she felt the air grow thicker.

"Maybe we should…"

"He can't get out," Eve said, her voice no longer that of the excited child she had been before, but one which resonated with the confidence of a predator eyeing a rival. "He wants to, I can see that," she said, turning her own head slightly to match his and smiling wickedly at him. "He wants to get out and rip my head off, but he knows he can't do it on his own; not that he'd do anything without being told." The male took a slightly longer, deeper breath than before, telling Eve that his heart rate had increased with a slight surge of adrenaline. She knew he wanted to kill her, but she also knew that he wasn't allowed to. She didn't tell Rebecca, but she longed for the chance to fight him again.

"Who is the other one?" Rebecca asked, breaking the spell between the two killers. Eve turned away without a second glance at Shadow and stepped past the empty cell to see a female watching them from a sitting position on her bed.

"She won't come to the glass," Eve said, "not for me,

anyway." The female, Reaper, eyed them with no trace of emotion at all.

"What about the empty cell?" Rebecca asked.

"I didn't know that one's name," Eve said, "but I know he was hard to kill."

"He was hard to… *what*?" Rebecca shot back, shocked at the words that came from the girl's mouth. Eve smiled at her and giggled again, returning to the persona she normally used around the corporal, who realised with sudden and worrying clarity that she hadn't broken through to the girl one little bit.

"He was *very* hard to kill," Eve said again, "probably harder than both of these two. I cut his head off in the end; that definitely worked."

Rebecca's mouth opened and closed as Eve giggled again and ran off towards the climbing equipment. When Rebecca turned back to the glass, she screamed a yelp of fright and staggered backwards because Reaper had moved in total silence to stand up against the glass only inches from her face.

"Host," she said, the sound muffled by the thickness of the glass. Her eyes bored into and through Rebecca's own as she failed to understand what the frightening woman meant. "His name was Host," she said, blinking once and turning around to walk back to the bed and sit down again. Rebecca, her spine chilled by the encounter, retreated to join Eve and tried to remember that the girl was quite possibly the most dangerous person she'd ever encountered.

CHAPTER TWENTY-SEVEN

SUNLIGHT

Nathaniel had read the report of corporal Howard's second day underground, annoyed that the girl had immediately begun to manipulate the person sent to keep her company. He corrected himself, knowing that he had intentionally placed Howard there to gather intelligence and chided himself for thinking that his enemy would do no less.

Eve had used her relationship with Howard to test the limits of her knowledge, and when she had revealed that she knew the identity of Cohen, then the girl had success-fully figured out that Rebecca Howard was no babysitter.

Still, he was glad that he had put her in and not some intelligence operative, as he was certain that Eve would see through that ruse in seconds and maybe even kill them. Corporal Howard's innocence, coupled with the fact that she actually knew very little of their operations below ground, gave just enough away without compromising their position. It had worked, he convinced himself, because it had uncovered Eve's comparative *lack* of inno-cence, and reminded him that she was no mere child to be shaped and trusted; she was a killer, and she was their enemy.

With all that in mind, Nathaniel opted not to break his word and rescind his promise of letting her go outside. Corporal Howard was sent to escort her back to the elevator, where two uniformed guards put a hood over her head and turned her away from the access panel so she couldn't see the digits typed in to use in any subsequent escape attempt.

In spite of the oppressive security measures, Eve still sounded excited. She admitted freely to having been on the streets of the Citadel before but only once in daylight and only for a few minutes before she was captured. She asked question after question until Rebecca was forced to tell her to wait and see, and that she would explain everything when they got outside.

The elevator doors opened and a squad of black-visored troops greeted them behind a smiling man wearing an outfit similar to the Chairman's. Eve's hood was removed, and she eyed the squad with a wicked smile, recognising that these weren't the run-of-the-mill patrol types but a highly-trained team.

"Major Stanley," she said in greeting, surprising Rebecca that she knew the Chairman's new right-hand man. The girl seemed to hold none of the skin-crawling sense of unease that *she* felt when around the man.

"Good morning, Eve," Stanley said, "a few rules from the Chairman and you'll be permitted one hour in the Citadel. One, you don't leave the walls and go out into the city. Two, you *will* stay in sight of these troops and make no attempt to evade the drones that will be following you." He smiled as he drew out a small tablet and turned it around to show her. "Three, if you break any of these rules, this room will be flooded with incendiary. You know what that is?"

Eve looked up from the live image of Cohen sitting on her bed reading to look Stanley in the eyes and nod slowly.

"Four," he went on, producing a thick collar like a necklace, "you'll be wearing this. If you do anything we don't like, then your head will follow hers. Understood?" Eve nodded again, standing still as her wrist restraints were removed and the necklace locked into place with a high-pitched whine sounding to signal its activation. Stanley stepped aside grandly and smiled.

"Enjoy," he told them, adding, "one hour."

Eve walked towards the exit and sunlight, not waiting for Rebecca and certainly not waiting for the soldiers; it was their responsibility to keep up with her, not hers to wait for them. Rebecca caught up with her and spoke quietly as she kept pace.

"I didn't know about any of this," she said, "I swear it."

"It doesn't matter," Eve told her without any attempt to disguise her true feelings, "I get to go outside and that's all that matters."

———

Nathaniel watched from the separate command centre he'd ordered opened up for the specific purpose. He had six stealth drones, not tethered to Eve but all manually operated by experienced drivers, as well as a standby force of over a hundred troops ready to deploy and seal off any area inside the Citadel.

He didn't want to kill Eve, didn't want to hit the switch that would send an electrical impulse to the detonator inside the ring of explosive fixed around her neck, but if she was willing to sacrifice the life of Cohen in a bid for freedom, he simply couldn't allow that to happen. Better to have her dead than back with the enemy.

He was banking on her compliance based on Cohen's life being in the balance, but he hadn't got to be Chairman without learning to plan for contingencies. He corrected himself, thinking that he didn't get to *stay* Chairman without planning all the angles.

He watched as the girl emerged into the sunlight reflecting blindingly off the concrete of the promenade. He watched as her eyes evidently began to adapt and she lowered the hand shielding her face to stare up at the lines of statues adorning the grand street and began to walk away from the main building. He bit down his panic, panning out on one of the cameras to see the soldiers spreading out to line the two sides of the wide thorough-fare as everyone else went about their business without giving them a second look. Some stared at Eve, sensing that she was somehow different from the frightened, ever-watched population as the girl marvelled up at the first statue she reached.

Around him inside the command centre, the efficient muttering faded away to white noise as he watched in close-up how the girl's face registered marvel for what had been created there.

He missed the relevance as they stopped at the statue of the third Chairman of the Party. He didn't see Howard's nervous glances left and right at the soldiers as Eve stood directly in front of the place where she had been leaving the handwritten copies of her assignment notes for some unknown courier to spirit them away into the hands of the Resistance.

He saw what he wanted to see; a girl kept underground and fed vitriol by his enemy. A girl he still hoped he could bend to his cause, if only for the poetry of sending her against her creators. He watched her as she looked up at the statue and shook her head slowly from side to side and toyed with the explosive around her neck.

"I don't like it," he said, eyes narrowed at the screens, "something isn't right. Move in the standby force to form a close cordon; she knows her own people are watching her."

———

Nathaniel wasn't the only one watching closely. Deep underground less than a mile away from Eve, Fly tapped at the keys of a fold-out keyboard left behind when Mouse disappeared.

"I'm in," he said, "they're covering her specifically with a handful of drones, from what I can see… and they're all linked to the main server…" he tapped furiously at the keys a few more times until exclaiming, "Got her."

The screen above him flickered to life, showing Helen, now in charge of a shambles that had so recently been a fighting Resistance, an image of one of their greatest weapons, who she had never met.

"That's Eve," Fly said.

"Okay, how long until we can get our people in position?"

"Hang on," Fly told her, "you seeing this?" He pointed at the screen unnecessarily as the close-up shot of Eve showed her fiddling with a thick cord around her neck and shaking her head slowly.

"Seeing what?" Helen asked, annoyed.

"She's telling us 'no'," Fly explained, "she's showing us the problem."

"Which is what?"

"I'm guessing it's a bomb around her neck or something," Fly said, "something that would make breaking her out impossible."

"Our intelligence said nothing about her being booby-trapped when she came outside," Helen protested, "we were expecting soldiers, but bombs?"

"We need to abort," Fly insisted, "pull our people back and just watch. We'll have to wait to get her back because I don't like this. I don't like this *at all*." Helen hesitated until Fly told her again that she should abort. She nodded, dropping her head in frustration as her first act in Command was to turn a rescue operation into surveillance.

"We know she's alive," Fly said, searching for the silver lining, "and we know she's still got a brain between her ears."

"So, we watch," Helen said, pulling up a chair with a missing wheel that threatened to tip her out when she sat down.

"We watch," Fly agreed, as unhappy as she was.

CHAPTER TWENTY-EIGHT

THE ACCORD

They argued long into the night over who had what honours and who should lead which part of the offensive. The only thing the Dearmad and the Nocturnals agreed upon was that the time was finally right to combine their people and end the Party which had cost all of their ancestors so dearly.

Blake, as she had been called according to her uniform, had told others that her name was Nadeem. She had been taken away in tears, with blood from the man who'd had his throat cut in front of her soaking her uniform. It was curious to Adam that if the man was her enemy and loyal to the Party, why it upset her so much that he had been killed.

After the Dearmad had taken their time questioning her and finding no resistance at all in her answers, Mark was permitted to interrogate the captive on behalf of the Nocturnals, whose only senior member was embroiled in complex war-gaming with the king and his advisors.

Adam went with Mark, more to satisfy his burning desire for information than to offer any tactical assistance.

He found the door barred by two warriors, each holding short spears and who had evidently been warned ahead of their arrival, as neither moved to prevent their entry. Stepping inside a chamber much the same as the one he had so recently been held in, Adam looked down at the woman huddled in the darkest part of the small space, who shook when the door opened.

"We're not here to hurt you," Mark said in a low voice as he entered, showing empty hands as a reassurance to her. "My name is Mark and this is Adam. We're with the Resistance." At the mention of the Resistance, the big, bright eyes in the beautiful but marked face looked up from behind a tumble of greasy hair which stuck to her forehead.

One look at her had told Adam that she had been mistreated by the Dearmad, that they had opted for a physical approach to questioning her. That unkindness angered Adam in a way he fought to control, making him spin on his heel and walk back outside to the two guards.

"Who did this to her?" he demanded. Both men glanced at one another and ignored his question. "I said," Adam snarled, stepping close to the bigger of the two menacingly, "who did this to her?"

"You talk to the king," the other one answered, eyes fixed on a point on the opposite wall. Adam stepped back, releasing a breath to calm himself and snatching the water skin from the belt of the speaker before going back inside.

He found Mark crouched near her, her tears flowing as she sniffed and sobbed weakly. Sinking to his knees beside him, Adam uncorked the leather bag and offered it to her. She looked up and her eyes met his, checking for the trap in the offering. Seeming to find none, she reached out tentatively and took the skin to bring it to her lips and drink. Having satisfied her thirst after a few long gulps, she poured some of the liquid into her hands and rubbed at her face with it. Smoothing back her hair and letting out a sigh that appeared to strengthen her resolve, she sat up a little straighter and looked at them both.

"What do you want to know?" she asked. "I told them everything, but that didn't stop them trying to beat more out of me."

"We won't do that," Adam promised, sensing an annoyance from Mark who he suspected would be willing to employ such tactics if it aided him.

"Start with who you are and what you do for the Resistance," Mark interjected.

"My name is Samaira Nadeem," she told them, "I was the adjutant to the Chairman," she paused, hesitating before speaking her next words. "And I was the one who gave the orders that got you two out of the Citadel."

———

Mark and Adam sat in silence after she had finished speaking. Both had interrupted at first, wanting to jump ahead in her story to the parts that they were most interested in but she calmly recounted the last few months of her life to bind both of them under a kind of hypnosis, during which they hung on every word she said. Even though she was dirty and bruised, both men recognised her unique beauty, and both could see how she would be a perfect agent to be placed among the senior officers of the Party; regardless of their situation, men would always say more than they should when faced with a woman as stunning as Nadeem was.

She explained how she had escaped, how she had fraudulently given the orders for her move to the Frontier and for the transport that allowed for their escape. She continued to describe how she had created a new identity for herself and gone north instead of south, at the end of which, both men were left astonished by her bravery and temerity.

She became upset when she spoke of how she was captured; not for herself but evidently distraught at the loss of those under her unlawful command.

"They weren't bad people, you see?" she explained. "Most of them working for the Party are doing it for their standard of living, not out of any hatred for others. Of course, there are the die-hards," she went on, her eyes glazing over as she was probably remembering the death of the man who had attacked her for her treason, "and the fanatics, but they aren't everyone."

"So," Mark said, knowing and understanding what she spoke of but feeling less inclined to be as empathetic as she was, "they'll know about you by now."

"Without a doubt," Nadeem said sadly, "I'd say my cover is well and truly blown."

"And your family?" Adam asked, "Would the Party go after them?" Nadeem smiled sympathetically.

"I don't have any family left," she told them, "so nobody else has to suffer for who I am."

"You saved our lives," Adam murmured as the true scale of their underworld finally hit him, "and risked your own to do it. Thank you." Nadeem fixed him with a look that was part amusement and part relief and smiled. Whatever the emotions behind it, she radiated such control over both of them that even Mark was sold on her.

"Come on," he said as he groaned to climb to his feet, "let's get you fed and cleaned up."

Neither guard dared to stop them, even though one of them seemed to want to protest until Mark leaned down to face him and told him to stay exactly where he was. They walked away, Nadeem moving slowly as though her entire body hurt, and they escorted her to the chamber Mark had been allocated to use the shower. He apologised that the clothing he had would be too big for her, but she smiled and thanked him with the lightest of touches to his arm, saying that anything clean to wear would improve her life at that moment.

They waited outside in awkward silence as the sounds of water splashing reached their ears. Neither wanted to imagine in great detail what the scene inside would look like; not in front of the another, at any rate.

"What are you smirking at?" Mark asked Adam, startling him out of his daydream and making him fire a guilty look at his mentor.

"Er, nothing."

"Good," Mark said, "you're married, remember?"

As much as Adam wanted to stay with the woman and protect her, Mark insisted that he go and find Dren to see what was happening. He reluctantly left, promising to find them in the place where they were served food, and returned to the king's hall where he found the arguments still raging. Catching Dren's eye, he saw her nod her head to join him.

"The king is inclined towards caution," she whispered in his ear, "but his people want war."

"What about the others?" he asked. "The… the *Nua*?"

"They also want war, but only if it is profitable to them."

"And us?" She smiled wickedly.

"We have always wanted war, but we have never been strong enough without the support of the Dearmad."

Adam stayed crouched close beside her, hearing the whispered translations as the negotiations unfolded. The Dearmad king tentatively agreed to commit his forces so long as the Nua matched with their own people. Both sides spoke of territory and resources but Dren stood and gave a long, almost aggressive speech, of which Adam caught only a few words. When she sat back down, she explained that the mainland belonged to the people there, minus the enemy, and that with them gone, all of them could flourish above ground and rebuild their lives.

Eventually, painstakingly, an accord was struck and the agreement to attack at the next new moon was made. Taking their Resistance ally with them, and with a final sour glance from the defeated challenger who came to see them leave, Adam and his people climbed back aboard their boat to carry the news home.

CHAPTER TWENTY-NINE

A DEMONSTRATION OF POWER

Helen had expected more of a transition than she had enjoyed when she took charge of Command. She'd hoped, if that day ever came, to continue the fight on a small scale until something huge changed that would usher in a new era in their history.

What she had not expected was for that event, that huge something, to happen only weeks after she embarked on that challenge.

The plan to rescue Eve from the clutches of the Party had been aborted. It was the right decision to make, but it still stung her as a failure. They had watched, seeing the girl taking in the sights of the Citadel in all its concrete, grey glory, before she walked back inside the building and out of sight of their piggy-backed video monitoring. Fly had assured her that there were positives to be taken from it all, in spite of their people being withdrawn. Had they not been, they would have been slaughtered, given the level of protection placed on Eve. Fly pored over the recorded footage again and again.

"She's definitely warning us off," he said for the fifth

time in as many minutes. "That thing around her neck has *got* to be some kind of redundancy to kill her if she goes out of their sight."

Helen said nothing, having assured herself of those assumptions many times over. "Is that our agent with her?" Fly, having checked, assured her that it was. "Did she try to set us up?"

"I don't think so," Fly answered hesitantly, "it's just as likely that she didn't know about the security measures. Would you tell our liaison if we had one of them captured?"

"Probably not," Helen admitted, having lived her entire life dealing with compartmentalised information "So what's the plan?"

Fly paused again, thinking about any answer he might give.

"We wait for a better opportunity," he said with a shrug. "There's literally zero chance of getting inside, which makes getting out again not even worth considering. If it was any other building, we could probably do it, but there? Underground? Not a chance."

She thanked him, checking her watch in the dim light and calculating that if she left now, she would get three hours sleep at best before she had to be up and going to work to maintain her façade of normality.

———

She had a little over two hours in the end before the harsh, robotic screeching of her alarm tore her out of the shallow slumber. She washed, dressed, ate and went to work to go through the same monotonous actions as always, with only the boredom of the repetitive work enabling her to remain undetected. Had she been in any other line of work, her exhaustion might have attracted attention to her and invited a closer scrutiny that would have been less than ideal, given her nocturnal role.

When the final klaxon sounded to signal the end of the working day, she shuffled in line out of the security check-points and stood motionless as she was subjected to a search she would describe as anything but thorough. Heading towards the tower blocks and her simple, drab residence she felt a nudge to her right side and instinctively recoiled slightly as she was jostled by passing workers moving faster than she was in their eagerness to be home and off the streets before curfew.

Slipping her hand into her jacket pocket on the side she had been bumped revealed a rolled-up piece of paper which she clung tightly to and resisted the urge to take out and read. It stayed inside her pocket until her front door was locked.

Bread, cheese, candles.

The scrap of paper containing the innocuous list of things to buy from the commissar wouldn't attract even the slightest interest from any over-zealous Party solider deciding to up their monthly quota of random stop-and-searches on a citizen. To them it would mean nothing, especially as all their meals would be provided to them at a time dictated by their regime, but to her it meant so much more.

Bread and cheese, the two staples of her barely adequate diet, meant that word had reached them from the Frontier. The addition of candles, found in the resi-dence of almost all citizens due to the enforced power outages when the Citadel frequently redirected energy to the headquarters building, told her that the news was urgent.

Such a simple communication. So child-like in its face-value subterfuge that the simplicity was its brilliance. Ignoring the exhaustion that evaporated in the face of her excitement, she threw on her coat and snatched open the door of her residence.

Only to find her own face reflected in the black visors of two Party soldiers, one with their black-gloved hand raised and poised to knock.

"Ms Randal?" a voice asked from behind them, locking her stunned body in place with her mouth open. A man not wearing a masked helmet like the others stepped forward to stand before her, only fractionally too close to be comfortable in normal circumstances. She felt anything but comfortable then, and his false smile and cruel eyes threatened to break her resolve before they had even begun questioning her.

She considered turning away, considered running back inside and throwing open the window to launch herself into the fresh air outside the tower block to fall to her death, but her mind screamed at her to stay calm. Logic kicked her in the back of her head and yelled at her that if they knew who she was, knew *what* she was, they wouldn't have been about to knock on the door; they'd have come through it with weapons raised to subdue and overwhelm her, to drag her away, never to return.

"Yes?" she said, swallowing and sounding only just as frightened as the situation dictated.

"Sergeant Major Du Bois," the smiling man said by way of introduction. Helen Randall had lived her entire life under the heel of the lower levels of the Party's military might, and not once in all that time could she ever recall being given a soldier's name who wasn't an officer.

"If you'd accompany us," he said, straining a little as though the effort of remaining polite was churning his insides up like a cement mixer, "we have a few questions for you." It was delivered as a polite request, but the words were undeniably a statement; as though a pre-destined sequence of events was unfolding and none of them had the power to change fate. Like it or not, the undertone told her, she *would* go with them.

"What's this about?" she asked, remembering to act as though she was just a construction line worker and had no secret existence that gave her more insight than she sometimes wanted.

"Just a routine follow-up," Du Bois said without lowering the guard of his fake smile, "checking in on everyone who wasn't at their workstation yesterday morning."

"I was sick," she began to protest, "I'm still not we…"

"I don't know the specifics," Du Bois interrupted her, "I just have a list and your name is on it. This way, please."

Helen sat in the darkened rear section of the Party transport vehicle as the tyre noise and whine of the electric motors powering them permeated the armoured body to reach her ears. The smiling man who wore no helmet sat opposite her, still smiling as though he had been stuck in that position when the wind changed, just like her mother had told her when she was young. The other two guards, obviously the smiling man's personal muscle – not that he looked like he needed any – sat worryingly close to her on either side to pen her in.

"Won't be long now," smiler said in a tone that was measured to sound reassuring but lacked any kind of real empathy behind it.

He was correct in his false assurance, because the whining sounds faded, and the vehicle stopped after less than a minute longer spent gliding through the streets of the Citadel. She climbed out, surprised that she hadn't been searched and that her hands weren't secured in restraints, expecting to meet a squad of soldiers under the shadow of the Party headquarters building, but instead found herself at a nondescript concrete building with nobody else in sight.

Du Bois, without looking behind him, walked straight up to a grey door set deep into the grey wall and tapped in a six-digit code to make the door buzz and pop open a fraction. Helen tried to hide her frown at the low-tech security and managed to wipe the expression from her face before he turned to look at her. She followed him inside, hearing the door shut behind her and turning to see that the guards hadn't followed them in. A light set into the ceiling blinked on, probably activated by a movement sensor, to shine artificial light on a simple table and two chairs. Du Bois took one with a groan as believable as his smile and offered the other to her with a flat hand.

"So," he said as he pulled a small tablet from the leg pocket of his uniform, "you reported that you were unfit to perform work duties due to illness at… oh-six-twenty-two, that right?"

"I don't remember the time but…"

"And you stayed in your residence all day due to this illness?" Helen fought the urge to freeze up, forced her face to not betray her and stuck to the lie.

"I slept on and off all day," she said, "still felt awful this morning but I couldn't afford another day of reduced rations so I…"

"So you *didn't* leave your residence?" Helen swallowed. She knew that her tower block had very few cameras working, and Fly had assured her that her route down the stairwell and into the basement was clear of any surveillance.

"No, like I said I went back to b…"

"Because a work party overseer visited your residence at zero-nine-fifty-four and reported that you didn't answer the door to him." Du Bois stopped speaking abruptly, intentionally letting her think that he would continue, so making any response she gave sound as though she was hesitating.

"Like I said," Helen responded calmly, but not *too* calmly, "I went back to bed. He could've been hammering the door down, but I was sweating up a fever and probably didn't hear him."

"Probably?"

"I guarantee I didn't hear anyone knocking on my door," she said firmly, showing enough worry at being whisked away but trying to stay walking that tightrope in case she gave anything away. Du Bois stared at her in silence for a count of five long, torturous seconds before putting back on his false smile and letting out a breath in a chuckle.

"Probably the lazy bastard didn't want to climb the stairs," he said, "we'll take you back in just a moment if you wait through there," he said, indicating another door. She rose uncertainly, thanking him and walking towards the door to place a tentative hand on the level to open it and step through.

The hood, made of rough material that stripped the skin from her lower lip as it was dragged over her face, smelled like she wasn't the first person to wear it. She didn't resist; didn't give them any reason to beat her or taser her or break a bone just to ensure compliance. It seemed that her lack of panic took all of the fun out of it for whoever was given the task of securing her for whatever lay in wait next, because they sighed in disappointment and toned down the severity of the violence, before securing her wrists in restraints behind her back and dragging her away.

———

Harvey paced the damp underground room much to the annoyance of the twins who, in contrast, waited with statue-like patience. Fly tapped intermittently at a keyboard without speaking.

"She should be here by now," Harvey complained for the third time in as many minutes. "Something's wrong."

"You don't know that," Jenna chided him, "not yet, so do us all a favour and shut the f…"

"He's right," Fly cut in quietly, "look." He pointed unnecessarily to the screen to the right of his display, showing a dark transport van parked outside Helen's residence block shortly after the time he had tracked her back from piecing together her journey home from archive footage. They huddled around to watch as she willingly climbed in the back of it, not restrained and not wearing a hood, as was customary for any citizen taken for questioning.

"We're screwed," Harvey said flatly.

"Not so fast there," Fly told him, "she only knew there *was* a message; not what it said."

"And what does it say?" Harvey shot back, having had the information withheld from him by the remains of project Genesis and not fully understanding that he had the power of Command over them.

"It says they're coming, and the war is about to start."

"And you don't think the timing of Helen being taken is a concern?"

"No," Fly told him after a pause, "because she's on an active list of everyone not reporting to their work assignment yesterday morning. They've taken fifty-two people in for questioning, so there's no reason to think they've singled her out."

"So, what do we do?" Harvey asked, the sheer drama of the simple message hitting him like a transport at full speed.

"We wait. If she doesn't come back and the others do, then we know they've got her, and we act accordingly."

———

Helen sat in the tiny holding cell, counting. She counted slowly to sixty, every two numbers ticking off inside her head equating to a breath in and the following two being the breath out. She continued like this until the number in her head translated to four hours and seventeen minutes, before the red light above the door turned green and it burst open to admit a pair of faceless guards who took up position either side of the door.

She raised her head, ignoring the soldiers and watching the portal until a figure stepped inside. That man, dressed in a uniform that wasn't a uniform, stood before her as another soldier brought a simple metal chair and placed it in front of her own.

The man sat, sweeping the tail of his unfastened brown leather coat behind him to expose the empty holster on his right thigh. He made a show of not looking at her, of tapping away at the tablet in his hand as though she were an insignificance, until finally he looked up at her and smiled.

His smile, unlike that of the disturbing man who had renditioned her to this place, was genuine. Unfortunately for her, not that her face betrayed the belief, his smile spoke of a man who had already won.

"Helen Randall?" he said, making a show of looking at the tablet again as though she wasn't the main focus of his night.

"You know I am," she said, trying again to mix the right amount of calm with just enough overt fear that she hoped would make her believable, "what's this about?" The man smiled again, sadly this time as if he was disappointed that she wanted to continue playing games.

"My name is Major Stanley," he said, "and I want to show you something." She said nothing, waiting for her opponent to show his hand before she responded. He stood, turning his chair so that he sat beside her and paused as she recoiled slightly. He made a noise in his throat; amusement and derision in equal parts. Lifting the tablet for her to see, he swiped from right to left repeatedly, showing her footage of other people in similar holding cells to the one she occupied. Some sat in corners, huddled and rocking. Others banged at the doors and wailed to protest their innocence. The scenes repeated, over and over, until he lowered the tablet to tap at it again.

"You're spotting a theme, I imagine?" Stanley asked conversationally, raising the tablet for her to see once more. "See if you can spot the odd one out." She looked, seeing her own image played in fast-forward. She barely moved, as she knew she hadn't for hours. Her equal measures of calm and panic had been grossly underplayed, it seemed. The tablet was passed to the soldier who had brought the chair, who took it and left the room.

"So, you see my dilemma?" Stanley went on as he leaned back comfortably in the chair. "I have fifty-two people who missed their work assignment yesterday morning when something very important happened inside the Citadel. Of those fifty-two, fifty-one of them are losing their minds. They've offered up names, places… all manner of information in an attempt to save their own skins and be let go. You haven't said a word. Why is that?"

"Because I've done nothing wrong," Helen assured him after the briefest of pauses, "and I don't know anything that would help the Party." Stanley sat forward abruptly, snapping the fingers of his right hand as though she had said precisely what he had wagered her to.

"And *that's* the issue," he crowed. "Everyone thinks they have something to offer, unless they had, let's say, *allegiances* they wouldn't betray…"

Helen's mind raced, trying to get two steps ahead of him before she answered and failing to come up with any idea, no matter how weak, in good time.

"You see," Stanley said as he stood and walked slowly behind her, "we see and hear almost everything that happens inside the Citadel. I say almost because we obviously miss some things, like the fact that unregistered children are born underground and that normal, everyday people, much like yourself, lead double lives when they entertain a foolish notion of one day overthrowing their rightful leadership."

Helen said nothing, which prompted the arrogant major to lean over her shoulder and whisper menacingly in her ear.

"You wouldn't know anything about that, would you?"

"You mean the Resistance?" she scoffed, "They're a myth. Something the old folks tell their grandchildren if they're lucky enough to have them."

"So," Stanley said as he stood upright again, "you think me paranoid?"

"I didn't say that," Helen told him, "I just don't know

that what you're saying is real. You know more than me, obviously."

Stanley laughed softly. It was a cruel laugh and not one of mirth. "Cohen said that too," he told her in a quiet voice. As much as she tried, as much as she forced her body not to respond to the chemical cocktail his words had caused to wash into her bloodstream, her nostrils flared, and she sucked in a sharp intake of breath.

"Who?" she tried to say, but it was too late. He had her, and he knew it.

CHAPTER THIRTY

EXPENDABLE

Eve went back to her room, turning to say her farewell to Rebecca, who she knew would go back to her life above ground.

"Wait," she said, "don't you want to stay for a while?"

Rebecca looked taken aback, clearly lost for words as her mouth opened and closed.

"I… I could, I suppose…" Eve's face lit up and she threw her arms around the young woman, ignoring the tensing she felt in her body out of fear. Not all of it was false, however. She longed for company, and despite clearly being the focus of Corporal Rebecca Howard's current assignment, she found herself growing attached to her. Of all her studies, of all the time learning a different perspective on the history of their home, none of her teachings had included basic psychology.

If it had, if she had learned less about how to manipulate people with weapons and more with her mind, then she might have understood more of what was happening inside her head. She craved attention. Acceptance. Had been isolated for so long that she would make friends with just about anyone, and Rebecca had shown a vulnerability in front of her which disarmed her more than she could have understood.

"I'll have to get permission," she warned Eve, extricating herself from the crushing embrace and pulling the device from her back pocket. "You go on ahead," she told the girl, "I'll catch you up regardless." Eve went reluctantly, looking back over her shoulder to see if the woman was following. Rebecca made a show of tapping at the screen until she was certain that Eve was out of sight before pressing a single icon and lifting the device to her ear. The call connected almost immediately and was answered with a single word.

"Yes?" the Chairman's voice snapped.

"It's done," she said, "it's a go… you're sure you can guarantee my safety, Sir?"

"Corporal," Nathaniel's voice resonated back to her, "if I'm right about this, then I won't have to." The call clicked off without another word and Rebecca took a steadying breath before putting on an expression of excitement and following Eve's direction.

Rebecca used her authority to have food brought to Eve's room instead of them having to eat in the subterranean canteen with all the other evening workers. They ate, watched movies of the Party heroes of the past and laughed at how ludicrous their exploits seemed.

Rebecca sat on Eve's bed behind her and brushed her long hair until it was as silky as water, allowing Eve to do the same to her. Their conversations ranged over various topics, and when the subject landed on the opposite sex, Rebecca admitted to having had a few relationships but that none of them had proved long lasting.

"What about you?" she asked the girl. "Nobody you like?"

"There was one boy," she said, "I wasn't supposed to know but people always spoke about us like we were, I don't know, *bred* for each other or something…"

"Where is he now?"

Eve's expression dropped. "No idea," she responded quietly, "he came with me when I was caught, but… no idea." She resumed the gentle brushing of her hair with more melancholy than before, her hand moving the brush more slowly than before.

The timing couldn't have been more perfect.

A dull, muted explosion rippled along the hallway far from the room they occupied, causing their heads to turn in silent unison towards the door.

"What was that?" Rebecca asked, her voice tense and wavering.

"I don't know," Eve responded, standing up with an entirely different bearing from any the older woman had seen her use before. "Stay here," she told her firmly, crossing the short distance to the door in one pace, before pulling the handle and finding it locked. Without asking, she whipped back and snatched the ID card from Rebecca's belt to tug it free before she cold protest.

"I mean it," she said as she swiped the card and pulled the door open, "stay here."

Moving fast, sunk low to the ground on bent legs to pad barefoot along the abandoned corridor, Eve tuned in to her other senses.

Smoke. Far away but unmistakable. There was something else in that faint waft, something acrid as though the smoke was from an explosion and not a fire. She saw nothing, or at least nobody, seeing as the working day was well and truly over. Still, she knew there would be a strong contingent of guards down there for her benefit. Indeed, she'd be disappointed if there weren't, and those soldiers should have responded to what she was sensing.

The sound of boots running hard on the polished floors drifted to her from ahead and to her left in the direction of the main elevator she had ridden in previously. She froze, waiting to detect in which direction they were running, instead of assuming it was the forces stationed down there responding. The echoes of the interwoven corridors threw her senses out and made it impossible for her to figure it out, so she went with her gut. Running ahead instead of taking the direct path left, she moved fast to come at the elevator from the other side in the hope that she wouldn't encounter anyone on the way.

"Fan out," growled a voice from around the corner she was hiding behind, "find the old woman; she's the priority. The girl doesn't know enough to be a danger." Eve's eyes went wide as the words made sense to her.

Cohen!

She turned, bare feet squeaking on the ground, and set off fast back towards the cell where she had seen her mentor sitting quietly in ignorance. Her mind raced as she ran, head whipping side to side to throw her hair in her face as she searched the deserted hallways for enemy. Off to her right, she could hear the sounds of sporadic gunfire thumping the air in single shots, until one long burst of automatic fire prompted a strange silence that was merely the absence of loud noise.

Rounding another blind corner at speed in her haste to reach Cohen's cell before the attackers did, the skin of her feet made more squeaking protests as she found two of them at the door with their backs to her. Neither turned to look at her, but both stood back and flattened themselves against the wall either side of the door as a small charge detonated and the portal flew open violently. Eve leapt forwards, urging her body to move her fast enough to stop whatever was happening.

If she hadn't heard the words, hadn't read the cruel-heartedness in the tone of their leader, she might have felt a sense of elation at the rescue mission she had given up on hoping for. As if to underline her fears, both men filled the ruined doorframe and lifted their guns to their shoulders.

"It's her," one said flatly.

"What the he…" Cohen's voice snapped, before both guns spat flame and bullets to stop her speaking forever. Eve's mind froze even as her body continued to streak along the corridor. She heard a scream; a high-pitched shriek of murderous rage and pain that seemed to come from everywhere and nowhere at the same time. The scream stopped as she twisted her body in mid-flight to raise her right knee to just the right spot for it to connect with a sinewy crack against the jaws of one man. He dropped like water, spinning slightly to his right with the impetus of her attack, to bounce him face-first off the scorched door frame and backwards into the corridor. As the other man's eyes followed the path of his comrade, his mind seemed to catch up with events and he began to raise his rifle towards where she was crouching on the ground.

She spun, staying low and shooting out a leg at the right moment. It wasn't a sweeping kick designed to take the man's legs out from under him and topple him to her level, but instead her right foot stamped out to connect with his leg higher up.

The strangled cry of unfathomable pain drowned out the crunching of the lower leg bones practically separating from the upper ones. His leg ruined but still upright for the time being, the man's gun barrel wavered in her direction as he began to topple backwards. Eve added her body weight to his slow momentum, simply slamming her shoulder into his chest as she snatched the gun aside to send him sprawling backwards to leave the weapon in her grip. He slid to a stop, hands already fluttering at the leg dangling at a horribly unnatural angle and sucked in a breath to scream in pain. Eve glanced inside the room, all immediate threats taken care of, and looked down on the small, frail frame of the woman who had raised her.

She had never been overly kind to Cohen, preferring to be a constant pain to her as she bore the brunt of all of Eve's frustrations, but seeing her now with her torso in bloody ruin and her lifeless eyes looking up at a spot on the ceiling, Eve felt nothing but loss and sorrow for the small woman.

That loss, that sorrow, evaporated under the intense heat of her anger. She spun around, advancing on the man whose leg she had wrecked and dropped both knees onto his chest. Flicking her hair over her shoulder to lean down in some ghastly approximation of passion, she locked eyes with him just as she would have done with a lover if she had ever known one. That eye contact was fleeting and brief as his brain told his hands to do something foolish and make them scrabble at a holster to retrieve another weapon. She shifted her position, trapping his moving hand under one sharp kneecap, and turned his own gun that she still held in her hand on him.

His eyes widened, recognising his death in her face, but her own eyes stayed unnervingly calm. She regarded the gun briefly before switching her gaze back to him, finding it vulgar and loud with none of the skill and grace her own sword had given her. Her sword, lost to her now, would have taken this man, this *coward,* to pieces with such ease that merely holding the dull metal of the gun offended her. She tossed it aside derisively as her hands explored the pouches and pockets on her victim's chest. Slender fingers resting on what she hoped was the hilt of a knife, she drew it out to find her hand holding a long, flat-bladed screwdriver.

"It'll do," she said to herself, shoving the tip of the tool through his ear as hard as she could and feeling the hot wetness of blood seeping out as the man's eyes went dull like a pair of lightbulbs burning down when the power failed.

Standing, bloody screwdriver still in the grip of her right hand, she looked left and right up and down the corridor before throwing one last glance at Cohen in the hopes that the woman had forgiven her for how she had been.

Forgiveness covered, she set off towards the noise of sporadic gunfire in search of revenge.

The small detachment of soldiers stationed down in the depths of Special Projects after the working day was complete had been unprepared for any external threat to their post. They were there primarily, or so they believed, to prevent an escape from within. Their eyes were on the video monitoring of their 'guests', as their Chairman called them, and not on any external threat as, realistically, the chances of a hostile force getting through the main building of the Citadel to attack them so far below ground were so small they weren't a consideration

When the locked doors of the elevator opened and three devices were tossed into the guard room to explode in searing flashes of light and noise, filling the rooms with acrid smoke, they responded as they had been trained and came out fighting. Half of them were cut down by gunfire immediately until their commander, a lieutenant with a reputation for possessing a respectable level of skill, ordered them out of the other doors to flank and coun-terattack.

By the time they had formed a defence and engaged in a sporadic firefight, more than half of the attackers had already spread out into the underground complex on the hunt for their true objectives. The lieutenant knew nothing of that, having lost his surveillance eyes and ears when the explosions went off to rob them of their command centre, but he did his best to lead his men in the desperate fight.

Eve heard their gun battle and avoided heading directly towards it as the echoing sounds of more boots running on the hard ground alerted her to danger behind. A brief glance over her shoulder told her that four of them, all dressed in Party uniforms but not carrying the standard weapons and somehow looking out of place, as if they had stolen the costumes, were aiming their guns at her.

Springing to her side to roll on the ground and rise effortlessly to her feet, she heard the terrifying sounds of bullets whining off in ricochets from the concrete pillar she had hid behind. Voices shouted orders to advance on her and, looking down at the blood-streaked tool in her hand, she knew she couldn't close the gap between her and them without dying.

Changing her plan in a heartbeat, she fled along the corridor to swing left and right at the unmarked turns until she found the open area of the gymnasium. The lights began to flicker into life as her movement was detected, making her fling her unbound hair left and right again as her head whipped around to find the control panel. Seeing it twenty paces away and heading for it at a dead run, she hit the switches to kill the lights and plunge the wide, open area into near-darkness, illuminated only by the dim glow of the corridor beyond and a few emergency lights high on the ceiling.

Eve took a few seconds to think and get her bearings,

recalling everything that had been in the big room before the lights had gone out and allowing her to map the area through memory alone. She set off for the apparatus, instinctively seeking the high ground like a predator, when a thump of flesh on glass caught her attention. She stood still, looking at the two occupied cages of the disturbing creatures she had fought before, finding that one of them was upright and fixed her with an intense look.

Eve hesitated for half a second before running over to stand face to face with Reaper. The silent young woman, face set in a mask of resting hostility, stared at the girl.

"Someone's broken in," Eve hissed at her, "they've already killed… they're here to kill us," she said. Wordlessly, Reaper's eyes moved to the spot on the wall where the override panel to her cell was, holding up a sequence of fingers with both hands for Eve to see in the low light.

This time she didn't hesitate. She didn't know why, not for certain, but she believed in that moment that her genetically engineered enemy was an ally.

"Four, six, six, three, nine, nine, eight," Eve muttered to herself as she pressed the numbers on the pad deliberately. The door popped and slid aside, leaving her unprotected from her foe. Reaper stepped out, showcasing her superior height over Eve and paused for a breath to look down at her. Her eyes darted away, looking towards the corridor where voices could be heard shouting, and turned back to nod for Eve to follow her. Both young women ran for the apparatus and leapt to climb up from the ground in readiness to ambush their attackers.

The seconds spent waiting for them to arrive, for them to decide on what to do and for them to begin spreading out to search the open area felt heavy and slow after the rush of her escape from them. Off to her left she could sense Reaper moving stealthily, like the cats she had seen hunt mice and rats underground, moving to better position herself for the fight to come.

"Lights?" one of the men hissed in what he intended to be a whisper, but which carried far and clear in the dark.

"Don't know," another answered, "did you see a switch?" They continued to advance in a ragged line heading towards the elevated positions of two unarmed killers as they spoke, giving away their positions and state of mind. They were frightened of them. Frightened of the dark.

And they had good reason to be.

"Go back to the entrance and find a swit… *argchh!*"

"Grant?" a voice shouted, "Grant, stop messing about! Where are you?" That voice neared Eve's position and stopped, spinning around with his gun barrel raised as he searched for his comrade. From off to her left, the choking noises subsided quickly, and she didn't waste time imagining what Reaper had done to the one called Grant. Torn his throat out, most likely. With her teeth or her nails.

The one below her breathed loudly, raggedly, as though panic was rising inside him and threatening to boil over the top. She heard him take two steps towards the point where the noises had come from, before he walked into a metal upright supporting the framework she was resting on lightly to send vibrations up the tubes and through her body.

Her eyes, accustomed to darkness in the recent past so easily forgotten, made out the shape of him below her. She stood, tucked her arms to her sides and hopped lightly to fall downwards like a spear. Landing two paces away from him she ducked to crouch low on the ground as he swung his gun barrel around wildly to face the small noises she made. Crabbing on all fours sideways, a sight that would've seemed more like a demonic possession than anything else, she removed herself from the danger of his gun and made ready for her attack.

Standing tall, taking one elongated step towards him, she sprung lightly from her left foot to wrap her right knee around the back of his head. Gripping his neck tightly with her calf she flung her upper body backwards and down to rip him off balance and choke a cry from his lips before his instinctive need to preserve his breath kicked in and he went silent. Her hands met the ground just where she expected it to be as she braced herself and used the impetus of her body to throw him down hard onto his back, intending to break his neck and crush his larynx with her leg as they landed. As he fell, his finger squeezed the trigger of his gun to light up the big room in eerie strobe-effect flashes of orange and white before it went dark again. In the confusion of the light and noise, Eve had released her hold on him to land on her feet and roll backwards to come up in a crouch.

"Over there!" a voice yelled, followed immediately by more gunfire aimed in her direction.

"No!" was all the man she had attacked could shout before his body was outlined by the muzzle flashes to make his silhouette dance grotesquely, as the round hit him and punched through his body. Eve rolled away as fast as possible to get to her feet and sprint in a wide arc and be well away from where they thought she was.

The world erupted into blinking daylight as one of them had found the lighting control panel. Eve, still running, angled her trajectory to attack the nearest gunman who had his back to her; felling him with a brutal punch to the base of his skull and stamping a heel down hard onto his throat the second he hit the ground. More gunfire sounded – single shots fired from a pistol – and she glanced over to see Reaper shoving the struggling form of another attacker towards the shooter as the bullets failed to penetrate his body to offer her a slither of protection. Eve could tell that she wasn't going to cross the distance in time before her human shield fell down dead, and she spun the handle of the screwdriver in her hand to cock back her arm and hurl it as hard as she could.

The screwdriver, having not been designed for that purpose, resisted the throw because of the imbalance of weight and the fact that the wide handle offered up too much resistance in the air. Had she thrown one of the slim daggers she used to own, it would have sailed true and pierced the neck of the shooter easily. The screwdriver, still protesting its use as a lethal weapon, struck him hard with the handle on the bone of his eye socket. It was enough, and Reaper dropped her dying burden to advance on him before he could bring the gun to bear on her again. She delivered a series of bone-crunching kicks to various anatomically vulnerable points on his body, and he dropped to his knees before she fell on him and gripped his face, wearing an expression of pure savagery.

His screams, animalistic and high-pitched, tore the air as her thumbs bored deep into his eye sockets. Eve, who had begun running towards her to help, stopped in horrified awe at what she was seeing. Cutting an enemy's head off with a sword was one thing but gouging out his eyes with her thumbs was a gruesomely disturbing sight for her.

She didn't have to endure it for long, as another loud report cut over the screams. Reaper, expression of brutality and hatred disappearing instantly, seemed to lock her eyes onto Eve's in a final second before she fell to her side, hitting the ground with an uncontrolled crack where her skull slammed down unprotected, Eve watched as the blood welled out from her body.

She turned to the entrance, seeing a man holding the

gun that had killed the monster who had turned out to be her ally, and her blood ran cold as that same gun was placed very deliberately against the side of Rebecca's head. She took an automatic step towards this new enemy, prompting him to shove the barrel hard against her friend's skull and shout a warning at her.

"Don't," he snapped, "stay where you are." Eve thought about responding, thought about asking who they were and what they wanted but her mind had already connected those particular dots. They were Resistance – they *had* to be – and they had come to protect their secrets at all costs. They would kill her, just as they'd killed Cohen, because they were both expendable. As the gun slowly turned on her, she considered making a final play to rescue Rebecca, to kill the man holding the gun, when she knew the result of any action would lead to both of them dying.

She closed her eyes, waiting for the end, as the single gunshot rang out.

CHAPTER THIRTY-ONE

WAR GAMES

"Just like that?" Adam asked, "We just *take* the Frontier?"

"Yes," growled the king, fixing his son-in-law with a look that spoke of much confidence but far less patience.

"What about their strong points? Their back-up forces?" Mark cleared his throat and paused, making Adam guess whether he was warning him to shut up or if he actually had something to say.

"They've been doing this a long time," Mark finally said as calmly as he could without embarrassing him. Dren, having entered the room in total silence, scoffed loudly from behind Adam to make him jolt as though touched by a tiny current of electricity.

"We *have* been doing this a long time," she said caustically, "we have been doing this from the first days of our lives. We have been *doing* this for generations. *We* are ready, it is *others* we have been waiting for." Adam shifted uncomfortably, having figured out that the one person on the planet he shouldn't disagree with had failed to answer the specifics of his questions.

Dren fixed him with a look, throwing her hands up in

mock surrender as he clearly wasn't going to accept her generalisations. Turned to her father with the slightest bow of her head, she spoke in low, rapid words of their own language too fast for Adam to understand any of it. The king, doing as his daughter asked, turned to gesture at the wide table for two of the attending warriors to step forwards and grip the edge of the tabletop.

With a heave of effort, the flat surface came free and was shuffled to one side where it was rested against the wall of the chamber. What it had revealed underneath was an intricately carved relief of the entire south west region. Delicate strokes of some old tool showed the craggy shore-line where it met the water, and even that water seemed to come alive in the low light underground and the shadows moved over the smooth, carved waves to give it the effect of being alive like the sea itself.

Adam, in awe of the craftsmanship, couldn't help himself and leaned over to run his fingers over the physical map and marvel at how his fingertips caught on the polished wood. As if the skill and artistry of the original carvers wasn't enough, a holographic display burst into life from a projector set high into the cavern's ceiling. Red and blue shading appeared over the carved map, depicting the battle lines between the enemy and the rightful inhabitants of the land. Icons showed buildings, strong points, weak points, and troop numbers.

Dren stepped forwards, glancing slightly up at the king, who held out a hand, extending his upturned palm to invite her to speak. With a gracious nod, she gave the city people an up-to-date briefing.

"Their numbers are concentrated at five major points along our borders," she began, indicating the five collections of red icons on the display. "Each location houses the support forces for certain areas, and each of those comes under the command of a single officer." She looked at Adam and Mark, now joined by Mouse, who was regarding the display as though it was nothing new to him. Adam guessed the intelligence briefing was already filed away in his brain and tuned back in to hear Dren's words.

"The plan, as soon as the sun begins to set, is to attack each area in two places. We do this in great strength to make them think that each attack is the main one and make them deploy all reserves to strengthen their lines. When we are certain that they have committed their people, we attack… *here*." She pointed to an area on the map further behind the disputed territory safely located a few miles away from the trenches.

"How do we…?" Adam began, stopping himself and, smiling at Dren, continued, "You have tunnels leading there?"

"We have a tunnel," she said, returning his smile. "Our main forces will continue to make it appear that we are mobilising in force, but the true attack will be at their command centre." The king stepped forward, filling the space with his deep, gravelly voice.

"Here, we take away their eyes and ears," he said. Adam glanced at Mark, who gave him a slight shake of his head, meaning that he would explain later and not to interrupt.

"We break their radios and their computers," he went on. "They will be alone in the dark and they do not cope with the dark like we do." He nodded to his daughter to continue.

"We were born in the dark," she intoned solemnly, "and they were not." Adam swallowed, hoping that nobody was looking at him with the same contempt as they had for the Party soldiers. He was born in the dark, only a different kind of dark; an artificial one. The skills of the

Nocturnals were passed down through generations, which made him feel more like a laboratory experiment than before. He rolled his shoulders to push away his anxieties, knowing that he had proven himself in both environments and was just as lethal as they were.

"And when their command and technology is taken out?" Mark asked. "What then?"

"Then we finish them," Dren said savagely, her fist held before her face clenched tightly, "for good."

"What do you need us to do?" Adam's mentor went on.

"Very little," she said, meaning no insult by her words. "We have been planning this day for many years, but if you prefer to be involved, you could be involved in the main attacks." Mark nodded, almost bowing, as though thanking her for the honour. Dren turned to Adam.

"You will be with me, attacking their command..." she glanced away from him, over his shoulder, before he could answer, "... and you too." Adam looked behind him to see a shocked Mouse, unaccustomed to being addressed directly in the company of kings and war chiefs.

"M... me?" he stammered.

"Who better? You know their technology well. We could use you." Mouse looked from Adam to Mark and back again, as though either man would say something for him. It wasn't that he was afraid of going to war, not at all, but more that he was overwhelmed that they considered him worthy of the elite. He cast his eyes to the hard-packed dirt floor and mumbled something that he hoped would sound like a respectful acceptance.

"It is agreed, then," Dren stated.

"It is agreed," the king responded. "The day is set for two nights' time."

"Why wait?" Adam blurted out, remembering himself and bowing his head to show respect to the king.

"The Nua need time to bring their ships to the colder seas," Dren explained, "and the Dearmad must cross the water in their boats under darkness and hide in the empty lands of the west until all of their forces are joined."

"Oh," Adam said apologetically, "okay."

"In two nights' time, then," Dren said in a tone of voice that seemed to end the briefing, "we attack, and drive these invaders from our land forever."

CHAPTER THIRTY-TWO

THE TURN

Eve opened her eyes. She'd heard the gunshot but felt nothing. She was still on her feet, not thrown down in violent agony as she'd expected she would be, and instead of seeing her own death, she saw the body of the man holding the gun to Rebecca's head slump down to the floor with a gaping hole where his nose had been only moments before.

Nathaniel stepped into the light, the heavy revolver in his outstretched hands with a wisp of smoke drifting lazily from the barrel. He held it out firmly, stepping confidently like a man accustomed to handling the weapon and taking a life, swinging it between the two remaining terrorists in case either of them made a move. He stepped close to Rebecca, who still stood unsteadily with tears streaming down her pretty face, to shield her body from the attackers.

"Reaper," he barked, "report." Hearing the words, Eve's eyes fixed on the eerily silent young woman to find her still and more silent than before. She glanced at the two remaining enemies with a coldness, seeing how both were stunned into indecision. One very slowly lowered his rifle with the hand taken deliberately away from the trigger to show he had no intention of using it.

"Corporal Howard," Nathaniel said in a low voice as his gun still covered both terrorists. "*Corporal Howard!*" The girl yelped and jolted a little as her attention returned to the real world. "Corporal, please remove the item from my back and give it to Eve."

She hadn't seen it until his words brought her attention to it, but something protruded over one shoulder, which was a different kind of black to the dark backdrop behind him. With a long, sonorous ring, a straight blade was drawn from a scabbard to glint in the poor light. Rebecca hesitated for a moment, looking at the Chairman for a second confirmation that he meant to give the young killer her weapon of choice, but his attentions were fixed on the two men. Drawing back her arm she tossed the sword through the air.

Eve regarded it as it sailed her way, marvelling at the way the blade caught the light with each ballistic turn, before she stepped lightly forwards and plucked it from the air by the long handle. Rebecca had obviously intended for it to land safely on the ground, but Eve didn't want it so carelessly treated. She twirled the sword once, feeling the weight of it as though being reunited with a part of her own body, before letting it come to rest vertically behind her right arm.

"You had your orders, I suppose," Nathaniel snarled at the two men who seemed more confused and uncertain with each passing second. "You're supposed to kill the girl? Is that it? Stop her from telling your secrets?"

"Sir, I…" one of them began before another gunshot rang out to compete with the blinding flash from the muzzle. Before he had collapsed to the ground his comrade stepped up and began raising his weapon.

A ringing noise ended abruptly with the tip of the sword appearing from nowhere to sweep an arc through his neck. He stood still, eyes wide in shock and pain, before blood began to well at the invisible line where the razor-sharp sword had cut him. He choked once and dropped his weapon to clatter at his feet, just as the blood burst out of him as if his body had been taken by surprise and had forgotten to bleed. An arterial spray of hot, sticky blood erupted from his half-severed head to cover the girl, who seemed not to even close her eyes, let alone turn away to protect herself from it.

Turning back to Nathaniel and Rebecca, her face sheeted in blood, she slowly spun the sword again as though contemplating something.

"Thank you," Nathaniel said, sucking in a huge breath and deflating slightly. Eve took another step close to him and the catatonic Rebecca, blood still dripping from the tip of the sword held low in her right hand as though it was an extension to her arm. She waited, seeing no response to her holding the sword almost close enough to kill him before he could raise the gun. One more step was all she needed but something unfathomable inside her made her hesitate.

"No," Nathaniel said with a chuckle, "*really,* thank you." He held the gun out to the side and pulled the trigger before she could react, clicking the hammer forwards with a metallic ring and no answering gunshot. "That was my last bullet, otherwise I'd have killed both of the bastards as soon as I had the chance."

Rebecca chose that moment to collapse in a heap of sobbing tears as the stress of being held hostage finally overcame her. Both Eve and Nathaniel knelt beside her to offer comfort and as they did, the two adversaries' eyes met briefly.

It would have been the easiest thing just to flick her wrist then. To kill him. His eyes stayed locked on to hers and if he knew that was what she was thinking, he gave no indication of it.

"They *did* come to kill me," she said in a low voice, "and Cohen. They only got her." Nathaniel dropped his eyes for a moment before speaking.

"I'm sorry," he said, not mentioning the fact that Eve had never formally admitted to knowing the wizened old woman. "Do you see what I'm trying to achieve here?" he asked, his eyes pleading with her for understanding. "I need to find the rest of these people and put a stop to this."

Eve nodded, standing slowly and pacing back towards the body of the man she had killed. She stooped, careful not to put her bare feet into the widening pool of blood slowly creeping outwards from him. She wiped the sword blade slowly over his threadbare jacket as she looked at his face. She didn't recognise him, but then again, she was beginning to learn that she knew very little of what the Resistance, the *terrorists*, did.

She had been kept in the dark, figuratively and literally, and she was done being someone else's pawn.

———

Nathaniel slumped into the chair in his office and let out a satisfied sigh. Major Stanley poured two measures of neat alcohol into glasses and slid one across the desk as he took a seat opposite the man who had drawn the heavy revolver from the front of his left thigh and rested it on the polished wood.

"It worked then?" Stanley asked.

"Like a charm," Nathaniel answered with a ghost of a cruel smile. He pressed the lever with his right thumb and flicked the weapon to drop the cylinder out on its arm to shake it lightly.

Two spent casings fell away to ring a small tune on the desk until they came to rest. Nathaniel reached into a pocket of his leather coat hung on the chair back and dropped in a speed loader of a full six bullets to snap the cylinder back into the gun and restore it to the holster.

"Risky move," Stanley opined as he lifted the glass to his lips.

"What's risky about giving a lethal enemy a weapon when I'm unarmed?" he asked, deadly serious and intense as he stared hard at the junior officer. Both men stayed stock still for a few seconds before they laughed together and relaxed.

"Worked like a charm," Nathaniel said smugly. "The scum spent years perfecting a weapon for us to use against them."

"And all it took was massive destruction caused to sensitive equipment and ten soldiers sacrificed for the cause," Stanley said, his tone bordering dangerously on judgemental.

"Problem, Major?" Nathaniel enquired calmly. Stanley collected himself with another healthy gulp of the dark liquid in his glass.

"Not at all, Sir," he said before drinking again. "Not at all." He sipped his drink before chuckling and pursing his lips and lifting a finger to wipe away the errant drop of liquid.

"Which part?" Nathaniel asked, his own voice filled with amusement.

"The look on Howard's face. You were definitely right in keeping her out of the loop." Nathaniel smiled smugly and leaned back, silently congratulating himself on his own genius.

Outside the open door, in the outer office which had been her miserable work assignment until only a few days before, Rebecca Howard barely breathed as she listened to the two intolerable men gloating.

She was more dishevelled than she had ever appeared outside the safety of her own residence, but in light of having her life saved from the terrorists, she had chosen not to care about that and had come to thank the man who had fired the bullet which freed her.

Stepping backwards slowly as she fought the urge to storm in and confront them, she turned and crept away to write another urgent message for the Resistance.

CHAPTER THIRTY-THREE

INVASION

"Sir," came the insistent voice, "I'm very sorry to wake y…"

"What the hell is it?" Nathaniel growled as he threw the covers off his body with difficulty as his legs had tangled in the sheets. He had drunk heavily after returning to his residence inside the Citadel and a glance at the digital display beside his bed told him that he hadn't slept anywhere near enough to purge the alcohol from his system.

"Colonel James, Operation Centre," the intercom speaker crackled back at him, "I'm sending a detachment to bring you here." Nathaniel stood, glancing around for his clothes, which weren't in their characteristic folded position but strewn on the carpet where he'd cast them in his haste to fall into bed. He recognised the colonel by name but didn't know him well enough to have placed his voice if he hadn't given his name.

"I assure you that I'm more than capable of making my way to Ops, Colone…"

"*If* you'll forgive me, Mister Chairman," James interrupted with a hint of annoyance in his words, "but it's a matter of protocol. The Party has come under attack and you need to be protected." Nathaniel was saved from unleashing the first response that came to his mind as the odd sound of tyres on tarmac without any engine note crunched to a stop outside his open windows.

"I'll be there shortly," he growled, hitting the disconnect button on the intercom before any answer could be given. He threw open the wardrobe to select fresh items identical to the ones discarded on the floor, before pushing the heavy revolver home into the leg holster and striding from the bedroom to snatch up his leather coat from a hook by the door. He hadn't washed the sleep from his face or rinsed the booze from his mouth, and that discomfort only made his mood more sour as he rudely ignored the salutes thrown up by the soldiers sent to secure and transport him.

The journey was short, two minutes at most, but the door to the operation centre was open and guarded by half a platoon of soldiers in full combat gear. These weren't the run-of-the-mill types that walked around the city telling tales on suspicious citizens, but the real deal; the same as the team used to secure Eve on her foray above ground. These were elite soldiers and the door they guarded didn't look as if it would house an operations centre for a nation; it seemed more like a bunker set at the bottom of wide, stone steps than an eye-in-the-sky control room.

"What the hell is happening?" he asked the room loudly as he snatched a cup of steaming liquid from the hands of a startled captain. He sipped, wincing as the drink was too hot and contained more sugar than he thought was healthy. He shot a disapproving look at the captain, who had the decency to drop his eyes and apologise for how he took his coffee.

"Sir," a young man said as all eyes turned to him. He wore the insignia of a colonel but appeared younger than the captain who, until recently, had been the owner of a very sugary coffee. Nathaniel drank again, his eyes locked on the colonel, who he now recognised as James. He said nothing, letting the silence build in intensity until the younger man cleared his throat and gave the bad news.

"*'hemm*. Our forces have come under attack. We've lost contact with three of our northern mining facilities overnight. All of them have failed to observe the increased security check-in radio procedures…"

"And the Western compounds?" Nathaniel asked, all trace of hostility for the duty officer vanished in a heartbeat.

"Also not responding to our attempts to raise them."

The room was silent as all eyes were on their Chairman, waiting for orders to reduce their unease. If he hadn't still been feeling the effects of the alcohol swirling around his bloodstream and affecting his choices, he would have calmly given his orders and fought down the urge to lash out and express his anger and frustration. He was, however, still partly drunk, to the extent that the hand holding the coffee cup tightened so that the skin of his fingers turned white with the pressure. With an eruption of anger, Nathaniel roared incoherently and turned his body violently to throw the cup against the wall so hard and with such malevolent force that the trajectory was dead straight. The cup smashed into smithereens to shower hot, sweet coffee over anyone standing close enough.

Turning back to face the others, he tugged down the waist of his leather coat and took a breath, holding it for a few seconds before letting it out and fixing Colonel James with a blank look of control.

"Lock down the entire Capital," he said coldly,

"nothing in or out, no scheduled convoys, mobilise every single soldier and double the Citadel guard." James nodded and went to turn and relay the orders to the relevant people, but Nathaniel wasn't finished. "I want two entire regiments deployed immediately to the nearest outpost, one of the Western farming facilities unless I'm mistaken – and get me the commander of the Frontier at once."

James hesitated, his mouth half open as though he was about to speak but lacked the confidence to form the words.

"You've lost contact with the Frontier, too?" James just swallowed and nodded. Nathaniel leaned forward, gripping the edge of a desk with such force that the nearest officer took an involuntary step backwards.

"Get me Major Stanley," he said, needing a trusted and capable man to do his bidding, "and someone bring Colonel Barclay down here to relieve…" he waved a dismissive hand towards James, "…this man at once."

The room seemed to reactivate as people began working, leaving Nathaniel locked in a staring contest with the shamed Colonel James for a few seconds before the junior man decided against getting himself executed on top of his career aspirations suffering for being the bearer of bad news.

———

The feint attacks were believable, in that the soldiers guarding the cold trenches found themselves attacked without warning and slaughtered. The devils who rose from the shadows didn't kill everyone, in fact they killed very few outright, but the horrific injuries they inflicted on them made men scream out and clamp desperate hands onto deep cuts in the vain attempts to stem the arterial flow of blood and exist for just a few moments or minutes longer; so long as they could maintain the pressure on their wounds and help came for them.

Help did come, and when it arrived it found no enemies to kill; instead, it received desperate orders to reinforce other areas under attack and so the relief forces left decimated sections of the Frontier without reinforcements as they chased an invisible enemy, always arriving after they had melted away.

By the time the confused and garbled reports had been fed back to the Frontier headquarters, nestled safely behind the lines, and someone began to try and make sense out of it, a once disgraced captain assigned on rotation to the commander's staff suddenly saw his redemption in the mixed reports.

"It's a diversion," Captain Hastings said proudly for the attention of the senior officer. "Sir, it's a diversion. They aren't trying to break through, they're…" he stopped speaking as the lights went out and the emergency back-up kicked in to bathe them in an eerily soft, blue glow.

"You were saying, Captain?" the duty colonel snapped as he snatched up a weapon from the rack on one side of the room. A heavy crump noise rocked their underground room followed by a high-pitched whine that sent captain Hastings sprawling backwards into a desk covered in papers as his senses were assaulted. He blinked, trying to restart his brain as dark shadows flowed into the command centre and filled the air with the muted sounds of screams as men and women were cut down by the darkness.

Hastings righted himself, reached down with his hand to draw the pistol and aimed it at the nearest moving shadow, which was slicing and hacking at the man who had just spoken to him. He raised the gun, aimed, and squeezed the trigger just as a flash of steel flicked through his vision.

His hand sagged, his finger unable to pull the trigger as he realised his tendons had been severed. The bright metal flashed again, upwards this time. There was no pain, not at first, but Hastings watched in disbelieving horror as the hand holding the gun fell to the concrete floor.

He cried out weakly, clutching the bleeding stump of his right hand with his left and falling backwards again as a shadow appeared in front of his face, wide eyes bright in the reflection of the emergency lighting, and the shadow cracked a smile at him before a wickedly curved blade opened his windpipe and a second and third savage swipe released the contents of the arteries of his fleshy neck to the outside world.

Hastings managed another two seconds of incredulous staring at how fast it had all ended, and his hopes of earning some great honour and returning to the Citadel faded as quickly as his consciousness fled.

With their command structure gone and their communications no longer working, the men and women assigned to the Frontier as punishment were wiped out long before the sun began to rise. As their lines fell, held for so many generations against a foe they so arrogantly thought themselves at least equal to, so too did the Party's hold over the entire island as the simultaneous attacks began hundreds of miles away.

The Nua flowed from their boats onto the stony shorelines nearest the northern mining facilities, just as the Dearmad melted out of their hiding places among the craggy hills to flow downwards to the farming strongholds in the west.

By the time the sun had fully risen, as though decades of military dominance meant nothing, the total power of the Party was wiped out, with the exception of the forces inside the walls of the Citadel.

The day many had hoped for, the day their ancestors had talked about and prepared them for, had finally come. As the faceless soldiers of their enemy fell to the weapons of the people whose existence those simple soldiers were not even aware of, as the ground grew slick with blood and the frightened Citizens emerged into the chill morning to be told that they were free, so did the sun dawn on the first day of the revolution.

CHAPTER THIRTY-FOUR

TURNED

Nathaniel had feared something big would happen, that the Resistance had been underestimated by all his spies and by himself above all. He suspected a larger scale attack inside the Citadel, or perhaps even some form of uprising that would need to be quelled and would spark a string of public executions to restore order.

What he didn't expect, not even when the anomalous reports first came from the north, was to lose every other facility outside his main stronghold overnight. There were other pockets of Party troops still out there, some in transit between facilities and a large contingent on their way back to the Citadel, having been promptly ordered to reverse their course to reinforce their seat of power.

"Sir," a young radio operator called out, not to the Chairman, who he hadn't realised was in the control room, but to his immediate superior. "Transmission incoming from mining facility four."

"Put it on the main display screen," Nathaniel ordered from behind the young man, making him jump and turn in his seat to hang his mouth open at the sight of the man he hadn't known was in the room. Beside the Chairman stood a major, dressed similarly and radiating the air of a man whose coat buttoned up tightly over duties the young man didn't want to imagine.

"What are you waiting for?" his lieutenant snapped. "Do as the Chairman ordered." He pressed buttons and turned his chair to face the large bank of screens that dominated one wall. Nothing happened, and the tense silence seemed to gather weight as he pressed the buttons again.

"We've lost the video fee…" he began, just as the screen burst into life with an accompanying soundtrack of automatic gunfire muted by heavy doors on the other end of the connection.

"…able to maintain the perimeter," came the words just out of sync with the terrified face of the man shown on the screens. "They're inside the walls. Is anyone receiving this transmission, over?"

"Mining facility four," said the smooth radio voice of the lieutenant in stark contrast to his usual nasal twang. "This is the Citadel. Go again with your report." A look of naïve relief washed over the man's face as he thought merely making communications contact with the Citadel would mean he had a chance of survival.

"We were attacked before dawn," he said in a rushed, desperate voice. "We held them back for hours after some form of EMP device shut down our drones and communications. Somehow, they got inside and manually overrode the gate controls, they're inside the facility! We managed to restart the emergency power generators, but it won't hold out for long. Please advise…"

The lieutenant turned to look at Nathaniel, his raised eyebrows asking for permission to tell the truth, or for permission to lie. The Chairman wordlessly held his hand out for the headset the younger man wore and seated it carefully over his head before clearing his throat.

"Identify yourself," he said clearly and calmly. The man looked confused for a split second before regaining what little composure he still possessed and answered.

"Captain Fisher, Second watch."

"Captain," Nathaniel said in the same cool tone he had employed before, "this is the Party Chairman." He waited for the recognition to dawn on the face of the terrified captain he could see but then he realised the man was looking at a blank screen on the other end of the link. "You and your people have performed admirably. As we speak, a large relief force is heading your way; *hold fast to your position*, Captain, and I will personally pin the honour for Hero of the Party to your chest. You *must* fight them. Lead your soldiers into battle and do so for the glory of the Party." He watched as the fear seemed to wash away from the man, allowing his face to display a fierce pride and dangerous resolve in its place. He opened his mouth to speak, no doubt to recite a very war-like quote from one of the former leaders of the Party, remembered from his education for just such an occasion. The words never came as the screen and the distorted audio feed simultaneously went dead.

Nathaniel cleared his throat again, removing the headset just as carefully as he had placed it over his neat hair before handing it back to the lieutenant.

"The relief force, Sir?" he asked.

"What relief force, Lieutenant?" Major Stanley snapped with evident scorn. The young officer looked from face to face between the two men until it dawned on him. There was no relief force, nothing that their leader could actually do for the men and women there under attack, other than to instil in just a few of them the belief – no matter how false it might have been – that help was coming and that they went to their deaths fighting.

Nathaniel held his head high and kept his face a mask of cold control, but inside he screamed and raged at this enemy who was so rapidly collapsing what had stood for generations unchallenged.

"Drone down in sector sixty-four," called out another voice from the far side of the room, where the flying cameras were monitored. On that side of the large control room it was unlikely that they would be aware of the terrible drama which had just unfolded, and the voice calling out the report sounded almost bored. These weren't the specific reconnaissance platforms that were remotely flown by human pilots, but the automated grid searching type employed all over the Citadel and beyond.

"Where is that?" Stanley barked and he crossed the room with long strides.

"Er, south," came the stuttering response from another person unaccustomed to finding very senior officers looming over his shoulder.

"How far south?" Nathaniel asked, appearing over the other shoulder and tripling the man's anxiety in a heart-beat. Fingers tapped at keys to confirm the answer he already knew but wasn't confident enough to say aloud without double checking.

"Eighteen miles south by south-west. It's usually a technical malfunction of a bird flying into the dro…"

"I highly doubt that. Last recorded images," Stanley demanded, leaning down and resting a hand on the side of the man's console to further the sense of fear he wasn't enjoying. Fingers hit keys again as the footage was brought up playing in reverse. The black screen exploded with a momentary white flash before the rolling bed of green treetops began to pass by in reverse.

"Stop," Nathaniel said quietly, "take it back again and switch to thermal." The operator did as he was told, replaying the last few seconds of the drone's existence through a spectrum of vision alien to the human eye.

"There," Stanley said, jabbing a finger at the screen to distort the image.

"I saw it," Nathaniel answered, having spied the vague radiance of human shapes hidden beneath the tree canopy. He stood tall, turning around to find the officer supervising the drone banks and finding a female lieutenant hovering expectantly.

"Recall all standard drones," he ordered her. "High altitude units equipped with thermal cameras only." She opened her mouth automatically to explain that they didn't have that kind of equipment in regular rotation but clapped her lower jaw upwards just in time to trap the words inside.

She doubted that the Chairman, *the* Chairman – of the entire Party – would want to hear problems instead of solutions. She nodded her understanding of his orders and turned away to seek out her superior and get the less common drones in the air as soon as possible.

Behind her, Nathaniel turned on his heel and strode for the exit doors, leaving Stanley to skip a couple of steps to fall in beside him.

"What now, Sir?" he asked quietly. Nathaniel walked on in silence as though he hadn't heard the man, not breaking step as he walked through the doors which slid open ahead of him, forcing Stanley to duck behind him to avoid impact with the sliding metal and glass. He caught up again, ready to repeat his question, when Nathaniel turned to him and answered.

"Now," he said with a slight snarl of anger, "we

prepare for the Citadel to come under attack. And to that end, I'd like a personal guard."

———

Eve paced in her room, occasional glances lingering on the door handle which had never operated from the inside before. She was conflicted and confused. Upset and angry. Her confusion was mainly at being placed gently back inside her comfortable cell but still in possession of her sword, without either of the soldiers making any attempt to disarm her.

She didn't know how she would've reacted if they'd tried; she asked herself that question and not even her bullish immaturity truly knew the answer.

Would I have killed them? She questioned herself. *Probably not,* the sensible, coherent voice in her head told her. *You would've given them the sword without a second thought.*

That was what upset her – the fact that she figured out deep down that she would comply with what her captors told her to do, because she was no longer sure that they really were the bad guys. Her anger rested solely at the feet of the dead men who had killed Cohen and also, she thought with an unexpected stab of regret, for the bastard who had put a bullet in that silent psychopath who had turned out to be on her side, or who at least had shared the same goals as Eve did for a time.

She decided to test her freedom and reached abruptly for the door, expecting to find it locked, but almost released the handle and recoiled when it opened without much effort. She peered out, holding the sheathed sword behind her body in anticipation of seeing at least two armed soldiers with the guns almost at the ready position, should she pose a threat to them.

Empty.

Even more confused, she stepped back inside her room and gently closed the door, turning back to it and trying the handle again in case it was a mistake. Again, the handle moved with hardly any effort expended and opened her world up to the deserted corridor outside.

She hadn't seen or spoken to anyone in the aftermath of the attack. In fact, the whole subterranean floor had been almost abandoned, with only the occasional passing set of hurried footsteps heard or the arrival of food accepted; all, though, without any news or instructions.

She slipped out on bare feet again, her loose, comfortable clothing hardly in keeping with her body's movements and the straight sword she carried tucked vertically behind her back. Following her feet in the direction they usually went in after leaving her room, her ears began to detect voices ahead from the common area she normally ate her meals in when she was accompanied.

"…think she'll agree?" said the harsh voice of the man she recognised as being Nathaniel's regular sidekick.

"I hope so," said the top man himself, his annoyingly calm, flat tone of voice unmistakable. "I'd like to hope that she's seen who the real enemy are and will choose to do what's right."

"What *is* right?" she asked as she rounded the doorway, seeming to startle both men even though she caught a hint of the jolt being rehearsed.

"Eve," Nathaniel said, "good morning. Please come in." She did, slowly revealing the sheathed sword from behind her back as her eyes stayed glued to both men for a reaction to her possession of it. Neither man seemed to notice, as though the big revolver on Nathaniel's left thigh and the more angular handgun that Stanley carried on his right hip were of the same breed as her razor-sharp sword.

She slid the sword onto the table and looked at what was on offer, seeing a more basic spread than before and casting her eyes about for anything but the foul-tasting coffee the two men seemed to enjoy so much but finding nothing. As if intuiting what she wanted, Nathaniel turned to a low table behind him, twisting to retrieve a pitcher of the orange juice she liked and a fresh glass. Wordlessly he placed it before her and spoke.

"As I was saying to Major Stanley," he explained, "we find ourselves in a rather unprecedented situation and I hope you'll agree to help us – help *me* – with it."

"Help you with what?" Eve shot back as she poured juice into the glass and took a seat, still within reach of the hilt of her sword. The two men glanced in each other's direction for their eyes to meet, like they were collectively deciding either what or *how* to tell her what was going on. With a sigh, Nathaniel explained current events to her.

"The terrorists who attacked us here and killed... well, who killed a lot of people as it happens, aren't alone." Eve took a gulp of her drink as she watched the man, waiting for him to speak and enjoying how uncomfortable she made him feel, no matter how much he tried to hide it. "You might not know this, but we have other places than this city, than the Citadel. There are mi…"

"Mining facilities to the north," she cut in, "farming areas in the west, and the Frontier."

Stanley cleared his throat, not conveying any meaning with the sentiment but simply betraying that he didn't like people to know too much, especially when those people were what they thought of as traitors.

"Exactly," Nathaniel went on, "and overnight we've lost contact with all of them."

"Your radios stopped working?" she asked, a teenage splash of taunting in her tone.

"Yes," Stanley said stiffly, "when people used electro-magnetic disruption devices on them just prior to attacking." He saw her face turn towards his, a mask of neutrality which he misunderstood.

"An electro-magnetic devi…"

"A pinch," she interrupted. "A crunch?" she said, frowning to try and decide if she should correct her first recollection. "I've heard… them mentioned," she said, changing the flow of her words too slowly to pretend she wasn't going to mention a name of someone she no longer knew.

"So," Nathaniel said, almost as a question or an invitation for her to offer an opinion.

"So, I don't know anything about it," she replied defensively, "how could I? I've been stuck underground for who knows how long and I…"

"I wasn't insinuating that you knew anything about it," Nathaniel told her gently, "I'm asking for your help. I suspect the Citadel will come under direct attack very soon. Probably tonight."

"*My* help? How? Why?"

"I'd rather like to live long enough to fix this whole, bloody mess. To ensure that, I need people around me I know have certain… *skills*."

Eve understood what he wanted. Her conflicted senses about right and wrong and good and bad were a jumble of thoughts inside her head. The woman she could have trusted to tell her the way of the world was dead; killed by the people she had trusted and fought alongside, but who she suspected had also lied to her about the truth of history. Before her was a man who, quite literally, repre-sented the head of the snake she had been raised to hate through the same kind of indoctrination she always believed those children who lived above ground suffered at the hands of the cruel Party leaders. To allow herself more time to think, she fell back on some sullen, teenager-like behaviour.

"Why don't you use that creepy attack dog?" she asked, leaving Nathaniel with the clear impression who she referred to.

"Shadow will be beside me. However, Reaper is sadly…" he slowly rotated his hand through the air as though trying to coax his brain to summon the most appropriate word. He glanced at Stanley for help.

"Reaper's probably going to die," he said bluntly. "Even if she doesn't, then she won't be good for anything for weeks." Eve stared at him for a few seconds, just long enough to make him feel a little uncomfortable before glancing back to fix her eyes onto the point where Nathaniel's eyebrows almost met.

"So, you want me to replace her as your robot body-guard," she stated with a mocking edge to her words.

"No," Nathaniel told her firmly, his eyes boring into hers and making her feel the same discomfort Stanley had suffered, "I want you by my side so that when the bastards send their best assassins for me, I'll have one better fighting for what's right – for the *people* and not the desperate, selfish terrorists who would twist the freedom they think they can gain and send everyone into lawless chaos."

"And to do that," Stanley said with a groan as he hefted a black canvas bag off the carpeted floor and onto the table before unzipping it noisily, "you need to be wearing something a little more appropriate than pyjamas."

CHAPTER THIRTY-FIVE

THE CITADEL

Adam ducked low behind the leafy, green remnants of what he had been told was once a building but now just seemed to him to be an overgrown pile of rubble, half swallowed by the Earth. He felt uncomfortable being exposed in the sunlight, only having done so once before and finding himself unable to shake the sensation that the previous time had resulted in total disaster.

If he was uncomfortable, he couldn't begin to imagine how the Nocturnals felt. All of them wore the cowls of their clothing pulled up over their heads to shield them from the brightness of the sunlight, which to Adam was an uncommon sight but still wasn't bright by any standards he'd witnessed before.

In addition to their hooded, shrouded faces, he knew that they would be wearing the darkened goggles which turned his daylight into theirs and allowed them to see perfectly above ground. His hands felt clammy as he tucked the long, wide-bladed knives under his armpits to wipe his palms on his legs before gripping the hilts again. The source of his nervousness was hard to pin down, but he guessed it was mainly due to the oncoming column of soldiers approaching in a convoy of near-silent trucks around the next bend in the road.

Their ambush was a simple one; a Party troop carrier, liberated from the Frontier which they now owned entirely, was off the road just out of sight of the approaching enemy as though the original occupants had suffered some form of mishap. That would, so the plan went, cause the lead vehicle to stop and deploy troops to investigate, which would, again they hoped, bunch up the other vehicles and cause a hold-up, allowing the trap to be sprung.

In honour of his status, or at least the status of Dren, his small group had the responsibility of rapidly disabling the vehicle or driver of the last vehicle in line as soon as it came to a stop, so that the convoy was trapped in the killing field of their choice.

In spite of being quite adept at killing, he shuddered at the thought of the army he marched with slipping out of their hiding places to bring gruesome death to the unsuspecting enemy. He almost felt pity for them before he caught his dangerous change of attitude and reminded himself that these soon-to-be victims would kill him in a heartbeat. Moreover, they would hurt and oppress others who weren't able to fight back like he was.

Those few moments of distracted reverie allowed half of the column to pass his position before his mind shot into the present and he felt that familiar sensation of the cold drop in his chest as his body chemically prepared to fight.

His eyes stayed glued to the last vehicle in the convoy, running through the actions of breaking cover and disabling the driver, who he could already see had the window open to peer out and try to understand the reason they were slowing. Adam knew that the lead vehicle must have come to a complete stop by then, that the next five in line wold have concertinaed to stop nose to tail, but the further back he looked, he could see how the drivers had anticipated the change and begun to slow more gently.

Then his heart dropped.

The last vehicle in the long line, the one he had his eyes glued on, ready to act, wasn't the last vehicle at all. Further back, a length of maybe ten other trucks, came a smaller troop carrier like the ones which stalked the streets of the Citadel night and day, ready to disgorge a knot of so-called peacekeepers to crush any expression of individuality by the Citizens.

"We need to move," he hissed, not waiting for any response from any of the fighters around him as he slithered backwards and sheathed the wicked knives behind his back. He knew from the light sounds at his back that he had been followed, and he hoped that they recognised the danger he had foreseen and were coming to help.

Hugging the dead ground as much as possible on the approach, he stopped before the landscape levelled out and he would be exposed to the mirrored glass of the troop-carrying van's windscreen. Risking a glance behind him he saw that five others had elected to follow, although from the look on a few faces, he suspected that two of them didn't fully understand why. He saw the nearest man, a short, squat individual with a handful of short throwing spears tipped with devilishly sharp leaf-shaped blades and gestured for one of them. He was handed one without hesitation and hefted it in his right hand to gauge the weight only moments before he would be forced to employ it in real action.

"Pilum," the man growled, smiling at the weapon and nodding reassuringly like he was trying to sell it.

"If they get away, they'll report our position and strength," Adam explained. Blank looks answered him, which produced a wave of unease but a glance across the roadway showed that those on the other side had either followed suit or recognised the danger themselves. Dren was over there, he knew, along with Mouse, who was decorated with various contraptions to wage his own special form of warfare. But before he could spare them another thought, the vehicle was slowing and approaching their position.

Adam stood, heaved back his right hand holding the spear that he now knew was called a pilum, and launched it with a perfect arc at the window shielding the driver's head from the outside world.

The tip of the small spear punctured the glass in almost precisely the right position, its trajectory perfect to penetrate the man's neck just above his collar. But instead of going through, it stuck in the glass and quivered uncertainly.

Adam's mouth opened slowly to utter a curse of disbelief when the van slammed to an abrupt stop and began to move backwards.

"No, no, no," Adam yelled as he broke cover and ran to jump at the window, his flat foot extended to try and force the blade all the way through and stop the driver but he had timed the jump wrong and knew as soon as he'd reach the top of his arc that the van was moving backwards faster than he had anticipated. The sense of failure stung him deeply, until another feeling rose like heat from his gut.

The van was juddering to a halt.

Mouse, to his right with both feet set in a wide stance and his face a mask of ruthless anger so in contrast to his usual, apologetic manner, fired a kind of weapon from his hip that emitted no noise. That weapon, not one of his own design but modified from the devices the Nocturnals used to kill the Party drones foolish enough to fly over their lines, fried the electronics of the van's engine and brought it to a stop. Adam kept moving, wrenching the spear tip free and twisting it to try and force the hole large enough to achieve a killing thrust on the driver before a pistol barrel appeared in the small gap and the world erupted with the sharp, percussive cracks of gunfire. Adam rolled away out of any danger as the gap wasn't large enough for the soldier to turn the weapon towards him. Others tried to open the rear door but found them in lock down. Before Adam had begun to formulate the beginnings of a plan to pry them out of their protective tin can, the man with the pilums threw two in quick succession with accompanying grunts, embedding them in the flat panel sides of the multi-layered metal, before taking a short run up and using the spears as climbing holds to get to the roof. He turned, silent but for a double clap of his hands as a bottle was launched up to him by another warrior. Spear man took an exaggerated gulp of air and turned his face away as he popped off the lid of the large bottle to tip it up into the air vent on the roof and roll away.

Confused, Adam watched in silence until the muted screams of pain from inside the van made him understand.

The driver's door to his right burst open and a retching, coughing man stumbled out to gasp fresh air. Trying to gather himself, he looked at Adam through tear-filled eyes laced with red veins burst throughout the whites. He spluttered again, tried to raise the weapon which offered Adam little threat as he flipped the knife in his hand to catch it by the point ready to fling it into the soldier's neck. A curved blade appeared at the man's armpit like a ghost and sliced with such a quick, short action that the pain hadn't even registered until after the hand holding the gun dropped to his side.

He never felt the pain of the first cut because over his other shoulder came another curved blade that opened the major blood vessels in that side of his neck to collapse his feet out from under him. He fell, exposing the slight frame of Dren wearing a goggled expression that showed less than no remorse for taking a life. The other occupants fell from the vehicle to be cut down mercilessly and Adam's raised eyebrow and silent question were answered by Mouse.

"Hydrochloric acid and ammonia," he explained. "Produces something called ammonium hydroxide." He looked down and shuddered, making Adam unsure whether he was affected by the bloodshed or was, more likely he admitted, considering the chemical reaction of the two substances and what they would create. Dren spoke in short, guttural sentences to the other Nocturnals to send them to tasks securing the end of the trap before she led the way to the head of the column.

Each vehicle showed a similar scene, either with or without the chemical weapons employed to prise the soldiers out from their safe interiors, and each vehicle told a tale of a very one-sided bloodbath. At the head of the convoy, where the king commanded, he heard cheering as the helmet of a soldier was tossed high over the heads of the victorious ambushers.

Something about the head didn't seem right, Adam knew, and as the realisation dawned on him, he had to fight to keep the horror from his face.

The helmet still had a head inside.

"My father says," Dren told him, translating and startling her man, "that we are a half day from the walls of the enemy stronghold."

"Strongho… It's a city," Adam corrected her. "With

innocent people inside. He knows that, right?" She looked at him with an unreadable expression.

"Of course," she answered, before walking away.

As night fell, as the dull glow of the distant sun faded to the west, the high walls of the Citadel came into view and the sense of foreboding that the concrete labyrinth inside gave him returned as heavy as the darkness did.

———

Inside that looming target, and in spite of her surreptitious attempts to avoid being followed, Rebecca Howard stopped beside the statue of the former Chairman of the Party and regarded him with a blank expression for a moment, before lifting her foot to the raised plinth and miming the actions of tying her bootlace.

Forty paces away – far enough to be undetected but close enough to see that the laces of the boot weren't being re-tied – Sergeant Major Du Bois let out a low, cruel chuckle to himself as he saw the subtle movement of her hand to tuck something into a gap in the stonework.

He waited until she had gone, then waited another minute in case she was being followed by another traitor, and he sauntered over to retrieve it. He didn't read it, merely looked up and offered a mocking salute to the former glorious leader as though the long-dead man had assisted him somehow.

Taking the rolled-up paper wrapped in plastic first to his own quarters, he read the small writing over and over before leaving and requesting an urgent audience with Major Stanley.

CHAPTER THIRTY-SIX

THE ATTACK

It started quietly. Reports of suspicious movement and gatherings during curfew which, when the forces inside the Citadel were deployed to investigate, had vanished. Drones, every available piece of hardware, scoured the skies and streets as live feeds to the control rooms dropped out at irregular intervals.

Some of these signal failures were unexplained, but many had transmitted their last images showing ordinary Citizens throwing bricks at them. Such treason, such insurrection would normally result in everyone found outside of their residences being arrested, but there weren't enough soldiers on the streets to cope with the outbreaks.

The guns mounted over the gates stayed worryingly quiet as the enemy who had been detected marching on them refused to make a direct attack like an honourable adversary would; instead they ringed the walled city and hid like the vermin they were.

Nathaniel, wearing a blank mask that told the control room staff how unconcerned he was, raged inside with anger and fear as he was powerless to do anything but monitor the game board and move the pieces the best he could.

The doors opened and Stanley appeared on the threshold of the control room, eyes scanning left and right until he located the Chairman, who he summoned with an expression of wide-eyed urgency. Nathaniel walked slowly towards him, not wanting to spread panic with a rushed reaction.

"You need to see this," Stanley started before Nathaniel cut him off.

"Not here, Major," he said in a formal, low voice. Stanley recognised his error and impropriety, closing his mouth before any more words could tumble out to be over-heard. The two men walked to one of the larger confer-ence rooms on the same corridor and shut themselves inside. Mirroring the same low, controlled tone Stanley told the Chairman about the report he had been given, producing the evidence to support the claim. Nathaniel's only emotive response to the news was to inhale sharply through flared nostrils before he regained control of himself.

"Where is she now?" he asked.

"Downstairs," Stanley responded, meaning the lower sub-levels of the Special Projects program. Nathaniel nodded thoughtfully, turning towards the elevator and assuming Stanley would follow. Arriving at the correct subterranean floor, he stepped onto the still-scorched walkway and headed for where his newest recruit would be as he snapped his fingers towards the temporary guard post to summon an entourage. They fell in behind the two men, not knowing what they were being called for but knowing enough not to ask.

"Corporal Howard," he barked as he entered the room where the guard's armour and weapons were stored. The woman jumped in fright, spinning around as she fumbled with the heavy slide of a pistol she should have been acquainted with but evidently wasn't adept at handling. Guns snapped up into shoulders to pin her in threat but Nathaniel's weapon stayed in its holster. Instead, he crossed the room with his characteristic long strides and slapped the weapon out of her small hands with utter disdain before stepping uncomfortably close and fixing her with a hard stare. She quailed away from him, prompting his top lip to curl upwards involuntarily.

"Lock this traitor up," he ordered in a flat, emotionless tone; his rage subsided as quickly as it had risen. "She can be in the first round of executions after she's told us everything she knows."

He turned on his heel to leave but stopped in his tracks at the words she spat at his retreating back.

"She knows," Rebecca hissed with a touch of gleeful insanity in her words as though she could still triumph after her torture and execution. "She'll kill you."

Nathaniel glared at her for a few seconds before turning and storming out to the sounds of her screaming and struggling against the grip of the soldiers dragging her away.

"Eve!" Nathaniel called out as he banged a fist on the door of her cell. He was about to repeat the summons when the door opened and she stood confused before him.

"Eve," he greeted her almost grudgingly, his right hand floating free at his waist, should the need to draw his revolver arise. "Have you seen Corporal Howard?"

"She's not here."

Nathaniel stifled a sigh of exasperation. "Has she been here?"

"Not recently."

"*How* recently?"

"Not for a while."

The urge to rub the frustration from his face with both hands was strong but he took another breath and composed himself to deal with the obtuse youth.

"When exactly," he said in a measured tone, "did you last see Corporal Howard?"

"Yesterday," Eve replied with a nod and a smile of achievement. She guessed she'd given the correct answer as Nathaniel looked relieved. His hand, she noticed without looking directly at it, moved away from his belt buckle where it had been hovering unnaturally and the tension seemed to evaporate.

"Good. I'm afraid I have some bad news regarding the Corporal," Nathaniel told her as he snapped his fingers and waved his hand dismissively to send the accompanying soldiers away. "She was observed passing information to the enemy – to the terrorists – this morning." He waited as the look of horror on her face morphed into anger. "She will be arrested and dealt with afterwards, but…"

"After what?"

Nathaniel didn't hesitate one bit before answering. "After we've defended the Citadel against the attack. Now, if you wouldn't mind putting on your new armour, I'd appreciate having you close to me."

Eve paused for a while in the empty room, her eyes resting on the sheathed sword. She could almost sense its presence; as though the inanimate object held a life-force of its own which called to her. She reached out for it, detecting something like a weak electrical current the closer her fingertips got to it, which made her pause for fear of a shock. She huffed, ignoring the foolish notion, and snatched up the blade to stop the buzzing in her head and stalked from the cell to put on the armoured suit.

As she stripped off the loose clothing she wore,

prompting rapidly averted gazes and noises of discomfort from more than one soldier present, she slid her feet into the suit and began to work it upwards over her body. It fit her like it was moulded to her image, as though the fibres of the overlapping, thin sheets of armoured material somehow adapted to her form like a living thing. When she had it on, when it was closed up tightly to her neck, she moved her limbs to check for any restriction to her movement that could catch her unaware and put her at risk. She found none, marvelling at how something so heavy could feel so light when she wore it.

She slid the sheathed sword into a loop over her right shoulder, slipping the blade free with only just enough room to draw it from that position, and wielded it in a few lazy arcs before she reversed the tip and slid it back. Picking up a handful of knives from a weapons rack she slotted them neatly into the custom holders on both thighs much like the ones she had worn when she'd fought for the other side.

A soldier appeared beside her, his cheeks flushed with awkwardness as he mumbled a greeting to her before offering out a handgun, grip first.

"Newest model we have," he said. "Fires a sub-soni…"

"Don't care," Eve snapped, cutting him off. "Those things are useless to me."

She turned to walk out, feeling graceful and powerful again, but annoyed at an itching discomfort above her left hip inside the suit. Ducking aside before she reached the exit, she unzipped the upper body and reached inside awkwardly to remove a scrap of thick paper. Glancing at it she saw scrawled, hurried handwriting and quickly closed her fist around it to hide it from sight.

"What have we got?" Nathaniel asked loudly as he stepped back inside the control room. Eve hung back, walking just ahead of Stanley and feeling his eyes burning into the close-fitting suit. Shadow stayed glued to the Chairman's side, similarly armoured and doggedly obedient to the extent that she almost felt embarrassed for him.

"The walls are breached," answered an officer trying his hardest not to seem terrified, "but we can't see where. They must've got over somehow because all gates are secu…"

"They went underneath," Nathaniel interrupted him calmly as he picked up a tablet and swiped over captured images from drones before they went down. "Pull back all forces to strategic locations and order the reactionary force to defend this building." He stared at the officer who hadn't yet moved to comply, raising an eyebrow with sufficient force to startle the man into relaying the orders.

"Sir," said a voice from beside Eve as an older woman approached.

"Colonel Barclay," Nathaniel responded, "any word from the soldiers I ordered to return to the Citadel?"

"None, Sir," she said flatly, which in itself was an answer that spoke far more than just the two words she used. Nathaniel's mouth set into a tight line as he recalculated his plan, given that the entire relief force was assumed dead or captured. "They don't seem to have much in the way of co-ordination," she explained. Nathaniel looked at her silently, waiting for the rest of the information and conveying his mild annoyance at having to wait for it. "The reported contacts are random and sporadic," she said as she brought up a map of the city on her own tablet to show him.

"They're harassing us," he told her, not needing to look at the map to understand their tactics. "They should realise that they can't win any stand-up fight against us, so they're nipping small chunks off instead of trying to bite out our throat." Barclay nodded in understanding, agreeing with the assumption he had just made, and closed the map on her screen with a tap.

"So we consolidate, we wait out the darkness, and if we aren't victorious by morning, then we burn out every tunnel under the entire Citadel with chemicals and surround ourselves with…" he trailed off as an idea evidently dawned on him. "Fetch up all of the prisoners we have and secure them by the entrance."

"Sir?" she said, shaking her head and turning away to call out the orders.

"Let's see the bastards come in guns blazing when they have to kill their own to get to us," he murmured to himself.

Eve, the scrap of paper screwed up tightly in her hand and her face desperate to contort in rage, felt her right hand twitch as her body wanted to reach for the sword and end the whole conflict there and then.

The hurried message from Rebecca had confused her at first, her mind wanting to reject it, but everything fell into place now. She still had a job to do, she knew, and that job, that purpose, was the same as it had always been.

She took a step forward, her hand fluttering as the logical part of her mind still told her that to cut him down there would be suicide, when Shadow's eerily dead eyes locked onto hers. He began to step towards her, to block her path, when a shout rang out loudly.

"They're here! They're outside the building!"

CHAPTER THIRTY-SEVEN

ENDGAME

Eve, resplendent and feeling powerful in her new armour, held the sword in its sheath in her left hand. She could feel the balance of it, even without the blade uncovered, and felt it vibrate in her grip like it had before, as though it longed to be free and take lives as much as she did. She was among the finest of weapons standing ready to defend the people of the Citadel, but that defence required just a little more deception first. The rain began to fall heavily, the distant sky illuminating with occasional flashes of lightning as though the weather knew the enormity of what was about to happen.

The attack had begun just as she had anticipated, and all over the city, patrols had been going off the grid every few minutes. The drones, the *army* of drones that would have blacked out the sky in places had it not been a moonless night, found nothing of their attackers, as she knew they wouldn't.

They were inside the walls. The advanced parties of skilled killers like her, sneaking around under the streets like rats using the old tunnels that were the biggest weakness to their defence. She had heard the Chairman order them all found and burned out, but time was not on their side and the routes of access too many to prevent some of them getting in.

She had been them, was *born* one of them but she didn't want to go back to a life spent underground again. Didn't want to be kept in the dark, to go hungry and to be eternally bored with her existence. She would fight, and she would live a better life after this night was over.

Blocking the steps to the Citadel's headquarters with just a handful of soldiers at her back, she watched the darkness ahead through the driving rain and the intermittent flashes of streetlighting that lit up the wet, gloomy streets like lightning.

The soldiers, with all their technology and weapons, couldn't see what she saw. She saw those shadows in the near distance ripple and move. Dissolve and reform in different places, and she knew they were coming. She made no move to warn the soldiers; faceless drones as human to her now as the flying cameras were. She heard the whistle of metal flying through the night air just as a flash of light gave them a snapshot of their coming deaths in the form of shrouded figures moving fluidly to close the distance.

As the first blades began to hit home and drop them in choking, gagging waves of death she turned away to get back inside the imposing building and end it.

"Where are you going?" one of them snarled, reaching out and grabbing her wrist as she reached for the door. She opened her hand, splaying the fingers out wide and instantly feeling the grip on her falter. Turing that hand over she forced the soldier to either release her or be forced off balance, and she knew that choice would be difficult as it meant logic fighting against instinct.

Without training, without hours and days and years

spent honing that logic into an instinct of its own, those moments of hesitation could spell death.

He didn't release her, instead yelping in fright as he bent at the waist to lean over sideways instead of letting her go and bringing up his weapon. The sword, still held sheathed in her left hand, shot forwards to jab the hilt hard under the man's chin to sprawl him backwards to choke from the shock and pain of the strike. Gunfire erupted behind her as the soldiers began to unload their weapons at the shadows.

She turned away, reaching once more for the doors but finding a face behind the glass which, for the first time ever, showed an emotion.

Shadow, staring back at her from the inside the building, smiled.

———

Adam and Dren were among the second wave of fighters to reach the Citadel. Already ahead of them the sounds of battle raged in a one-sided gunfight as they weren't yet close enough to hear the singing of blades and the butcher's sounds of the injuries they inflicted.

A handful of soldiers defended the front of the building, fighting a desperate defence as bodies piled up ahead of them. Adam stopped at the corner of a building and ducked behind the concrete, reaching out to snatch at Dren's arm and tug her into cover with him just as a line of bullet holes appeared in the wall behind where she'd been running. Her big eyes met his in silent thanks before they both ducked away again under a hail of more gunfire which threw down three of their own.

"This way," he yelled over the noise, pulling her around the building to loop in and not run down a killing corridor of bullets. He scaled a drainpipe with ease, reaching the low rooftop and turning to help her up. She didn't need any assistance and was hot on his heels to drop low beside him and glance around as her knives appeared in her hands again.

He led her onwards towards danger as the sounds of weapons fire intensified, dropping over the edge of the roof to land beside a huddle of black-clad, helmeted soldiers preparing to launch a counterattack.

Blades hissed as the two killers spun and sliced, opening up arteries and stabbing deep into the unprotected parts of their victims' bodies between the armour plating. Dren needed no instruction on how to kill the faceless soldiers of the Party as she'd been doing it longer than he had, and their synchronicity, almost a symbiosis as they attacked, devastated the soldiers in seconds.

"There," he said, pointing towards the doors to the building and setting off at a run before his legs faltered and he slowed. Dren looked at him, opened her mouth to ask if he had been shot, when she followed his gaze to see what had disarmed him.

Standing in front of the doors, wearing the black armour of their enemy, was Eve.

————

Eve stood still; her eyes locked on the emotionless orbs of the inhuman creation designed as an answer to the problem she posed. She reached for the handle of the door, pulling it towards her and stepping back to give herself the space she needed to wield her sword, when he attacked.

Launching his body in what seemed like blind rage against the glass he slammed the door into her to throw her backwards, forcing her to go with the momentum and roll back to her feet. He was on her before she could regain her full height, slamming the buzzing baton in his right hand down towards her unprotected skull in a brutally savage blow which she managed to defend against by raising the still-sheathed sword to absorb the energy. It knocked her backwards again, forcing her to throw her body into another roll which she turned into an attack by rising up and extending her right foot to connect under his armpit on the next downward swing of his weapon. The impact jarred him, sending him backwards a pace as he shook out the stunned limb and allowed her time to get to her feet again. He smiled at her again, tossing the baton lightly through the air to catch it in his other hand, which wasn't affected by her kick.

Eve curled a lip at him, hating the bastard for so obviously being ambidextrous, and rose to sweep the long, straight blade from the sheath and level it at him. Lighting flashed again, making the cold steel extension of her arm glow as his electrified club did, as the two regarded each other for a few beats.

He attacked, lunging low to her left to so obviously invite a wild swing with her sword to his unprotected left flank so he could twist inside the reach of her blade and connect the weapon with her body and end it all in the opening second. He seemed to know all along that it would come to this; like their final duel was an inexorable eventuality which he had been relishing since the first time he saw her.

As she knew, truly knew for the first time in her life, that this was what she was alive for, she recognised that he too held the same belief; only his was one which had always been with him.

"Traitor," he spat as she moved to make the cut before springing lightly backwards so that his baton jabbed into thin air. She was stunned for a second, not thinking that he could speak and being taken by surprise not only by his words but by the hateful vehemence of his tone. The falling rain sizzled on his baton as the two circled one another and he shook out his numb right arm to reach behind his back and draw another baton. He activated it with an almost casual flick of his wrist to double the sizzling, crackling noises of the weapons which she sensed were turned up to a lethal maximum.

"Animal," she shot back. "*Drone*." The second insult made him frown as though he considered her choice of word to liken him to the mindless, controlled machines that buzzed through the city. He smiled again, making Eve feel the anger rise in her chest like acid and she had to fight the urge not to launch into a wild attack. They continued to pace in a mirroring circle before he reversed course with the speed of a striking predator to swing one baton upwards in a sweeping arc as his right hand shot a straight jab at her chest. She skipped backwards again, trying to gauge his speed and ability before deploying her own tricks, but she wasn't filled with confidence.

His style was close-quarters and deadly, whereas hers required more space in which to dance her sword and her body to cleave limbs and heads from bodies. Twice more he attacked her directly, never forcing his assault too far but only to test her reactions as she assessed him.

A storm of bullets passed between them like metal wasps intent on a goal and not concerned by the duelling pair. Both of them ignored the passage of the lethal projectiles.

"Is that why you didn't help when your own people attacked that dungeon you call home?" she asked him, goading him with the confusion of human emotions he didn't possess a full understanding of. "Reaper did, but she was always better than you."

Shadow snarled and lunged to his right in an exaggerated move, forcing Eve to swing the sword across her body to deflect the double blow of his weapons. He pressed his attack this time, recovering to move directly at her and swing blow after blow to force her backwards as her sword twirled to parry the electrified metal. He jumped, one baton jabbing straight out at her as the other was arcing downwards over his head. She didn't bother to block either as the combination was designed to break the defence of her single weapon; instead, she ducked and rolled forwards out of his way to swing the blade backwards blindly and cut at where his left leg should be. She knew when she was halfway through her swing that he had recovered from his landing and stepped lithely over the sharp edge of her sword.

She rolled again, rising to her feet and turning to face him as her wet hair clung to her face to partially blind her on one side. Flicking her head to try and shift the obstruction to her view she saw him coming low towards her and twisted desperately out of the way, only to receive the faintest of brushes from the tip of his baton.

Fire coursed through her body, locking her muscles up for a split second and pushing a waving sensation of instant fatigue throughout her entire body to take her breath away and leave her shaking. She staggered backwards, one hand clutched to her right flank where the electricity had barely connected with her, and fearing the weapons even more. She retreated fast, her free left hand reaching down to snatch two of the throwing daggers from her thigh to launch them one after the other at him. He swung his right shoulder back and turned his head to watch the knife pass him by, but her aim on the second throw had been perfect.

As he avoided the first throw, she had sent a second knife at his opposite shoulder, only the speed of the throws prevented her from winding it up to anything near full speed. The dagger hit home, embedding its tip in the hard flesh of his upper arm but failing to puncture all the way through.

He slapped it away, dislodging it and turning a glare on her so filled with rage and humiliation that she took another step backwards involuntarily. Still feeling her muscles spasm and ache, she readied herself for what she feared would be their last tangle before her stunned body failed her. She looked around, searching for an escape and seeing none. Behind her the surviving soldiers poured continuous gunfire at the Resistance fighters as they contracted into a dangerous huddle and before her, blocking the route back inside the headquarters building, stood her unbeatable nemesis.

He attacked again, ruthless and savage, forcing her backwards with each desperate parry before she could retreat no further and ducked to lunge under his swinging arm with her sword snaking out ahead of her. The edge caught, biting into his suit in the same place she had landed her first kick to made him hiss in anger and pain as the two staggered away from one another.

Emboldened by her lucky cut, Eve stood tall and took up a fighting stance. Her eyes flickered over his right shoulder, and it was her turn to smile.

CHAPTER THIRTY-EIGHT

THE COLLAPSE OF ALL THINGS

Shadow saw the fleeting switch of her gaze but dismissed it, failing to sense the source of her renewed energy and focusing only on his decision to end his game with her. He advanced, confident and almost casual as he closed the gap to her unmoving form, to draw back his bleeding right arm ready to smash the baton into her body, determined not to stop until he had fried her heart with the current flowing though both weapons.

His blow never gathered the full momentum, instead failing before he had even begun to add the power of his body weight to the swing.

Eve, still holding the pose with her sword levelled at him, also held her smile as the next flash of lighting reflected from the wide blade of two big knives behind her attacker. The butcher's sounds came again, this time forcing Shadow's eyes wide in shock and disbelief as the weapon fell from his numb fingers and his eyes followed the source of the growing agony to see a knife blade protruding upwards from his right bicep. He snarled, the sounds he made nothing but incoherent rage as he brought the baton in his left hand around to swing wildly in the direction his grievous injury had come from. As he did, he felt his grip on that weapon falter in time to turn back and see a short, wickedly curved blade slice deeply through his left wrist.

He staggered, showing more shock than pain on his face as he squinted to make out the two shapes suddenly illuminated by another vicious streak of lightning. His legs failed him, dropping him to one knee as his weak right hand gripped at the ruin of his left wrist, as if he could somehow stem the gushing flow of his blood, which was washing away in the heavy rain with a finality that told him he wouldn't recover.

The taller of the two shapes shot a hand towards him to grasp the embedded knife hilt and rip it out of Shadow's right arm, spilling another gushing wave of hot blood to further weaken him. Slow footsteps behind foretold his death as he twisted his head in time to see the lateral swing of the long blade before… nothing.

"Took your time," Eve gasped, doubled over and breathing hard to recover from so nearly being fatally electrocuted. She elected her usual caustic sarcasm to cover the elation she felt at seeing him alive.

"Been busy," Adam said. Eve's eyes turned to view the girl smaller than she was step forwards and offer a respectful bow of greeting.

"You are as great a warrior as Adam tells me," she said in an accent Eve had never heard before. She stumbled over her words, mumbling a weak acceptance of the praise as she tried to fathom who the small woman was. From her stance and poise and the way she so expertly handled the blade, she was clearly a fighter, but she was smaller than Eve and close to a head shorter. There was an unspoken air of awkwardness as Adam glanced around but whatever had happened would have to wait.

"We have to end this," she said as she stood upright with difficulty. "Can you deal with them," she waved a gloved hand towards the surviving soldiers, "and I'll deal with the rest?"

"The rest?" Adam asked, confused. Eve saw it then; saw the look exchanged between the young man she had felt almost the same as and the small, big-eyed and beautiful creature beside him.

"Time to cut the head off the snake," she told them, accepting the fate of her chosen course. Without another word, she turned and began to jog stiffly towards the doors until her cramped muscles eased and her movements once more became cat-like and dangerous.

Eve ran for the elevator to take her back to her target, leaving streaks of rainwater on the floor, the squeaking of her feet accompanying each step. She only had half a plan for how to achieve her goal, how to succeed in her suicide mission, and she knew that speed and confusion were key.

Bursting from the elevator after the agonisingly slow upwards journey, she half fell onto the nearest of two soldiers posted to the corridor.

"They're inside," she gasped, her soaked hair clinging to her face as she leaned her weight onto him.

"Who is?" snapped a terrified female voice from behind her. "*Them?*" Eve looked over her shoulder, still leaning on the first soldier as she gauged the distance to the female holding a rifle half aimed in her direction. Eve tried to speak, doubling over in a faked fit of coughing, with both hands on her thighs before she rose with a dagger in each hand. Her left hand, unaimed as she was so close she couldn't miss, buried the blade under the man's jaw and make him jerk as he gagged on his own blood. Her right hand, gloved fingertips deftly releasing the blade at the perfect moment, sent it in a flat arc to snap back the woman's head before she could even signal her hands to pull the trigger. Both bodies dropped simultaneously as Eve stood tall and strode for the control room.

She barely waited for the sliding doors to open as she fell inside, staggering to regain her feet as though she had barely made it back in one piece.

"You need to get out of here," she croaked, her eyes locking onto Nathaniel's as she spoke across the crowded room to him alone. Nathaniel glanced once at Stanley, giving him the smallest of nods, before walking towards her. "They're inside the building," she coughed. "They killed Shadow." Stanley made a noise of exclamation as Nathaniel raised both eyebrows in shock. She staggered towards the elevator, slowing to allow both men to get ahead of her before the bodies of the two soldiers came into sight. Both men froze, turning at once back towards her as the sharp sword was drawn over her shoulder with a singing hiss.

Stanley, stepping forwards bravely as he had done before to protect his leader, thrust his left forearm out ahead of him and moved to slap his right palm into the control to activate the ballistic shield. As the metal fanned out like an opening flower, his right hand was already reaching back to draw the pistol from his hip.

Eve swung, the timing and placement of her sword's edge perfect as the shield reached its full display only a fraction of a second before the arm holding it was severed from the body to clatter to the floor.

Stanley, gun in hand and wearing a mask of pure horror, failed to pull the trigger in time before the blood gushed from the stump of his left arm and took away his ability to remain upright. Still reversing the blade to finish it all, Eve's eyes located her last target just as she knew she hadn't been quick enough.

Masked by Stanley's actions in stepping ahead of him to activate the shield, Nathaniel's right hand swung across his waist to draw the heavy revolver from his left thigh and turn the barrel to fire two rapid shots from the hip. Stars exploded in Eve's eyes as her breath was hammered out of her body by the two huge impacts to her chest. She gasped as she fell backwards, toppling as her knees gave way to slam her down onto her back and stare up at the white ceiling tiles while she fought to force breath into her lungs.

More gunshots flashed to deaden the sound in the corridor as the accompanying bright flashes hurt her sensitive eyes. Only instead of feeling the same crippling impacts, she felt only the curious sensation of a heavy weight landing beside her. Turning her head, she looked into the rapidly blinking, pain-filled eyes of Nathaniel.

———

Following their own agenda, members of the Resistance invaded the Citadel via another entrance and fought their way upwards after liberating every prisoner held there. Armouries had been ransacked and fierce gun battles raged on different levels of the imposing headquarters building, before the vanguard of their assault gained the control room level.

The woman at their front, stunning in her unique beauty even when soaked to the skin and sporting a fresh cut to one side of her forehead to compliment the bruising and swelling of her other injuries, saw the broad back of the man she recognised instantly. She heard the two gunshots and saw Eve thrown backwards, and without hesitation, she pulled her stolen rifle into her shoulder and fired a burst into the

Chairman. He toppled to fall beside his victim, but Samaira Nadeem didn't take the sights of the weapon away from him until she was standing over the blood-slicked carnage.

Stanley, twitching as his blood pumped weakly out of a cleanly cut stump, made her feel a stab of regret that she wasn't the one to kill the cruel letch of a man, but she dismissed him as dying and used the toe of her boot to try and flip the Chairman onto his back. She managed it on the second attempt, stamping her right boot down onto the hand that still held the revolver to prevent him from lifting it in one final act of defiance.

"Corporal," he coughed, blood covering his lips, "Corporal Nadeem. Or is it Captain Blake?" he began to chuckle weakly. Samaira ignored his words, feeling distinctly uncomfortable, not for having riddled his body with bullets, but for how he seemed to find the whole thing amusing. She wanted to ask him what was so funny, wanted to ask how he felt about his entire world falling down, wanted to ask how it felt to be the *last* chairman of the Party and felt a stab of regret that he wouldn't be there to see it pulled down.

"Get a medic up here," she shouted over the sound of gunfire as some in the control room still thought the fight could be won. "And tell whoever's in charge there that they can order all troops to stand down or I'll personally promote their second in command by shooting them in the face!" She continued to shout, demanding a medic be found to keep Nathaniel alive to face a public execution.

Eve's breathing began to feel less painful. It was still agony to move her ribs, but her repeated checks of her fingertips showed no blood where the bullets had hit her. The armour, so pliable and free, had held up to the power of close-range bullets and not penetrated her chest. Her ribs were shattered, at least that was how they felt, but when she realised she wasn't going to die and that what she was experiencing was just pain, she fought through it to roll onto her side.

Nathaniel's lips moved, barely any audible sound coming out and forcing her to lean closer.

"Don't... don't let them hang me... like a common criminal..." he pleaded through breathless whispers.

Eve considered his request, at least what she interpreted it to mean, and thought of how empty his death would feel if she stood and watched someone else take his life. Her decision made in a heartbeat, she reached down to pull the last remaining dagger from her thigh and lifted it to his neck. Leaning over into his ear she whispered, "This is not... a kindness. This is for Cohen."

"Where's that medic?" Samaira yelled as she slung her rifle and knelt beside the man to soak her knees in his blood. She swore, began pushing on his chest with both hands but it was pointless. Blood pulsed out through the holes in his back and the small puncture wound in his neck which had sapped his lifeforce away quicker than the gunshots had. His head and body rocked under the force of the chest compressions, making his lifeless gaze wander as his eyes were no longer fixed onto Eve's. His facial expression was thankful, as though her exacting revenge for a life taken had been a blessing to him; had somehow preserved his honour and dignity.

"Let's get you to a doctor," a kindly voice said, making Eve roll away from the dead man and look up into a bruised and swollen but kind face belonging to a woman she didn't know.

"You're Eve, aren't you?" she asked. Eve nodded numbly as the pain racked her from moving her chest.

"I'm Helen," the woman said, "and I'm the leader of Command."

Eve didn't care. Her part was done, she hoped, and for the first time in her life as she was half carried away from the four bodies lying dead in the corridor, she wondered if the death toll had been worth it.

———

One man who didn't heed the call to lay down his weapons and return peacefully to headquarters was the vicious man who enjoyed the torture and subjugation of others more than anything else in the world. Other pleasures had been taken from him, courtesy of the catastrophic damage done by the electrified baton applied to a very sensitive area, but he filled that gap with a renewed appreciation for causing pain to others.

The Party was done as far as he was concerned, and he decided to abandon the Citadel the second he heard the orders to surrender. He aimed for the north of the city, planning to escape towards the other Party-controlled enclaves and keep moving in any direction other than the south west.

He had hurt too many Citizens, tortured too many men and women for them just to allow him to be part of whatever chaos they looked forward to. He knew that retribution would come soon, and he knew that it wouldn't be pain free.

Throwing as many supplies into a troop carrier as he could cram, he pulled himself behind the wheel to start the silent engine and roll the tyres over the wet tarmac to escape via one of the smaller gates in the wall, well away from where the worst of the fighting had taken place.

In the end, it wasn't one of the elite soldiers the Resistance had created who caught him. It wasn't one of the warriors born underground and raised to hate everything about him. It was a pack of ordinary people; everyday Citizens, the likes of whom he saw as insects to step on from his position of power and authority. The van was blocked in, trapping him and forcing the decision to come out fighting. He didn't have space to use the rifle, so he fell from the cab with his pistol drawn. But before he could line up the first target and issue his threats so that they would let him go, multiple hands seized his and pulled the gun from his grip before he could resist.

Sergeant Major Owen Du Bois did not die well.

He was beaten, stamped on and crushed by the fists and boots of the downtrodden men and women he saw as something less than human. Unwittingly, they demonstrated his biggest fear as the last thing he ever experienced after the sensation of his bones breaking; that fear was that if any of the Citizens ever performed a head count, they'd realise that they were the majority.

They were the people.

And the people now ruled their island.

CHAPTER THIRTY-NINE

AFTERMATH

After the executions of those soldiers and officers accused of crimes, and after the executions of those Party members refusing to accept the new democratic system, and after the executions of collaborators and anyone else who didn't seem elated that their ruling dictatorship was over, so many people tired of seeing death that the Citadel seemed half empty and deflated.

The new regime promised fairness. Promised democracy, which was a concept in need of explaining to many, and they promised an end to the cruel routine enforced by their former puppet masters.

Construction, maintenance and the production of food and provision of services had ground to a halt, causing a shortage of just about everything after a week. Those who didn't want to go back to work in their old placements were offered inducements and better conditions, but in the end some people who flatly refused to play their part were arrested and locked away until someone could decide what law, if any, they had broken.

Those soldiers willing to serve the new regime were

given back their weapons on trust, and even without the emblem of the Party adorning their now helmetless uniforms, the city still felt somehow under guard. Drones still flew to protect the population, at least that was the official news sent down from the newly occupied Citadel headquarters, but many whispered that they were still seeking out Party officers and their collaborators, and were using the drones mostly for the purpose for which they had been invented.

Many left the Citadel in those first few weeks, packing up whatever provisions they could gather and helping themselves to any of the abandoned vehicles left around the city to break out and live their own lives free from anyone's rule.

In the end, many of them considered the loss of life had resulted in merely replacing one system, one regime, one form of rule for another.

The world still turned much as it had before, only to many the addition of democracy and freedom into their lives meant less security and more hunger. Freedom, the leaders said, came at a price. The price the people paid was much the same as the currency they had traded in under Party rule, and for the majority there was little difference in their lives after liberation.

Some left, only able to do so because their numbers forced those few nervous guards on the gates pointing west to choose between mowing down a crowd of unarmed civilians and turning their backs.

They headed for the rich farmlands between the Citadel and the western enclaves, and began to carve out their own way of life in the hope that the new government wouldn't seek them out and force them back under the banner of protection.

Far to the south west, on a rocky cliff overlooking the dark grey seas below turning white where the waves crashed onto the rocks, three people sat in quiet contemplation.

"Where do we go now?" Eve asked to nobody in particular.

"Wherever we want," Dren answered. The two young women had grown close in the week spent tending to Eve's injuries, which even weeks afterwards had barely begun to feel normal.

"Our part in this is done," Adam said, speaking in a voice that made him sound suddenly so much older and wiser than he had before. "We existed in the dark; that space between good and bad where other people don't go. That world doesn't need to exist any longer, so we have to find a new purpose."

"And what purpose is that?" Dren asked her husband – a fact Eve struggled to comprehend even then. Adam shrugged.

"I don't know yet," he sighed wistfully. "All I do know is that our purpose in life, all of our purposes, have been to end the regime. We've done that, but nobody left us any instructions on what to do if we ever succeeded."

"Isn't that the point?" Eve said. "There are no instructions now; we can do whatever we want to."

Adam lay back, despite the dampness of the grass and the slightest hint of rain in the air, choosing to treat the day like a warm summer.

"For now," he said, "I choose to do nothing."

"And after that?" Dren teased, nudging him in the ribs and prompting a grunt.

"After that? As much as I hate the sea, I want to see who else is out there."

FROM THE PUBLISHER

Thank you for reading *Erebus,* book two in Defiance.

We hope you enjoyed it as much as we enjoyed bringing it to you. We just wanted to take a moment to encourage you to review the book on Amazon and Goodreads. Every review helps further the author's reach and, ultimately, helps them continue writing fantastic books for us all to enjoy.

If you liked this book, check out the rest of our catalogue at www.aethonbooks.com. To sign up to receive a FREE collection from some of our best authors as well as updates regarding all new releases, visit www.aethonbooks.com/sign-up.

JOIN THE STREET TEAM! Get advanced copies of all our books, plus other free stuff and help us put out hit after hit.

SEARCH ON FACEBOOK:
AETHON STREET TEAM

ALSO IN THE SERIES

Genesis

Erebus

Phoenix

Printed in Great Britain
by Amazon